DEATH IN TH

Born in 1893, Anthony Berkeley (Anthony Berkeley Cox) was a British crime writer and a leading member of the genre's Golden Age. Educated at Sherborne School and University College London, Berkeley served in the British army during WWI before becoming a journalist. His first novel, *The Layton Court Murders*, was published anonymously in 1925. It introduced Roger Sheringham, the amateur detective who features in many of the author's novels including the classic *Poisoned Chocolates Case*. In 1930, Berkeley founded the legendary Detection Club in London along with Agatha Christie, Freeman Wills Crofts and other established mystery writers. It was in 1938, under the pseudonym Francis Iles (which Berkeley also used for novels) that he took up work as a book reviewer for *John O'London's Weekly* and *The Daily Telegraph*. He later wrote for *The Sunday Times* in the mid 1940s, and then for *The Guardian* from the mid 1950s until 1970. A key figure in the development of crime fiction, he died in 1971.

DEATH IN THE HOUSE

ANTHONY BERKELEY

THE LANGTAIL PRESS
LONDON

This edition published 2010 by
The Langtail Press

www.langtailpress.com

Death in the House © 1939 Anthony Berkeley

ISBN 978-1-78002-018-1

Contents

1. Death in the House 1
2. Cabinet Pudding 10
3. Brown Sauce 19
4. Much Ado and More Talk 28
5. A Minister Rises. 37
6. A Minister Falls 46
7. Suspicion at the Board of Trade 54
8. Assassination Is Not So Dull 62
9. A Conscience in Labour 70
10. Inside Information 78
11. Introducing Our Mr Lacy 86
12. Thorny Problem. 95
13. Scent and Sensibility 104
14. Danger in Downing Street 113
15. Bombshell in Whitehall 121
16. Agitation of a Home Secretary 129
17. Financial Fade-out 139
18. Chat in the Chamber 148
19. A Minister Shows His Mettle 157
20. The Bill Is Presented 166
21. Postscript to Politics 178

chapter one

Death in the House

'The House will hardly expect me to recapitulate the long story of troubles which have occurred in that unhappy country during recent years. The tale would even be tedious, for before a piling of tragedy upon tragedy the intelligence revolts, and finds tragedy itself tedious. But of late matters have reached a head. I need hardly refer to the disastrous attack a few weeks ago upon the Viceroy himself. The details will be fresh in every memory. But this I do emphasise, with all the power at my command: that outrage is deplored by responsible Indian opinion of every shade no less than it is deplored here.

'And that brings me to the crux of my remarks. It is precisely in response to the demands of that opinion, not to mention the urgent pleas of the rulers of the native Indian States, that His Majesty's Government has determined to introduce this Bill. We are resolved no longer to tolerate an agitation fostered and fomented not by the legitimate aspirations of the natives of India themselves, but by outside interests (and by this I mean national as well as individual interests – so much I may say, candidly and advisedly) in direct antagonism to the interests of India herself. Against these sinister activities India appeals for our aid. We cannot deny that aid.'

The Secretary of State for India grasped the lapels of his coat in the characteristic attitude which had been the joy of a hundred cartoonists and swept, with a stern, impersonal eye, the crowded benches before him.

The House of Commons seemed to be holding its breath. There had been notable, even epoch-making, Bills introduced before, but never had a speaker been accorded such a breathless, almost fearful attention. It was as if every member were personally dreading some devastating catastrophe, with that extraordinary gloating horror by which impending catastrophe is so often accompanied, as if a last-minute averting of the disaster would be almost a disappointment.

No sound but that of heavy breathing could be heard as Lord Wellacombe, after a brief pause, prepared to resume his speech.

'The Government has been accused, in quarters perhaps not altogether disinterested, of a certain weakness in its foreign policy. There will be no weakness here. Opposition to this will be strong and bitter. Mistaken idealists will find themselves ranged, in the name of liberty, with the most shameless self-seekers who see in the Bill a threat to their own personal advantages. But so long as it holds the confidence of this House, the Government is determined to carry it through in the teeth of all antagonism; and, once passed into law, it will be effectively and ruthlessly administered, without respect to person or people. It *must* be passed into law!

'Perhaps I can best explain the effect that we anticipate by the following illustration. The high-class Hindu is – is – the high-class Hindu...'

The steady, confident tones faltered for a moment. A little gasp went round the House, like a long, in-drawn 'A-a-ah... !'

The Secretary of State for India lifted to his lips the glass of water in front of him, and those who were nearest noticed that he did not set it down squarely upon the table again, but tilted it at a slight angle so that part of its contents was spilled. The action was curiously like that of a short-sighted man, which Lord Wellacombe was certainly not.

As if refreshed, he began to speak again.

'The high-class Hindu is in this peculiar position, that he –'

Lord Wellacombe's voice ceased abruptly. He rocked unsteadily on his feet for a moment or two; then his knees seemed to fold up beneath him and he fell full-length on the floor with a horrid crash.

In an instant all was confusion.

The other occupants of the front bench sprang forward and turned the fallen man upon his back. He was quite conscious, and seemed to be trying to rise. The others gazed at him helplessly in the inevitable way of the layman, be he dock labourer or Minister of the Crown, when confronted with sudden, inexplicable physical disaster. Other members, pouring down over the benches, made a rapidly growing circle round the prostrate man and then stood, gazing speechlessly and, to all appearances, no less vacantly than the apparently half-witted spectators at any street accident.

'Give him air,' commanded the member for West Watford importantly, and elbowed aside the President of the Board of Trade to loosen the fallen man's collar and tie.

'I'm all right,' muttered the Secretary for India, weakly.

The member for St John's Wood pushed his way from a very back bench to the centre of the circle.

'Excuse me,' he murmured to the Chancellor of the Exchequer, who was sympathetically but ineffectively chafing Lord Wellacombe's hands. 'Excuse me; I'm a doctor.'

The Chancellor made way for him thankfully, and even the member for West Watford withdrew before professional competence.

The newcomer made a swift but experienced examination.

'Well?' said the Home Secretary, fussily. 'What's the matter with him?'

The member for St John's Wood looked up sharply. He did not like the Home Secretary, although they were on the same side of the House.

'The matter with him?' he repeated slowly, as if debating a fitting answer to this curious question. 'Why – I can't say.'

'You can't say?' echoed the Chancellor of the Exchequer. His tones did not carry a question; it was as if he had but received confirmation of a private conviction.

'Well, what do you think?' demanded the Home Secretary.

The member for St John's Wood gazed thoughtfully on Lord Wellacombe's distorted features. 'As a pure shot in the dark,' he hesitated, 'I should say he'd had a stroke. But I don't know. That is, unless – ' He broke off.

The Home Secretary was exchanging a significant glance with the Foreign Secretary.

'I *told* the Prime Minister,' he began.

'Yes, but not now, I think, Beamish,' interrupted the other, with an almost imperceptible motion of his head towards the Press Gallery.

'I mean, someone will have to go and tell the Prime Minister,' the Home Secretary turned off his indiscretion lamely.

A youngish, clean-shaven man in the forefront of those clustered round the body, nodded to the Home Secretary. 'I will,' he said, and turned at once to make his way out of the group.

The Home Secretary murmured: 'Thanks, Arthur.'

'Well, no good standing here like a lot of dummies,' remarked the First Lord of the Admiralty, briskly. 'Someone had better have a word with the Speaker. He'll have to suspend the sitting. And we'd better send for an ambulance at once and have the poor chap taken home.' He turned to one of the messengers who had come hurrying in immediately the collapse of the Secretary for India had become apparent.

'Yes, and who's going to break the news to his wife?' demanded the Home Secretary, almost peevishly.

In the Press Gallery the reporters were feverishly scribbling: 'Lord Arthur Linton, Under Secretary for India, hastened away from the distressing scene to acquaint the Prime Minister personally with news of the tragedy.'

The temporary object of the reporters' attention felt his mind racing in time with his body as he hurried across to Downing Street. The swiftness of the disaster, so far from numbing his perceptions, seemed to have intensified them. During the speech his eyes had never left his Chief for a moment, and he felt as if he could remember every minute intonation, gesture and mannerism.

'Damn it,' he muttered to himself, 'the doctor must have been right. It must have been a stroke. Anything else is too fantastic.'

But he remained unconvinced.

There was a curious sense of responsibility weighing on him, too. Somehow, he could not help feeling, he ought to have been able to avert the tragedy... the rectification of some omission... the adoption of some unforeseen precaution... but what could he have done that the others had not thought of doing? He reminded himself that Sir Hubert Lesley was reckoned to be the most efficient Commissioner of Police of the decade; certainly Lord Wellacombe himself had had full confidence in him. And yet Sir Hubert had not succeeded.

But how could Sir Hubert have succeeded against a seizure? That, of course, was an impossible contingency.

The front door of No. 10 opened in response to his ring.

'I want to see the Prime Minister, Dean,' he told the butler, somewhat breathlessly. 'It's urgent.'

'The Prime Minister's still in bed, my lord,' the butler replied, doubtfully. 'His influenza, you know. He's better today, but I don't know whether – '

'He'll see me,' Lord Arthur broke in impatiently. 'Please tell him that I've come from the House and that something very serious has occurred.'

'Very good, my lord. If you will step in here…'

Less than two minutes later Lord Arthur was being shown into the bedroom.

The Prime Minister, an elderly, white-haired man with incongruously cherubic pink-and-white features, was sitting up in bed, a dressing-gown round his shoulders. A look of acute anxiety replaced the usual placid serenity of his expression.

'What is it, Arthur?' he asked, before the door had even closed behind the butler. For that matter Dean had been in the Prime Minister's service for nearly thirty years, and there were some who opined that he knew more about his master's intentions than the Cabinet itself. 'You don't mean…?'

'Lord Wellacombe,' began Lord Arthur, awkwardly.

'Good God! Not…?'

Lord Arthur shook his head. 'Oh, no. Just a collapse. But right in the middle of his speech. Without any warning. His legs… well, they just seemed to give way.'

The Prime Minister sank back on his pillows. And for a moment there was silence.

'It's – it's incredible,' he muttered at length. 'You mean, he just collapsed?'

Lord Arthur turned from the window out of which he had been staring. 'Yes. But Davidson was there – St John's Wood, you know. He's a doctor. He diagnosed a stroke.'

'A stroke – yes!' The Prime Minister fastened eagerly on the explanation. He raised himself on his elbow and fixed his eyes on the other's face. 'It must have been a stroke, of course.' It was as if he were arguing against an invisible opponent.

'Of course, sir,' agreed Lord Arthur, tonelessly.

'There was nothing to indicate… well, a shot, or anything like that? No blood?'

'Oh, no.'

'The galleries? They were crowded, of course?'

'Yes, but Sir Hubert was to have them packed with his men, you remember. He absolutely guaranteed there would be no danger there.'

Again there was silence.

'I shall have to come downstairs,' said the Prime Minister, with something like a return to his usual energy. 'What about Beamish and Allfrey and the others?'

'I left them in the House, sir. They were going to see about an ambulance. I expect they'll be round here as soon as arrangements have been made.'

The Prime Minister nodded. 'Yes, sure to. Beamish certainly will. Yes, I must come down. We must have a Cabinet meeting at once.'

'Is it wise, sir?'

'You mean, from the health point of view. Prime Ministers can't afford to be ill like ordinary people, Arthur. And I'm sure Sir Gregory would have a fit if I called a Cabinet meeting in my bedroom.' Sir Gregory Lane was the Foreign Secretary, and a notable stickler for procedure. 'I'll wrap up, of course. Just push that bell beside the fireplace, will you? Thanks. Now you'd better go down. Mollison will be somewhere about. Tell him to get hold of Sir Hubert and ask him to come round here at once. And send Verreker up to me here.' Mollison and Verreker were two of the Prime Minister's private secretaries. 'Oh, and you'll probably find Isabel in the drawing-room. I wish you'd break the news to her for me. She and Lady Wellacombe are fond of one another. She'll want to go round and see her.'

Lord Arthur nodded and made his way to the door. As his hand touched the knob, the Prime Minister spoke again.

'Arthur.'

'Yes, sir.'

'It *must* have been a stroke. This business got on his nerves more than we ever imagined. When it came to the point, the suggestion was too strong for him. A kind of self-hypnosis, one might say. That's the only logical explanation.'

'Absolutely, sir,' Lord Arthur agreed.

Nevertheless, as he made his way downstairs he knew that the same thought had been in both their minds: that Wellacombe, dry, precise, yet with a burning enthusiasm for India and India's welfare, was undoubtedly the last person to suffer from nerves or to practise, however unwittingly, any form of self-hypnosis. That Lord Wellacombe could have 'suggested himself into a stroke' – for that in plain language was what the Prime Minister's words amounted to – was just as incredible as the other explanation, which neither man had voiced, was fantastic.

Lord Arthur hurriedly executed the Prime Minister's commissions, and the sound of a piano playing a Bach prelude showed him that the latter's guess as to his daughter's whereabouts had not been wrong. As he entered the room Isabel Franklin rose quickly from the piano-stool.

'Oh, thank goodness someone's come. I was strumming to show where I was. Arthur… is everything all right?'

Isabel Franklin was in the early thirties, half a dozen years younger than Lord Arthur; the two had known each other from childhood. She was not pretty; indeed, when bored she could look positively plain; but when her interest was roused and her intelligence or emotions engaged, there was an attractive piquancy in her face, with its high cheekbones and wide, mobile mouth, such as a woman whose prettiness is her only asset can never achieve. Her father was a widower, and for the three years during which he had been in office Isabel had acted as hostess for him and as housekeeper of No. 10. Two months ago her engagement had been announced to the First Lord of the Admiralty – a bachelor, in spite of his breeziness. The match was considered an excellent one, but Lord Arthur had not shared the Prime Minister's pleasure in it, any more than he shared the Prime Minister's opinion of the First Lord. So far as he knew Lord Arthur had never thought particularly about Isabel; he had taken her for granted as an old friend, and his political career, undertaken at the urging of the Prime Minister himself whose discovery he was well known to be, had kept him too busy for any other interests. The vehemence of his conviction that Isabel was far too good to be thrown away on any showy mountebank (for such he privately considered the First Lord of the Admiralty to be) had quite surprised him.

'No,' he answered her now, with the bluntness of an old friend. 'Everything isn't all right. You'd better prepare yourself for a shock, Isabel.'

'Lord Wellacombe's dead?' said the girl instantly.

Lord Arthur gave her a short account of the scene in the House, and emphasised the probability of a stroke.

'No.' Isabel was pale, but she spoke quietly. 'It wasn't a stroke. You know that as well as I do, Arthur. Oh, poor father! And Lady Wellacombe. She's devoted to him, you know. Has anyone gone to break the news to her?'

'I expect so, by this time. They were talking about it when I left the House.'

'Oh, talk,' said the girl, contemptuously. 'That's all half of them ever do. They're probably still talking, each trying to push an unpleasant job on to the other. I'd better go round and do it myself.'

She walked quickly to the door, but Lord Arthur stopped her.

'Isabel, I don't think you'd better go just yet. This has been a shock to your father too, of course, and he's talking about getting up at once. In fact, he's calling a Cabinet meeting right away. Wellacombe's collapse will make a first-class political crisis, as I need hardly tell you. And if he does die… well, we've got to face the probability. But do you think your father ought to get up? Couldn't you persuade him to hold the meeting in his bedroom? There's precedent for it. I believe Gladstone did.'

Isabel hesitated. 'His temperature was normal this morning, though the doctor said he'd better stay in bed a day or two. But I think he'd be happier up. No, I won't interfere. Besides, you can't rule a Cabinet divided against itself from a bed.'

'How do you know the Cabinet is divided against itself?' Lord Arthur asked quickly.

Isabel gave him a faint smile. 'I sometimes act as father's unofficial and extremely private secretary, you know. Of course, he never gives away State secrets, but most things we discuss rather freely; it helps him, I'm sure. For instance, you needn't fence with me about Lord Wellacombe's collapse. I've seen this. In fact, I agreed with father that it was just a piece of silly bluff... heaven forgive me!'

She turned away, overcome for the moment with emotion, as Lord Arthur took the folded piece of paper she held out to him.

He smoothed it out and glanced hurriedly through it. It was a copy of a document which was now at Scotland Yard – and being feverishly subjected, Lord Arthur surmised, to every possible test for gleaning evidence where no evidence appeared to exist.

> *To the Prime Minister and Members of the Cabinet:*
> *Gentlemen, – Take notice that you will not be allowed to proceed with the present Indian Restriction Bill which you are now contemplating. Not only is this Bill not wanted, but its whole spirit gives incalculable offence to a vast number of people of whom I am only the mouthpiece. We do not want it, and we will not have it. If the Secretary for India persists in introducing this Bill into the House of Commons, as at present intended, he will have to be removed. And similarly with anybody who attempts to take his place. This is a fair warning, and I must ask you gentlemen to believe that no measures will be shirked which we consider necessary to prevent this Bill from becoming law, even to the elimination in turn of the whole Cabinet.*
> *The Brown Hand.*

Lord Wellacombe died at a quarter to five that afternoon.

chapter two

Cabinet Pudding

'We warned him,' said the President of the Board of Trade, nervously. 'At any rate we can't reproach ourselves with not having warned him.'

'Precious little warning needed,' grunted the Secretary of State for War. 'From *us*.'

'He was a sportsman,' the First Lord of the Admiralty asserted breezily. The First Lord of the Admiralty was always breezy. He felt it a part of his duties. Once he had been Secretary of State for War, and then had cultivated a toothbrush moustache. It was confidently expected by his colleagues that should he ever be appointed Secretary for the Colonies, he would turn up at his office in a slouch hat and sheepskin plus-fours. 'Wellacombe always was a sportsman.'

'Aren't we tending to take for granted a state of affairs which we know cannot exist?' asked the Foreign Secretary, dryly.

'You mean?' prompted the Home Secretary. Mr Beamish always preferred things in black and white. He was accustomed to describe himself as 'a plain man' (other people sometimes described him quite differently), and insinuation and innuendo were to him anathema. For one thing he very rarely understood them. 'You mean…?' he repeated, as the other showed no sign of amplifying his remark.

'Why, that Wellacombe's death was not a natural one, of course,' replied the Foreign Secretary, in tones that were just not downright rude.

'Oh, I see. Yes, perhaps you're right. I mean, of course, the death must have been natural. We mustn't alarm ourselves unnecessarily. After all, we have not only Davidson's opinion but Sir William Greene's. I made a point of ringing him up before I came. He'd only just seen the body, of course, and was inclined to be cautious; but he had to admit that on a very brief examination he was inclined to believe that death must have been due to sudden heart failure.'

He looked round for approbation of his foresight, but the faces of his colleagues remained studiously blank. The Home Secretary was not a popular man.

'Never knew Wellacombe had a heart,' observed the Secretary of State for War.

'He hadn't,' uncompromisingly replied the Chancellor of the Exchequer, who had been the dead man's closest friend.

'Well, gentlemen, it isn't very much use discussing that point yet awhile.' The Prime Minister, sitting by the fire and wrapped incongruously in dressing-gown and rugs, looked with uneasy eyes round the gathering he had called together. The Cabinet was present in full strength, and nerves were a little jumpy. 'If the police have finished with the body, Sir William is probably performing the autopsy now. There will be an analysis later, of course, by Sir Angus MacFerris. Till then it is little use speculating. In the meantime we have Sir William's opinion, as Beamish says and as Sir William told me on the telephone half an hour ago, that at a first glance the appearances are not inconsistent with death from some kind of a stroke.' The Home Secretary looked a little crestfallen that his interesting news had been thus forestalled.

'What I want to decide,' the Prime Minister went on, 'and that as quickly as possible, is who is to take Wellacombe's place and see the Bill through the House.'

He looked round, but for a moment nobody spoke. Then:

'Have you still got that absurd note, Prime Minister?' asked the President of the Board of Trade in his high voice. 'It would be interesting to hear its terms again – in the circumstances,' he added, with a nervous little laugh.

'Certainly I have it,' the Prime Minister returned, with unusual irritation. 'In fact I have copies here with me of all three. The originals, of course, are with the police.'

'Three?' echoed several voices.

'Three. The first two you have already heard about. Another arrived this morning. It was lying on the mat just inside the front door here. From the fact that one corner was actually under the door, according to the best of my butler's recollection when he picked it up, the police are inclined to think that it may have been pushed under the door instead of put through the letter-box in the usual way; but they can suggest no explanation of why that should have been done. I will read it to you, gentlemen – though I must repeat that this is *not* the business for which we are assembled,' added the Prime Minister tartly, with a glance at the President of the Board of Trade which caused that important gentleman to blush like a schoolboy.

In a voice completely devoid of expression the Prime Minister read:

To the Prime Minister and Secretary for India.

Gentlemen: It is obvious that you have not taken our warnings seriously. We regret the necessity of removing so distinguished and honest a public servant as Lord Wellacombe, but you are leaving us no choice. He will die in the middle of his speech in the House of Commons this afternoon. In case his personal affairs are not in order, he would be advised to see his lawyer before he leaves for the House.

We sincerely hope that Lord Wellacombe's death will be enough to show that this Bill must be dropped. We would very much regret having to eliminate, in turn, the whole Cabinet.

The Brown Hand.

'Eliminate the whole Cabinet! Good God, this fellow's got a cheek,' laughed the First Lord, heartily, but his mirth did not ring altogether true.

'Precise enough, in all conscience,' remarked the Lord Chancellor. As a lawyer, the Lord Chancellor could appreciate precision. 'It was a clear mind that formulated these letters.'

'Infernal fanatic,' muttered the Secretary for War.

'No doubt,' agreed the Lord Chancellor, mildly. 'But then fanatics so often are clear-minded. That's the real danger of them.'

'You – er – showed... that is, Wellacombe saw this third letter?' asked the Minister of Agriculture and Fisheries, somewhat hesitantly.

'Certainly,' replied the Prime Minister. 'We discussed it this morning. Naturally Lord Wellacombe disregarded it entirely.'

'Yes, yes.' The First Commissioner of Works drummed on the table with his fingertips. 'He could hardly do otherwise. But still...'

'In the middle of his speech!' suddenly boomed the Minister of Labour. 'You see? That's a point, eh? Not *before* his speech, or anything like that. In the middle of it. And Wellacombe did collapse in the middle of his speech, didn't he? Now how on earth could this chap have known he'd do that, unless he took steps? Killed him, in other words. Sorry to put it in plain words, gentlemen, but plain words never did anyone any harm. I'm saying Wellacombe was murdered, by the writer of these letters. Who's going to contradict that?'

The Minister of Labour had a reputation for being bluff. He was bluff with workmen who were contemplating a strike, and he was bluff with employers who were contemplating locking out workmen who were contemplating a strike. And somehow or other during his régime there had been singularly few serious strikes, and no lockouts. In consequence the Minister of Labour had been convinced that bluffness pays. He was bluff now even with his wife, to that lady's vast irritation. The Minister of Labour also seldom allowed one to forget that he had had a Board School education. He had found that, properly handled, a Board School education pays better in these days than any public school and University career. As a matter of strict accuracy the Minister of Labour had been educated at a Grammar School and lived in daily dread of his political opponents discovering the fact.

The Prime Minister took the situation at once in hand. 'No one is going to contradict, or agree with you, Robinson, because the rest of us require proper evidence before coming to any categorical conclusion like that.'

'Ridiculous, in any case,' muttered the Secretary for Air, just not *sotto voce*. 'Murdered in the House itself, right under all our noses. Fantastic!'

'Still, the – the police haven't been able to throw any light on the letters, Prime Minister?' queried the President of the Board of Trade, with his nervous little giggle. 'No news in that direction at all?'

'None, Lloyd-Evans,' replied the Prime Minister, shortly.

'Slack lot, the police,' asseverated the First Lord. 'Better get on their tails and ginger them up a bit, Beamish.'

'I'm sure,' retorted the Home Secretary with some warmth, 'that in so far as they come under the authority of my department, the police are perfectly – '

The Prime Minister waved a protesting hand. 'We are here to discuss the matter of Wellacombe's successor, gentlemen; not the efficiency of the police. The question we have to decide now is, who is to step into poor Wellacombe's shoes tomorrow and take the matter up where he left it?'

'Tomorrow?' echoed the President of the Board of Trade, uneasily. 'You really mean to go on with the Bill immediately?'

'Certainly.' The Prime Minister's tones were testy. 'We have these next few days earmarked for it on our programme, and the business of the State cannot be held up for any private individual. Much though we may feel Wellacombe's loss ourselves,' the Prime Minister's voice became more gentle, 'and deeply though we may be mourning him, we cannot let our personal feelings stand in the way of Government. Our duty is perfectly plain.'

'You don't think...' The First Commissioner of Works glanced round as if seeking support. 'You don't think it would be better to hold things up, till we have the result of the analysis?' he asked, delicately.

'Hear, hear,' agreed the First Lord, somewhat unexpectedly. 'No point in rushing things. Let's know where we are first.'

The Prime Minister looked at his future son-in-law with a certain surprise, but only remarked mildly: 'To hold things up would be a confession of weakness which the Government must at all costs avoid. In spite of the efforts of ourselves and the police, there is no doubt that rumours of these threats against us and the Bill have been spread. The Press has loyally printed nothing about them, but I am in a position to say definitely that has not been through want of knowledge. To back down now, because it would appear superficially at any rate that threats have not been without foundation, would be an exhibition of miserable pusillanimity to which I could never consent. The second reading must go forward as before.'

The Prime Minister's words were enough. No one ventured to dispute his authority.

'Well, have you anyone in mind for Wellacombe's successor?' asked the Secretary for Air, bluntly.

The Prime Minister did not answer the question in so many words.

'I was thinking more for the moment of asking one of you to take nominal charge of the Bill and see it through the House.' He looked inquiringly round the circle. 'I should like to hear any views that may be held.'

There was an uneasy pause. From the expressions on the various ingenuous political countenances it was clear enough that every Minister was feeling awkwardly that perhaps he ought to volunteer for this singularly unwelcome duty, and at the same time consoling himself with the reflection that, upon his soul, it really was a bit too far outside his proper sphere for *him*.

'I have learned that Wellacombe had written out his speech in full,' the Prime Minister dropped into the silence. 'It would merely be a question of reading it out. The debate, of course, can be handled by the departmental Under Secretary.'

Still nobody spoke.

The Prime Minister swept another look over his colleagues. A curious thought occurred to him: this was a parish council, met to decide a question concerning the parish pump. Were these really the first Ministers of the Crown, this undistinguished lot? Apart from the Foreign Secretary, the Lord Chancellor, and perhaps one or two more, there hardly looked a man among them fit to be anything more than a churchwarden or a rural JP. Just façade – and behind it nothing but wind. Were these really the best that the country could produce, to govern it? And he himself, just a very ordinary, rather tired old man: what was he doing, being Prime Minister of the greatest Empire the world had ever known?

'I'm only asking for a volunteer to read the introductory speech,' he said, wearily.

'I'll take the job on if you like, Prime Minister,' said a voice from the other side of the room, and half a dozen breaths were expelled in a simultaneous sigh of relief.

The speaker was the Secretary for the Colonies, a square, taciturn person who hitherto had not opened his mouth.

'Thank you, Middleton,' said the Prime Minister, quietly, but his eye was more eloquently cordial. The Colonial Secretary had been another of the Prime Minister's own discoveries. Oddly enough, too, he really was a Colonial.

Unlike most politicians, who speak whenever they get the chance and seldom relevantly, the Colonial Secretary spoke with reserve and when he did it was to the point.

'I'd better have a look at that speech of Wellacombe's as soon as possible,' he said, briefly. 'I'd like to go through it with Lord Arthur. Are they both handy?'

'Arthur's waiting downstairs,' returned the Prime Minister, cordially. 'He has a copy of the speech with him.'

'Good! Then if you don't want me for anything else?'

'Mr Prime Minister!' The Secretary for the Dominions, a large, swelling gentleman with a considerable presence, interposed with dignity and waved a big, white hand to keep the Colonial Secretary in his chair.

'Yes?'

'Without in any way making this a personal matter, I feel on reflection that it is I who ought to take Wellacombe's place. Our departments after all are the most closely allied. I shall be happy to volunteer to do so.' Though one might not have guessed it behind his imposing mien, the Secretary for the Dominions was feeling more than a little annoyed with himself. He had possibly missed a big chance. There would be extra-special publicity for the man who stepped into Wellacombe's shoes. The Press knew about those ridiculous threats, and they could be trusted to play the game and hint discreetly at the courage required to take over Wellacombe's job. It was all nonsense to suppose that there really was any danger, of course, but there would be no harm in dropping a word of dignified defiance to one or two favourite journalists. Besides, it *was* his prerogative. India was practically a Dominion. The Secretary for the Dominions had always felt a little jealous of the Secretary for India.

'That's very good of you, Lavering,' said the Prime Minister, hiding a smile. The motive behind the offer was perfectly plain to him. 'But Middleton's already volunteered.'

'I'm quite indifferent, if Lavering wants to do it,' Middleton said, carelessly.

'It is hardly a question of "wanting,"' replied the Secretary for the Dominions, heavily. 'I merely consider it my duty. I was, indeed, just about to offer when Middleton spoke.'

'Exactly,' soothed the Prime Minister. 'But as Middleton did speak, I think we had better leave it at that.' The Prime Minister stroked his chin with a thoughtful air. 'And it might be wise if we kept the identity of Lord Wellacombe's successor a strict secret.'

'Decidedly,' the Home Secretary agreed, officiously. 'Very much better.'

'There is not the least need for anyone to know, outside ourselves and Lord Arthur,' the Prime Minister went on, disregarding this support, 'right up till the moment when you get up to speak tomorrow, Middleton.'

'Just as you like, Prime Minister, of course,' the Colonial Secretary assented, a slight smile on his rather grim face as if to intimate that he would tolerate these precautions but was quite unimpressed as to their necessity. '*I* won't mention the matter, at all events.'

'No, I know that,' agreed the Prime Minister, with just so much significance in his tone as might have given the Secretary for the Dominions cause to reflect, had he not been too busy nursing his chagrin.

'Then if you'll excuse me...' The Colonial Secretary rose from his chair.

'Good luck, Middleton,' muttered the President of the Board of Trade, who was given to displaying emotion at inconvenient moments.

'Yes, good luck, old boy,' echoed the First Lord, with manly sentiment.

Middleton grinned sheepishly.

Before he could reach the door, the bell of the telephone extension rang sharply. At a nod from the Prime Minister, Middleton went to the instrument and lifted the receiver. He listened for a moment, said 'Hold on,' and carried the telephone on its long flex across to the Prime Minister's chair.

'It's Mollison, sir. He says MacFerris is on the line, with important news.'

There was a dead and anxious silence as the Prime Minister spoke, in his usual quietly conversational tones.

'Yes. Put him through. – Yes, Sir Angus? This is the Prime Minister speaking. – Indeed? That was very expeditious. – Already? Yes? – Good! Yes, tell me, please.' There was a long silence. 'Good heavens!' The Prime Minister's voice was shocked. 'You're absolutely certain? – Dreadful! – I see, yes, of course. Well, ring me up the instant you discover anything else. You've informed the Commissioner of Police, of course? – Yes, very well. Goodbye.'

The Prime Minister hung up the receiver and handed the instrument back to the Colonial Secretary. He looked at the strained expectancy on the faces of his Cabinet.

'Gentlemen, I am afraid this is more serious than we dared to fear. Sir Angus tells me that he has little doubt that Wellacombe's death was not a natural one. Sir William Greene sent him round certain portions of the body at the earliest moment, and though, of course, he has not yet had time to make exhaustive tests he has already detected the presence of an unidentified alkaloid, which almost certainly caused death. In other words, poor Wellacombe was poisoned.'

No one spoke.

The Prime Minister turned a worried gaze on to the Colonial Secretary.

'I can hardly take advantage of your offer, Middleton, made in ignorance of this new development.'

'Naturally my offer stands, Prime Minister,' Middleton returned, almost brusquely. 'Unless,' he added with malice, 'Levering still wants to do his duty.'

The Secretary for the Dominions gave him a ghastly smile.

The First Lord spoke up with nautical candour, as man to man. 'Prime Minister, shelve the Bill. I don't say chuck it altogether, of course, but shelve it at any rate till the police have had a chance.'

'That,' said the Prime Minister, firmly, 'is quite out of the question.'

chapter three

Brown Sauce

'It's worrying me, Arthur. Even apart from poor Wellacombe's death, the whole business is most disturbing.' The Prime Minister ran his hand through his rather long white hair and gazed anxiously into the fire. 'We've had enough trouble with the Indian extremists in their own country, but they should bring their terrorisation methods over here…'

It was the middle of the next morning, and Lord Arthur had snatched half an hour from his work of coaching Middleton in order to hurry round to Downing Street for a short and unofficial conference with the Prime Minister. The meeting was taking place in the library, where the Prime Minister, swathed in rugs but fully dressed, was ensconced by the fire. Whether in her capacity as sick nurse or as private confidante, Isabel Franklin was present too.

'You think it's the Indian extremists then, sir?' Lord Arthur asked.

'I suppose so. That's the view Scotland Yard takes, and it's the logical one. Dear me, dear me, why can't these poor wretches believe that we're all honestly trying to do what we think best for their country? But that's always the way in politics. No party has ever deliberately and maliciously supported a policy which it knew to be unsound; but few Oppositions ever give a Government credit for purity of motive… and no Opposition newspaper. Don't ever go in for politics, Isabel. It's a disheartening as well as a dirty profession.'

'As I've always told you, father, I shall offer myself as a candidate the day you retire,' Isabel returned briskly. 'We may as well carry on the family tradition of providing at any rate one disinterested member of the House.'

The Prime Minister smiled at her. 'Not if I can help it will you ever be elected, my dear. A daughter can be a terrible responsibility, Arthur. Never have one of your own.'

'No, Arthur will have one of somebody else's,' responded Isabel tartly.

Lord Arthur looked at her in some surprise. Cheap wit was not in Isabel's line at all. She smiled at him, and he smiled back.

The worried look which had for a moment left the Prime Minister's face returned.

'Well, it's like this. After sitting up all night Sir Angus has still not succeeded in identifying the alkaloid in poor Wellacombe's body. But from certain indications, which I'm afraid were too technical for me, and from the symptoms of his collapse, particularly the curious way his legs folded up at the knees, he tells me he's strongly inclined to suspect curare.'

'Curare!' echoed Lord Arthur in astonishment.

'There's a precedent,' said the Prime Minister, with a wan smile. 'Don't you remember the attempt to poison Lloyd George with curare during the War? They were going to introduce it by means of a nail in his shoe, weren't they?'

Lord Arthur was trying to remember what he had ever heard about curare. It did not seem to be very much.

'I suppose it's the sort of poison Indians would use?' he said doubtfully. 'I thought it was a South American one.'

'I think it's used fairly generally throughout the East too. Apparently the Malays mix it with snake venom, to quicken its action; and Sir Angus is inclined to think that may have been done in this case.'

'That glass of water he had,' Lord Arthur said suddenly. 'Could it have been in the carafe?'

'Curare kills by being introduced into the bloodstream,' Isabel put in quietly. 'I went round to the British Museum Reading Room and looked it up for myself, as soon as Sir Angus had rung up father. Apparently you can swallow it with impunity. It has to be introduced through an open wound.'

'Exactly,' nodded her father. 'And I've already had a preliminary report from Sir William about the open wounds in the body. He's going over it again, very carefully, because it seems that the stuff can be got into the body through quite a tiny puncture. Let me see.' He pulled a sheaf of papers from his pocket and selected one. 'Yes, there were three or four slight wounds. A little cut on the cheek, made no doubt when he was shaving. Apparently a tiny pimple cut off on the side of the neck, also made when shaving. A scratch on the ball of the thumb. And an abrasion on the right shin, as if he had knocked it against something. According to Sir William, none of them seem very hopeful.'

'The stuff couldn't have been smeared on his razor, I suppose?' Lord Arthur meditated. 'Not very likely. He'd have stropped it clean.'

'In any case, the time factor wouldn't fit,' said Isabel. 'It must have been administered within fifteen minutes before he collapsed, probably ten.'

'But he'd been in the House at least ten minutes,' Lord Arthur objected. 'Let's see, he'd been speaking for about five minutes, and I should say he'd come in about five minutes before that.'

The Prime Minister nodded. 'That's been verified, as near as possible.'

'But, good heavens, you surely don't believe the stuff was actually administered in the House itself?'

'It looks uncommonly like it.'

'What does Scotland Yard say?'

'Well, I've only had a word or two with Sir Hubert myself, but according to Beamish they're completely puzzled. In fact they're strongly disinclined to believe that the administration can possibly have been made in the House. Apparently they had Wellacombe under the strictest observation from the moment he left his own front door, and they say there wasn't a split second when anyone could have inserted the stuff into him.'

'What's the fatal dose, sir?'

'Very small. Thirty milligrams, or less,' Isabel replied.

'Don't they smear it on arrows?' Lord Arthur asked vaguely.

'I didn't understand from Sir William that there were any signs of an arrow wound,' said the Prime Minister, with feeble jocosity.

'It doesn't always kill, on an arrow,' Isabel put in. 'It just paralyses the limbs, one by one, beginning with the legs. Apparently the savages take advantage of that and torture the victim to death.'

'It killed all right, in this case,' said Lord Arthur gloomily.
There was a pause.

'Well, I suppose I must be getting back,' Lord Arthur said.

'Don't go for a minute or two,' Isabel answered quickly. 'That is, of course, unless you must.' She glanced meaningfully towards her father.

The Prime Minister was staring into the fire. He shook his head. 'I can't understand it, I can't understand it. Wellacombe was perfectly all right when he left his own house. According to the doctors he must have been. Sir Hubert tells me two of his men were on his heels all the way to the House. He spent an hour in his own room there, going over his speech.'

Lord Arthur nodded. 'I was with him part of the time.'

'Exactly. And no one else. And there was an attendant as well as one of the Scotland Yard Special Branch men outside the door. Unless someone or something was concealed actually inside the room, no harm can have come to him there. He was under observation right till the minute he passed the Speaker's Chair, and then he came under the observation of other men in the galleries. There was no chance. The whole thing's incredible. There's nothing to make a start from.'

'Who was sitting beside him?' Isabel asked. 'Haven't they any suggestion at all?'

'Lloyd-Evans was on one side of him and Pelham on the other.' Mr Pelham was Chancellor of the Exchequer and had been leading the House during the Prime Minister's illness. 'Neither of them can throw any light on the affair at all. Wellacombe spoke to both of them before he rose, and both agree that he appeared perfectly normal. They listened carefully, of course, while he was speaking, and neither heard any sound which could be regarded as in the least significant. Naturally they've each had long interviews with the Scotland Yard men, but frankly they can't help us at all; Sir Hubert is entirely satisfied of that.'

'Isn't there *any* clue?' asked Isabel helplessly.

'So far, none. Of course the police have taken possession of a number of things with which Wellacombe came into contact towards the last: his pipe, for instance, his tobacco pouch, and so on. They'll all be analysed. But even if traces of poison are found and we discover the vehicle, we're still confronted by the much greater problem of how it was placed there.'

'And who placed it,' Isabel added dryly. 'Had Lord Wellacombe any private enemies?'

'A certain number, my dear, of course. That is the inevitable lot of the politician. And, of course, the fanatics on one side are apt to look on the leading men of the other as inhuman, malicious monsters, of whom the world would be much better rid than not. There have been plenty of political assassinations before now – Spencer Perceval, the Prime Minister, for instance, over a hundred years ago, and the Phoenix Park murders. But somehow I feel this is in rather a different category. If it really was carried out by the writer of those Brown Hand letters or his associates, it is a definite attempt to deter the Government from its intentions by means of terroristic methods. One cannot possibly over-estimate the gravity of such a threat.'

'You must take every opportunity of making it public that no amount of threats, or even action, will have any effect on the Government,' Isabel told her father.

The Prime Minister smiled slightly. 'That will be done, my dear. In the meantime the Commissioner is having a list compiled of all poor Wellacombe's known enemies, as well as of all the people, friendly or otherwise, with whom he is known to have come into-contact for at least twenty-four hours before his death.'

'That's a big job in itself,' commented Lord Arthur absently. His eyes were on Isabel. He was frankly surprised by the grasp and decision she had shown. His admiration was half reluctant. Lord Arthur was not the type of man who admired women easily – or willingly.

'Quite big,' agreed the Prime Minister. 'And how are we getting on with – ' he broke off ' – with Wellacombe's successor, Arthur?'

'Very well indeed, sir. He's quite mastered all the essential points already. But I wish…'

'What?'

'I wish you had given me the chance of introducing the Bill, as Lord Wellacombe's understudy.'

The Prime Minister looked at him. 'No, Arthur. I thought of doing so, of course, and I knew you would be ready if I asked you. But in the circumstances I felt it essential that a member of the Cabinet should do it. I needn't explain why. If no one had volunteered, I should have taken on the job myself. I'd have done so in any case but for this accursed 'flu,' added the Prime Minister, not without anticlimax.

Isabel's eyes shone. 'That's the way to talk,' she approved fondly. 'I gather, by the way, from the pause you made just now that I'm not to know the name of Lord Wellacombe's successor.'

'No one is to know it,' her father assented. 'We're keeping that a close Cabinet secret. Nobody, outside the Cabinet and Arthur here, will know who is going on with Wellacombe's speech until the man himself actually gets up to do so.'

Isabel nodded. 'That's sensible. You mean, at least, they won't be able to get at *him*?'

'Precisely. Of course, we can't say even yet with absolute certainty that Wellacombe's death was caused by... come in!'

The Prime Minister interrupted himself in response to a tap on the door.

The butler entered with a salver on which reposed two unstamped envelopes. He tendered them to the Prime Minister.

'They are both marked urgent, sir, and Mr Lloyd-Evans asked me to bring you one of them direct, so I thought perhaps in the circumstances...'

'Thank you, Dean.' The Prime Minister nodded his assent to this short-circuiting of one of his private secretaries, to whom in the normal way all communications addressed to the Prime Minister would first be taken.

Dean approached Isabel. 'Mr Comstock is here, miss,' he said in a low voice. 'I have shown him into the drawing-room.'

'Oh, yes. Tell him I'll come in a minute or two.'

The butler left the room and the Prime Minister tore open one of the envelopes. He read the contents and frowned. Then, glancing first at his daughter and afterwards at Lord Arthur, he observed:

'I'm afraid there are some cold feet in the Cabinet already.'

'They want you to postpone the Bill,' Lord Arthur said quickly.

'Yes. You knew?'

'Well, I was approached to sign something...' Lord Arthur looked uncomfortable.

'This letter, no doubt; it's signed by several people. Who approached you?' The Prime Minister spoke peremptorily.

'Mr Comstock, sir.' Lord Arthur glanced uneasily at Isabel as he mentioned the name of her fiancé. 'Comstock' was the name of the First Lord of the Admiralty. Isabel met his look with an expressionless face.

'You should have told me. This must be stopped at once. Some of these people – ' He glanced at the signatories to the document in his hand. 'Some of these people may be talking. We can't have it said that there is division in the Cabinet on such an issue. They ask me to call another meeting and put the question of postponement to a vote. It's quite impossible. Ring the bell for Verreker, please, Arthur. I must deal with this at once.'

Lord Arthur rose. As he crossed the room towards the bell-push the Prime Minister opened the other envelope.

An exclamation broke from him as he read.

'What is it, father?' Isabel asked anxiously.

The Prime Minister looked at her with a face that had paled perceptibly.

'This business is even more serious than we believed,' he said, with a sigh. 'I'm driven to fear there is a leakage in the Cabinet itself.'

'In the Cabinet?' echoed Lord Arthur, startled, his hand still outstretched towards the bell.

'How else is one to account for this?' The Prime Minister read out in a voice that was not quite steady: '"If Middleton attempts to make that speech this afternoon, in accordance with what was arranged at the Cabinet Meeting yesterday, he will die as surely as Wellacombe did. This is the only warning."'

There was a silence.

'Good heavens!' exclaimed Lord Arthur, deeply shocked. 'You're right, sir. Somebody must have been talking.'

'In the Cabinet?' Isabel said. 'It's impossible.'

'I don't like to think it.' The Prime Minister looked grave and worried. 'Still, that certainly appears the only explanation.'

'And it is Mr Middleton who…?' Isabel hesitated.

Her father nodded. 'There can be no harm in your knowing now. Yes, Middleton was to take poor Wellacombe's place. But in view of this… Arthur, go and tell Verreker to ring him up at once and ask him to come to see me, will you? Of course, he must be given every opportunity to withdraw his offer now.'

Lord Arthur hurried to the door. 'If I know Middleton,' he said, 'that's the last thing he'll do. And I'll ring up Scotland Yard myself, shall I? Sir Hubert will want this new note as soon as possible. Is it signed "The Brown Hand" again?'

'Yes. It's just the same as the others. Oh, dear, I ought not to be holding it, ought I? It will have to be examined for fingerprints, of course. Oh, and Arthur! Keep this new development to yourself. I'll tell Middleton, but none of the others. Isabel…'

'Of course, father.'

As the door closed behind Lord Arthur, the Prime Minister sighed.

'I ought not to have read that note out aloud,' he said.

'You can trust Arthur,' Isabel returned quickly.

'Arthur, yes. And Middleton. And you, my dear. But whom else? Lane… Pelham…'

'Eric, of course,' Isabel said, a shade less quickly. Eric was Mr Comstock, the First Lord.

'Oh, Eric, of course, yes,' agreed the Prime Minister.

Father and daughter looked at each other. Both felt rather than knew what was in the other's mind; neither referred to it in words.

'I'd better go,' said Isabel. 'You're going to be busy.'

She rose, kissed him swiftly, and walked out of the room. The Prime Minister looked after her. That she was fond of him he knew, but Isabel was not a demonstrative girl; he was wondering when she had kissed him last.

The Colonial Secretary was the first arrival. Without wasting time the Prime Minister showed him the new anonymous letter and explained why he had sent for him.

'As you see, Middleton, our secret has somewhat mysteriously leaked out. I asked you to come round so that I could tell you that in the circumstances I consider yesterday's arrangement to be automatically wiped out.'

'You mean…?'

'That I can't possibly ask you now to make that speech.'

'You never did ask me,' the Colonial Secretary returned bluntly. 'I volunteered.'

'Quite so. Well, I'll put it more strongly. I think you should reconsider your offer, because I believe…'

'Yes?'

'I believe that your life is in danger. I'm quite sure,' the Prime Minister corrected himself, 'that your life is in danger.'

'And if I withdraw, who will take my place?' Middleton asked, with a grim smile.

'It might be possible to make some arrangement to obviate the necessity for anyone to take your place.'

'Do without the speech altogether?' Middleton frowned. 'That would look damnable like weakness.'

'It would *be* weakness,' the Prime Minister agreed equably. 'And therefore, my dear Middleton, if you wish me to speak plainly, I should take your place myself.'

'I have no intention of withdrawing.' Middleton's voice was brusque. 'None at all.'

'That is your considered decision?'

'That is all I have to say, Prime Minister.'

The Prime Minister looked at him, hesitating for a moment before he spoke.

'Thank you, Middleton,' he said.

He knew that Middleton would not wish him to say more.

chapter four

Much Ado and More Talk

Sir Hubert Lesley, Commissioner of the Metropolitan Police, was brisk, dapper, and efficient. Unlike some of his recent predecessors, he had never been a soldier but always a policeman, graduating through the Indian Police to the Chief Constableship of an important county, and thence to Scotland Yard. There was nothing about police or detective work that he did not know.

He arrived at Downing Street with a complete suite, consisting of the Deputy Commissioner, Sir Malcolm Burns, the Assistant Commissioner for the Criminal Investigation Department, Mr Willis-Carter, Chief Constable Nevilson, Superintendent John Armstrong, of the CID, and Superintendent Burrow, of the Special Branch. There were also a number of detective-inspectors, sergeants and constables, but these were left outside.

Only Sir Hubert himself and the Deputy Commissioner penetrated as far as the Prime Minister's library. The others at once set to work interrogating Dean, the butler, the Prime Minister's secretaries, Isabel, Lord Arthur, and anyone else they could find to interrogate.

In the library Sir Hubert gave the new anonymous letter a brief but careful examination.

'Humph, yes. So far as I can see, exactly the same as the others. Same paper and, so far as I'm competent to pronounce, same writing – not even disguised. I'll put my experts on to it, of course, but I doubt whether they'll be able to make any more out of it than the others. Nothing to go on, you see. Might have been written by any of London's seven million inhabitants. The delivery, that's our only hope.'

'My butler says it had been pushed under the front door,' said the Prime Minister.

'Lying on the hall mat, just inside the front door,' observed Sir Hubert, more correctly. 'Yes, well, that's hopeful. I've had three Special Branch men hanging around outside, to say nothing of the constables on duty – usual men replaced by detective constables. If it really was pushed under the door we ought to get him. They couldn't have failed to spot him. Yes, I think he may have put himself in the cart this time.'

'I sincerely hope so,' said the Prime Minister fervently.

'Well, Superintendent Armstrong has that in hand. Let's see, it was picked up about half an hour ago, and delivered to you presumably at once?'

'Dean saw it when he went to answer the bell to let in Comstock.'

'Ah, trust Comstock to be where the fun is. Never knew such a fellow. Always in the thick of everything. Yes, well, it'll be difficult to say the exact time of delivery.'

'There are always people coming or going in this hall,' said the Prime Minister, in a tired voice. 'It can't have been there for more than a few minutes.'

'No, of course. Well, I don't think there's anything more I can do here, Prime Minister. If you'll excuse me, I'll go and hear what the outside men have to report. Coming, Burns?'

The Deputy Commissioner, who had remained entirely silent during the interview, prepared to follow his chief.

'Oh, Sir Hubert!' The Prime Minister detained them for a moment. 'In a few hours Middleton will be speaking in the House. I want you to strain every resource in your Department to guarantee his safety.'

The Commissioner looked at him. 'We'll do our damnedest, sir,' he said.

The Prime Minister lay back in his chair. He felt a very tired old man, and tired of being Prime Minister, too. He was glad of a few minutes' solitude.

Outside, the Commissioner received his report. It was brief, decisive, and perplexing. Except for Mr Comstock and Mr Lloyd-Evans, during the period in question no person had approached the front door of No. 10, Downing Street.

'Damn!' said the Commissioner.

He waited for a few moments until the brief interrogations had been completed, then withdrew himself and his suite across Whitehall and back into Scotland Yard.

There, in the Commissioner's own room, a rapid conference was held. The results of all the interrogations were rapidly pooled, but nothing very helpful seemed to emerge. Superintendent Armstrong pointed out that the envelope appeared to have been trodden on as it lay on the mat, but whether by Dean or Mr Comstock it was impossible to say; in any case, there seemed small significance in the fact. None of the servants except Dean had anything in the slightest degree relevant to say. Both the Prime Minister's private secretaries who were actually on the premises at the time had been engaged on their own work, in their own rooms, and knew nothing. All the men on duty outside the house were agreed on three things − that they had kept a careful watch on the front door of No. 10 with frequent reference to their own watches, that during the ten minutes to which the inquiry had narrowed down no one but Mr Comstock and Mr Lloyd-Evans had approached the door, that it was quite impossible that anyone else could have done so and remained unobserved. In fact the only curious item in the whole affair was that Mr Lloyd-Evans should have done up his shoelace on the top step, walked quickly back into Whitehall, and then come back to the front door apparently to push something through the letter-box.

Mr Comstock, who had still been in the drawing-room with Isabel when the commissioner and his suite arrived, had already been interrogated, without much use. He had not noticed the letter lying on the mat when Dean let him in; he may have stepped on it so far as he knew; he remembered that Dean had stooped down just after admitting him and retrieved something from the floor, no doubt the letter, he had heard nothing about its contents till the police spoke to him, not even from his fiancée.

'Well,' said the Commissioner, 'someone had better go and see Lloyd-Evans. In fact, I suppose I'd better go myself. The man had the jitters, obviously, presumably over that letter of his; didn't know how the PM would take it; jeopardising political career and all that; hence the toying with the shoelace and right-about-turn into Whitehall before he could make up his mind to deliver; probably we'll find he had a quick one round the corner to work his courage up; then he walks slap up to the letter-box and shoves the thing in. I don't suppose he noticed anyone else while he was monkeying about, but we have to ask him.'

The Commissioner reached for his hat.

Mr Lloyd-Evans was at his desk at the Board of Trade. To the typists and messenger boys he was a great man, was Mr Lloyd-Evans; to the permanent officials he was a bore, as all Cabinet Ministers must be, but less of a bore than some because he never interfered with them and, on the whole, did as they told him; to the Commissioner he was a badly frightened man.

'Sorry to bother you and all that,' said the Commissioner, 'but there's something in the wind again. Did you know the Prime Minister has had another of these anonymous letters?'

'F-from the B-brown H-hand?' stammered Mr Lloyd-Evans.

'From the Brown Hand,' agreed the Commissioner grimly.

'Oh, dear! oh, dear!' Mr Lloyd-Evan's white hands writhed agitatedly together on his exiguous lap. 'They'll kill poor Middleton – I'm certain they will. The Prime Minister really should postpone the Bill, he really should. It's – it's murder to ask a man to get up and introduce it, when – '

'Why Middleton?' cut in the Commissioner.

'Middleton?' Mr Lloyd-Evans blinked at him.

'Why should it be Middleton who'll be killed?'

'Why, because it's Middleton – Oh!' The President of the Board of Trade pulled himself up with a jerk. He looked at the Commissioner with suspicion. 'You know, don't you?'

'I do, as it happens.' The Commissioner was thinking that perhaps it was not so surprising after all if a close Cabinet secret leaked out. Perhaps the surprising thing would be if a Cabinet secret were ever kept. Given a few Lloyd-Evanses… and the type was common enough… 'But if I hadn't, I should now.'

'If you hadn't obviously known, I should not have mentioned the name,' returned Mr Lloyd-Evans with dignity. The grip he had taken upon himself wilted as quickly as it had been born. The frightened look sprang into his face. 'Er – did you mention another of these anonymous letters? What did it say?'

'I'll tell you in a minute. But, first, Mr Lloyd-Evans, will you tell me this: why did you stop to do your shoelace up on the step of No. 10, Downing Street before delivering the letter you had for the Prime Minister?'

Mr Lloyd-Evans' eyes opened wide. 'Do up my shoelace? I'm quite sure I didn't.'

'What did you do, then?'

'Why, I just walked up to the front door, gave my letter to the butler, and walked away again. What else should I do?'

'That was the second time you were in Downing Street? I mean, after you came back from the Whitehall direction?'

'What on earth are you talking about, Lesley?' asked Mr Lloyd-Evans, huffily. 'I never came *back* from the Whitehall direction. I came from it. I was only in Downing Street once. And I can't imagine what all this talk about shoelaces is. Kindly explain.'

'Damn!' said the Commissioner again, and explained.

Mr Lloyd-Evans was indignant. He was also incredulous.

'Impersonating *me*? Fantastic! Preposterous! Why on earth should anyone want to impersonate me?'

The Commissioner explained again, rapidly and patiently.

'They must have got wind of the fact that you were to deliver this letter of yours in Downing Street, and no doubt they hoped that your double appearance, so to speak, wouldn't be noticed. And, after all,' added the Commissioner, stifling a smile as he contemplated the indignant countenance opposite him, rather like that of a peevish owl, 'after all, you wouldn't be so difficult to impersonate, with that moustache of yours and those spectacles. As an actor, you'll appreciate that.'

The President of the Board of Trade flushed angrily. In his young and more giddy days he had made quite a reputation as an amateur actor, and it had actually been a serious question with him whether he should bend his ambitions towards the professional stage or towards politics. Having chosen the latter he hated to be reminded of the former.

'Well,' he said coldly, 'if that's all the help I can give you – '

The Commissioner rose. 'Yes, it is. Thanks. Good morning.'

Back again in Scotland Yard he told his Superintendents of the interview.

'So the only blessed clue we can get,' he summed up, 'is that there are people working this thing who are right on the inside circle. Otherwise, how could they have known of this Round Robin of Lloyd-Evans'? Well, if that's all we've got, work on that.'

It was a busy morning in Ministerial circles. While Mr Lloyd-Evans was entertaining the Commissioner of Police at the Board of Trade, Lord Arthur, at the India Office, was called away from his coaching of Middleton to listen to a plea from the First Lord of the Admiralty.

Mr Comstock put the case with bluff frankness, as chap to chap.

'This thing's got to be called off,' he said. 'It's all round the place about Middleton now. You wouldn't sign our little petition to the Prime Minister before the news leaked out. It's up to you to make amends now. We can't send Middleton to his death. That's what it amounts to, you know. There's a strong feeling against it. The PM would never get a Cabinet vote in favour. You go and have a word with him, old chap. He might listen to you, when he won't listen to us. Tell him it's madness to persist with the Bill till these fellows have been caught. Give the police forty-eight hours. That's all: forty-eight hours. Damn it, they can't work miracles. But they'll have the lot of 'em within forty-eight hours, if I know Lesley. Come on, now, Arthur. You cut along and see the Prime Minister and – '

'I'm sorry, sir,' interrupted Lord Arthur, in formal tones. He disliked Mr Comstock for himself alone, apart from his dislike of him as the future husband of Isabel Franklin. (How could Isabel contemplate throwing herself away like that? How little one knows about one's childhood playmates!) 'I'm sorry, but it would be quite out of place for me to attempt to advise the Prime Minister.'

'Stuff and nonsense!' replied the First Lord, and began all over again.

At much the same time the Prime Minister was reluctantly receiving a deputation in his library.

The deputation was headed by Mr S P Mansel, MP. This alone was sufficient indication of the deputation's importance, for Mr S P Mansel was to the world of finance rather what an exceedingly prosperous outside broker is to the Stock Exchange: that is to say, unorthodox, adventurous, and quite improperly successful. There were indeed few financial pies, so long as they combined both magnitude and unorthodoxy, with, of course, the chance of large profits, in which Mr S P Mansel was rumoured not to have a finger, from shipping arms to Spain to obtaining concessions from insecurely throned Eastern potentates; and usually rumour was not very wrong. Mr Mansel was known to have been interesting himself lately in India, which no doubt accounted for his presence at the head of this deputation. For the rest he was a small man, slightly bald, slightly plump, slightly unimpressive for one with so many desperate financial deeds to his credit, with a manner quiet but a little fussy, and a reputation for ruthlessness which he deplored in public and justified in private. He represented West Watford.

Mr Mansel came to the point at once. In spite of the Prime Minister's orders and the precautions taken, the Cabinet's secret was now no secret at all. There was no member of the house which did not know all about the Brown Hand and the fate threatened to the introducer of the Indian Restriction Bill, and the House was perturbed for its Cabinet. The deputation represented no fewer than a hundred and fifty members, of all political parties, united to urge on the Government the advisability of postponing the introduction of the Bill until those behind the outrage on Lord Wellacombe were safely in jail.

Mr Mansel spoke briefly, but with earnestness and some degree of eloquence.

'My own position at the head of this deputation testifies to the serious view I take of the affair,' he told the Prime Minister, 'for it is probably known to you that my actual interests would be much better served by this Bill being passed into law as soon as possible. I have heavy commitments in India, but already they are less heavy than they were; for property belonging to my companies has been burnt, stores looted, and strikes proclaimed. Nothing would suit me better than the severest measures to restrict this anarchy. But I am not considering my interests. I am considering nothing but the lives of valuable public servants, which ought not to be jeopardised unnecessarily. To postpone the Bill for a few days would make no difference to our prestige even in India itself. There are ways even of dropping it altogether with nothing but credit. But we do ask you, Mr Prime Minister, most seriously to consider whether even a trifling question of prestige can be set against the lives of men who have served the country well and whom we wish to see continuing to serve it.'

'Gentlemen,' replied the Prime Minister wearily, 'I sympathise with the feelings of humanity which have prompted your visit, but I regret that what you suggest is impossible. No British Government could follow the course that you advocate. This Bill must and shall be passed through the House in the usual way, without delay. And I would remind you that each day's delay means the lives of literally scores of loyal Indian subjects. To set those against any possible threat to members of the Government is out of the question.'

In much the same terms, and at much the same time, the Foreign Secretary was dismissing yet another deputation, from responsible Indians who were in London at the moment. This was headed by no less a person than the Maharajah of Ghanjia, who put forward the argument (which the Foreign Secretary knew quite well to be a fact) that the nefarious activities against which the Bill was directed were being carried out by quite a small group of persons. The object of this group was to obtain the independence of their native country, nothing more and nothing less. They were working on terrorist lines, because they believed that terroristic lines paid; the example of Ireland was their inspiration. Apart, however, from the outrages for which they were responsible, they were negligible. The great mass of the Indian people did not desire severance from Great Britain, and could not be either persuaded or intimidated into desiring it; the native princes desired it less than anyone else. The proposed Bill gave the terroristic group an importance which they did not deserve. The Government in India already had adequate powers to deal with the agitators, if only it would use them. It would be not yielding to threats and force to shelve the Bill altogether and apply with vigour the powers which already existed.

The Foreign Secretary, answering for the India Office, regretted that in the opinion of the British Government the Bill was necessary; the Government's intention was to pass it into law as quickly as possible. Threats and attempts at intimidation were neither here nor there.

It might have seemed to a stranger in Downing Street that the Government was in a small minority, and the Prime Minister himself in almost a minority of one. Reports, however, from the party organisers indicated that the country as a whole, having by this time obtained more than an inkling of the facts, was united in support of the Government's firmness. The country, in fact, did not mind how many Ministers it sacrificed so long as terrorism was defied and intimidation ignored.

Perhaps the Prime Minister was able to find some consolation in this as he sat down to lunch after his harassing morning. Not even Prime Ministers, however, can always expect to enjoy their lunch in peace. Not half a dozen mouthfuls had passed his lips when he was summoned by an agitated secretary once more to the telephone.

It was the Commissioner of Police at the other end of the line, scarcely less agitated than the Prime Minister's secretary.

'That you, sir? Exceedingly sorry to interrupt your lunch, but thought I'd better report to you personally at once. We've discovered how it was done.'

The Prime Minister was torn between a horror of State secrets passing over the telephone and intolerable curiosity. Curiosity won.

'How?' he asked.

'Poisoned thorn,' replied the Commissioner briefly. 'We went over his clothing again with a tooth-comb; found it stuck under his coat collar; must have got pushed up there when he was moved. Rushed it round to Sir Angus MacFerris. He identifies the same stuff on it. Asked Sir William to make another examination of the body. He's just reported a minute puncture on left side of the neck; microscope shows traces of the substance round the puncture. What did you say?'

But the Prime Minister had said nothing. Visions of unprincipled natives, propelling poisoned thorns through blowpipes from the Distinguished Strangers' gallery, had left him speechless.

chapter five

A Minister Rises

Sir William Greene, Senior Pathologist to the Home Office, was a man of painstaking disposition, as, indeed, he had need to be. While his colleague, Sir Angus MacFerris, was at work in his laboratory nearly the whole night through, analysing everything analysable that had been brought to him, Sir William had been equally sleepless in reading up everything about curare on which he could lay his hands. It worried Sir William that he had never personally encountered a case of curare poisoning, and though he had imagined himself to have a sound enough working knowledge of the drug it was not long before he found that his knowledge did not work quite so well as he might have wished. Half a dozen telephone calls, which brought half a dozen equally eminent gentlemen out of their beds, confirmed his wish that the murderer had chosen any other substance out of the toxicological list.

Seated in the Prime Minister's library soon after lunch, with Middleton, Lord Arthur, and the Commissioner of Police in attendance too, Sir William explained his difficulties.

'Curares vary so much in strength, and consequently in effect. Different authorities give quite different results, and the recorded cases, both on animals and men, vary enormously. Naturally, the stronger the curare the more quickly it takes effect, and the more quickly death ensues. As regards this particular case, I must admit to considerable perplexity. From the vehicle employed, a thorn, one would have said that the curare must have been of a strength quite unprecedented to cause death; yet the time that elapsed before death seems to point to a very weak extract.'

'Didn't you suggest that snake venom might have been mixed with it, to quicken the action?' put in the Prime Minister.

'I did, to account for the rapid onset of the symptoms – if,' said Sir William, darkly, 'we are correct in relying upon the evidence that seems to point to the onset having been rapid. And I still think that snake venom or some similar substance was mixed with the curare, and this may well have hastened the symptoms; but it would equally seem to have delayed the death, for the best authority we have in this country on curare tells me that a latent period of forty-five minutes or thereabouts after the appearance of the symptoms means that the victim will probably recover. I think, however, that I have a theory which would cover this point.'

'Yes?' said the Commissioner, quickly.

'I should say,' replied Sir William, with maddening deliberation, 'that the intention was not to cause death. In this connection it is interesting to remember that in its native place, that is to say South America, curare is used far more as a paralysing or terrifying agent than as a means of death; though I am bound to add that the natives have an unpleasing habit of torturing their victims to death while they are lying helpless and paralysed by the drug. That, however, is neither here nor there.'

'Interesting idea,' commented the Commissioner. 'But if true, why did he die?'

Sir William shrugged his shoulders. 'He was not a young man. His heart was sound for his age, but…! Possibly there was a sudden respiratory embarrassment, which, in the absence of endotracheal oxygenation, is liable to prove fatal. One can't say.'

'Curare kills by paralysing the breathing system, doesn't it?' asked Lord Arthur.

Sir William inclined his head. 'Eventually, yes. The first symptom is a vague and general muscular weakness, rapidly becoming more intense, with collapse of the legs and arms, drooping of the eyelids, paralysis of the tongue so that speech becomes incomprehensible, the neck muscles unable to support the head, which lolls, and finally, of course, paralysis of the respiratory muscles, leading to death.'

Lord Arthur shuddered slightly. 'Not a nice death, either.'

'A singularly unpleasant death,' agreed Sir William equably, 'with consciousness active to the last.'

'You hear, Middleton?' said the Prime Minister.

'I hear,' Middleton replied grimly.

The Prime Minister glanced at the others. 'I asked you to come here, because I want Middleton to understand exactly the degree and the nature of the danger, and the measures which you, Sir Hubert, are taking to guard against it. Equally I want Middleton to realise that he has still time to withdraw, and none of us will think the worse of him if he does.'

'He's a fool if he doesn't,' said Sir Hubert bluntly. 'A danger you know and understand, yes: no need to funk that. But a danger you don't know and can't face... well, no man can be called a funk for side-stepping while there's time. Give us forty-eight hours, sir, and hold Middleton back till then.'

'No,' said Middleton, with his tight, unhumorous little smile.

The Prime Minister sighed. 'Well, shelving that for the moment, have you anything else to tell us, Sir William? Anything that can give Middleton any hint as to how to protect himself?'

Sir William leaned back in his chair, crossed his knees, and hooked his thumbs into his waistcoat. 'We-e-e-ll,' he said, and communed with the ceiling. 'Yes, there is one point. I mentioned the unlikelihood, not to say impossibility, of a single thorn being able to inject subcutaneously sufficient curare to cause death. But supposing there were more than one thorn?'

'Eh?' said the Commissioner. 'But there was only one. I'll swear to that. Since we found that one I've had the floor examined where he was standing, and every place where the body rested, in case anything dropped out of his clothing. There was no other thorn.'

'Nevertheless,' Sir William replied benignly, 'I have reason to believe there was at least one other thorn. For only a short time ago, thinking I would make another and still more exact examination of the exposed parts of the body, I found beside the scratch on the ball of the thumb, which I had already reported, another small puncture; and I have already been able to establish that both this, and the scratch itself, show definite traces of curare on the surrounding skin.'

'The devil they do,' observed the Commissioner, blankly.

'Yes,' said Sir William.

There was a silence.

'But how could thorns possibly have been used?' demanded Lord Arthur. 'I mean, presumably they must have been propelled somehow. A – a blowpipe is too fantastic. And one can't see a Member throwing them from the back benches, like darts. The whole thing's a nightmare.'

Sir William bestowed on him a quizzical look.

'But why assume that they were used on the floor of the House itself? Why shouldn't someone have – er – stuck them into the poor man as he was passing along a corridor?'

'Because of the time factor,' Lord Arthur replied, glibly, remembering the information Isabel had given him. 'Onset of symptoms within ten minutes, and – '

'Ten minutes?' interrupted Sir William. 'Not at all. The symptoms can make their appearance at any time, according to the strength of the curare, from five minutes till forty-five after the attack.'

'Then I'm all at sea again,' said Lord Arthur, helplessly; for when experts disagree, as it seemed that in the matter of curare they did, a mere layman had best keep quiet.

'Anyhow,' said the Prime Minister, 'let us take comfort from Sir William's theory that it was not intended to kill poor Wellacombe, and hope that the intention in the case of his successor is equally absent. Nevertheless, we should like to hear what Sir Hubert proposes.'

'Well,' said the Commissioner, briskly, 'I think I can guarantee him immunity at any rate until he's on the floor of the House; so if the attack was made on Wellacombe before he reached his seat and they're relying on the same plan again, we ought to be able to put a spoke in their wheel. He's to speak at half-past three, isn't he?'

Middleton nodded.

'Very well. Till 3.20, with your permission, Prime Minister, I shall keep him here in this house, remaining with him myself. It's just past a quarter to three now, so I'm afraid you'll have to put up with my company for the next half-hour, Middleton. At 3.20 a closed and, so far as we use 'em in this country, bullet-proof police car will come to a halt outside the front door, facing towards Whitehall. And when I say bullet-proof, I can promise it will be thorn-proof at least. Two of my best men will meet us at the entrance to the House; others are posted in the Yard, the lobby, and at every useful point. The other two and myself will accompany Middleton right up to the Speaker's chair, taking care that no person, not even the Chancellor of the Exchequer himself, comes within arm's length of him from the moment he leaves the car till the moment he passes the Chair.

'According to our time-programme, he should be in his seat by 3.28. Once he's there, he ought to be safe. Lord Arthur tells me he'll be sitting just behind. There'll be other Ministers on either side, and Lord Arthur has undertaken to get two Members whom he can trust absolutely on either side of him. That should make a fair screen for Middleton's sides and back. As to the rest, we thought it better not to close the Public Gallery officially, but I think any unknown member of the public who tries to get in this afternoon will find there is no seat left. I've made arrangements for enough Distinguished Strangers whom I can rely on to act as unofficial escort to any Distinguished Strangers whom I don't know personally, particularly foreign ones. All Indians have been given a strong hint that they would help us by keeping away. I don't know what more we can do – and I don't know how anyone with a blowpipe is going to get through that cordon,' added the Commissioner with force.

The Prime Minister nodded. 'That certainly sounds effective.'

'Good lord!' observed Middleton, with undisguised scorn.

'Do you really mean we're to be driven by this bluff to such lengths?'

'Middleton, my dear fellow, I don't for one minute believe it is bluff,' said the Prime Minister, earnestly. 'Neither does the Commissioner. We half assumed it was bluff before, and poor Wellacombe paid the penalty of our neglect. This time I intend to run no risks.'

'Then you really want me to conform with Sir Hubert's somewhat elaborate programme, Prime Minister?'

'I not only want you to,' said the Prime Minister, with the quiet authority which he knew how to use at times. 'I insist on it.'

Middleton shrugged his shoulders. 'Then, of course, in that case…' His tones were frankly sceptical. 'But personally I think we're making a mistake. We're letting this fellow, whoever he is, see that we're frightened by his threats. I should much prefer to walk over to the House from my own office, in the usual way.'

'No,' said the Prime Minister.

Middleton, having made his protest, subsided.

The Prime Minister turned to Sir Hubert Lesley.

'You've made no progress in tracing the man who left that note this morning?'

'The feller disguised as Lloyd-Evans?' The Commissioner shook his head. 'None, I'm afraid. We're up against a blank wall there. Unfortunately, you see, those spectacles and that drooping moustache of his make it easy for anyone with only moderately similar features and build to pass muster for a few minutes as Lloyd-Evans, with the help of the right sort of coat and hat. The reports agree that the man apparently put something through the letter-box, or pretended to, and then knelt down to tie his shoelace. Naturally, thinking he was Lloyd-Evans, my men paid no particular attention to him beyond noting his movements. Obviously the shoelace was a blind to push his note quickly under the door.'

There was a little pause.

'But why *under* the door?' Lord Arthur asked. 'Why not through the letter-box in the ordinary way?'

'Just what we've been asking ourselves, naturally,' replied the Commissioner. 'But we can't find the answer. Must have been some point in it, though not necessarily very much. These people have their kinks and fads, you know. Perhaps he thought that depositing his warning on the hall mat was a more dramatic way of doing things. Or perhaps he thought it might throw suspicion on someone inside the house.'

'It's queer, all the same,' Lord Arthur murmured, as if not quite satisfied. 'I should have thought that at all costs he'd have wanted to avoid being unnecessarily conspicuous.'

'Well, perhaps there's a pointer there. What if he wanted to be conspicuous? That would mean he was deliberately trying to throw suspicion on Lloyd-Evans himself. Though why he should want to do that, Heaven knows. Well, I've nothing more to report, Prime Minister, so no doubt you'd like Middleton and me to be getting along.'

'Yes, no doubt you'd better. Arthur, take Sir Hubert and Middleton down to the morning-room, will you? Isabel will be somewhere about. Tell her they're not to be disturbed. By the way, I take it that you and Middleton have finished conferring?'

'I think so, sir,' Lord Arthur replied, holding the door open for the other two to pass. 'He has the notes I made out for him, and the full text of Lord Wellacombe's speech. I don't think there's any more we can do together.'

The Prime Minister nodded dismissal, and the three made their way downstairs.

Downing Street outside was empty, but for the plain-clothes men. A hundred yards away the traffic in Whitehall made the familiar prosaic rumble. It seemed strange to Lord Arthur, as it did to the Commissioner, to realise that the life of their charge, a Minister of the Crown, was in danger. It seemed still stranger to reflect that the danger was a threat against the Government of the greatest Empire the world has ever known. It seemed strangest of all to reflect that the danger, hidden, baffling and deadly, was a real one and that the entire forces of the said Empire had hitherto proved inadequate to cope with it.

As if in answer to such thoughts the Commissioner remarked, as they turned into the morning-room: 'Anyhow, there isn't an Indian in this country that we haven't got the tabs on.'

'You still think it's an Indian then?' Lord Arthur asked.

The Commissioner shrugged his shoulders. 'India's at the bottom of it. That's plain enough. But as to who may be doing the actual dirty work…' He passed into the morning-room.

Lord Arthur hesitated for a moment, then went in search of Isabel. There was a bare twenty minutes to wait, and his nerves were on edge. Isabel, he thought, with her sound common sense and calm, might prove a sedative for them.

Isabel, however, was not at home. Dean told him that she had already gone over to the House, to occupy the seat she had bespoken in the Ladies' Gallery. After telling the butler that no one was to be allowed to approach the morning-room until after the two persons now in it had left the house, Lord Arthur made his way into Downing Street.

Unconsciously he found himself hurrying down Whitehall. There was plenty of time, but he felt suddenly that he must hurry. Something might be happening in the House; he ought to be at his post.

His post was on the second bench, just behind his Chief, so that if any information were wanted at the last moment he could go out and get it. Middleton would sit on the front bench, next to the seat occupied by the Prime Minister when the latter was there to lead the House. The Chancellor of the Exchequer, who was still acting as Leader, was already in his place behind the despatch box; beyond the vacant space which Middleton was to occupy was again Lloyd-Evans.

Lord Arthur glanced at Lloyd-Evans as he took his own seat. The man looked quite ghastly; he was sickly pale, and his forehead was damp. He seemed to Lord Arthur like a man in the last extremity of dread and terror; but what had Lloyd-Evans to fear?

The House itself was packed.

Every seat was occupied, and members jostled each other on the floor below the gangway. It was no longer a secret who was to step into the dead man's shoes that afternoon to continue the speech which had been so disastrously interrupted the day before, and all eyes were anxiously fixed on the vacant space on the Government front bench. Lord Arthur looked at it too, and shivered a little. It was only twenty-four hours since a fine, honest man had died there, in the course of his duty; already it seemed like so many weeks.

In a perfunctory way the House concluded its earlier business. Even the most truculent of Independents seemed unwontedly satisfied with the answer they received to their awkward questions. A curious hush made the low tones of Ministers strangely significant.

Just before Middleton was due, Lord Arthur felt a nudge from behind. Turning, he saw Mr S P Mansel leaning towards him.

'Call Middleton off,' he whispered urgently. 'For God's sake call him off. It could be done somehow. Otherwise it's death. I know it. You know I have interests in India. I have sources of private information too. These men mean what they say. If Middleton comes into the House, he'll die.'

Lord Arthur shook his head. 'It can't be called off now,' he whispered back.

The other's words had increased his anxiety. Mansel knew what he was talking about. A warning from that quarter was a genuine one. But what could be done now?

Suddenly a little whispering sigh went up from the crowded benches. Middleton had come in.

He sat down fairly and squarely in his usual attitude of alert stolidity, arms folded, eyes looking straight ahead. One would have said he was unconscious of being the focus of attention, but for the slightly contemptuous little smile playing round the corners of his mouth. Those who were watching saw him straighten up with something of a jerk, before smoothing down the back of his neck with his hand in his usual mannerism; a mannerism as familiar to the cartoonists as that of Lord Wellacombe's grasp of his lapels.

He had been sitting there scarcely thirty seconds before the Speaker called upon him.

There was a little susurration as pent-up breath was softly expelled. Then Middleton rose briskly to his feet.

chapter six

A Minister Falls

In the Press Gallery all was instant bustle.

Some of the reporters made their pencils fly over the paper, dashing off brief descriptions of the scene below them; others rushed away at once to telephone the news to their various papers that the speech had at any rate begun. It was as if the name of Lord Wellacombe's successor, perfectly well known to the reporters in advance, had, so to speak, been officially released. Within an unbelievably short time the news would be available on the streets, to be bought by an eager public who, in spite of official reticence, had now more than an inkling that something was amiss and whose curiosity had been further stimulated by hints in the morning editions from an otherwise loyal Press.

A request had in fact been sent round to editors that nothing definite was to be stated in print about the threats to the Government, and public alarm at all costs was not to be raised; but though the letter of the request had been strictly observed, it had not been held to cover the most tantalising and luscious hints that events of terrific national importance, not to say peril, might be expected at any moment. The result might well have been to rouse public excitement even higher than if the truth had been baldly and calmly stated; but in point of fact so many people had so good an idea of what the truth was, and were so busy passing it on to others still in ignorance, that the public, beginning to realise that it was only their Ministers and not themselves who were threatened, felt less of alarm than of a sporting interest in the whole business. The idea of the

Cabinet team going in to bat, as it were, one by one against an invisible demon bowler, appealed to their sporting instincts.

In the meantime matters in the House were pursuing their outwardly normal course.

Middleton began his speech with a sympathetic though noncommittal reference to his predecessor in the duty, delivered in his usual blunt, almost curt tones. The Government must not be thought lacking in respect for a great figure, he explained, in deciding to push ahead with their programme with no interval. The welfare of a great nation was at stake, and it could be served best only by this Bill being passed into law at the earliest possible moment; in such circumstances, whatever their private feelings might suggest, these must be subordinated to the larger necessity. The Government also, added Middleton flatly, wished to make it public that they were not to be intimidated by any vague threats, or by the very real opposition which existed in certain quarters towards the Bill, from carrying out what they felt to be their urgent duty.

With these few introductory remarks, which served to stretch the tensity of the House to still further lengths, the Colonial Secretary passed on to the more flowing periods of the prepared speech. With a word of apology for troubling the House with remarks which it had already heard once before, he began at the beginning and went steadily ahead.

As the speaker passed into the sentences which he already knew by heart, Lord Arthur glanced at his watch. The hands said twenty-six minutes to four.

By twenty to four there's a good chance, he thought to himself. By a quarter to four we ought to be over the danger-mark.

He glanced up at the Ladies' Gallery, but could not see Isabel behind the heavy grille. Bending forward with his elbows on his knees, he sat staring at the floor, trying to keep his eyes away from his watch.

Slowly the minutes passed. Middleton reached the point at which his predecessor had collapsed, paused for a moment with a touch of drama unusual in him, then read steadily on.

Twenty minutes to four came, a quarter to four, thirteen minutes to four, ten minutes to four. And then it happened.

At exactly six minutes to four Middleton's voice suddenly faltered. He seemed to look down with some surprise towards his legs, and there was an instant's pause while he obviously braced up his sturdy, stocky body against some unknown weakness. He began to read again.

But only for a few minutes. Then he paused again, and slowly lifted a hand towards his eyes, as if he were actually trying to lift up their drooping lids. He splashed a little water with a shaking hand from the carafe into the glass on the table before him. The glass slipped through his fingers on to the floor.

With an almost superhuman effort the Colonial Secretary could be seen to pull himself together. He struggled somehow through another sentence or two, his words becoming more and more blurred, while Members, leaning forward in their seats, watched him with an incredulous horror. Then from under his drooping eyelids he swept a haunted look along the Opposition front bench, muttered weakly a few jumbled words which only those sitting nearest could interpret as 'Not very well... must sit down a minute,' and staggered, his head lolling grotesquely on his shoulder.

The Chancellor of the Exchequer and the President of the Board of Trade both tried to help him on to the seat, but they were too late. Before he could reach it Middleton slumped down, his legs folded up underneath him exactly as had Lord Wellacombe's, and he toppled impotently to the floor.

As one man the House rose to its feet, the silence of awe and disaster stilling the comments of even the most determinedly loquacious. Lord Arthur scrambled over the back of the bench in front of him, followed by Mansel. They reached the fallen man at the same moment, and helped the two ministers to lift him into an easier position. The member for East Surrey reached the little group only a second later. They made way for him, and he grasped Middleton's pulse, while in uncanny silence the House watched, scarcely venturing to breathe.

It was the Home Secretary who put the question that was on everyone's lips.

'Well, man?'

The member for East Surrey looked at him with distaste.

'He's alive,' he said, briefly, 'but...'

Again that curious little sigh rustled through the House. The doctor's words had been spoken in little more than a whisper, but they had carried to every corner.

'The House is adjourned,' said the Speaker, in a low voice.

A tall, burly figure pushed its way without ceremony through the rapidly gathering groups on either side of the Speaker's chair. Sir William Greene had been waiting, filled with anxiety and impatience, in the lobby. Lord Arthur, seeing him coming, hurried to meet him. Together they made their way to the stricken man's side, the others falling back before the pathologist.

Sir William did no more than glance at the helpless man.

'It's all right, my dear fellow,' he said to him, in a curiously gentle voice. 'You're not really so bad as you're feeling. I know exactly what you're feeling. You're quite conscious and can hear and understand everything, but you can't lift a finger. It's alarming, and very unpleasant for you, but the danger's over now. We'll pull you through, at any rate. I'm going to have you taken out of here at once, and in half an hour you'll be pretty well normal again.'

He turned to Lord Arthur.

'There's an ambulance in the Yard, by my orders. Send one of the attendants for the stretcher and the bearers.'

Already the news was round that Middleton was to recover. The atmosphere had lifted instantly. Members smiled with relief, and one or two Ministers even spoke a word or two of encouragement and congratulation to the paralysed victim.

In less than a minute the stretcher-bearers had arrived, lifted the Colonial Secretary deftly on to the stretcher, and carried him with gentle gait from the Floor. It was not until they had actually disappeared from view that anyone thought to ask where Middleton was being taken.

'To the Secretary for India's room,' replied Sir William, shortly. The questioner had been Mr Beamish, the Home Secretary. He looked at Lord Arthur. 'Is Middleton married?'

Lord Arthur shook his head.

'Thank Heaven for that.' He made as if to follow the stretcher.

'But if he's all right...?' said the Home Secretary. 'If he's going to recover...?'

'He isn't,' returned Sir William curtly. 'Within a quarter of an hour he'll be dead. But I couldn't let the poor devil know that. Now I must go and make his dying easier. Ah, Lesley!' He joined the Commissioner, who had been waiting impatiently by the Speaker's chair, and they passed, talking rapidly in low tones, out of the Chamber.

Within half a minute Sir Hubert was back.

'Mr Beamish,' he said, formally, 'I have men at every exit. Have I your confirmation, sir, that no one is to leave here until further orders?'

The Home Secretary looked taken aback.

'Is that necessary?' he asked.

'In my opinion, absolutely,' replied the Commissioner in a wooden voice. 'Sir William agrees with me that Mr Middleton must have been poisoned in this Chamber, *here,* by a person probably still present. It is my duty to recommend to you, sir, that every single person here, on the Floor as well as in the galleries, be searched before leaving.'

The Home Secretary cast a harassed glance round. Preposterous questions about privilege leapt into his mind. To search the whole House of Commons, member by member! The idea was fantastic. And yet…

'Of course we must be searched, and I for one should insist upon it voluntarily.' The dry tones of the Foreign Secretary made Mr Beamish wince. 'The course is no doubt unprecedented, Beamish, but so is the situation. You will, of course, confirm the order.'

'Of course,' muttered the Home Secretary. He pulled himself together. 'Of course,' he repeated, firmly. 'And you'd better begin with the Government front bench.'

The President of the Board of Trade turned a palsied face to Lord Arthur. 'What's this? We're all to be s-searched? But this is prepost – ' He collapsed without warning at the other's feet.

'Good God! Another of us gone?' ejaculated the First Lord of the Admiralty, who looked almost as shaken as the President of the Board of Trade himself. No longer was there the least trace of the breezy sea dog about Mr Comstock.

The member for East Surrey made his second examination of the afternoon.

'No,' he announced. 'He's only fainted.'

'Now why,' the Secretary for the Dominions demanded of the Minister of Health, 'why should Lloyd-Evans faint?'

'Don't ask me,' replied the Minister of Health.

The Commissioner was quietly taking charge.

'There's no need to make an announcement, I think. If you gentleman will just file out in the usual way, my men will see to everything.' He spoke soothingly, as to a body of schoolchildren at an alarm of fire.

'And as the order is my responsibility,' said the Home Secretary, importantly, 'I will be the first. By the way, Commissioner, Sir William gave us no information. I suppose it was – h'm – curare?'

'Oh, it was curare all right. No, sir, please don't step there,' added the Commissioner to the Minister for Agriculture and Fisheries. 'We're keeping that space free.'

'Oh, I'm sorry,' muttered the chidden Minister, with a glance at the two or three plain-clothes men who had already marked out the area on the floor where the Colonial Secretary had stood and fallen and were now gently edging the great men off it.

To search the entire House of Commons sounds a formidable task. Actually, it passed off with remarkable smoothness, though it was nearly two hours before the last Member had filed up to the little groups of Scotland Yard men who were carrying out their task. By their faces these latter revealed that it meant no more to them than the searching of a petty sneak-thief or of any insignificant person pulled in for loitering with intent; but behind those stolid countenances there must have been an unholy joy at frisking a Minister of the Crown. However dignified a bearing one may try to preserve, to be searched by the police is an ignominious procedure at the best of times; and when one cannot help feeling that one is after all rather an important person, the ignominy increases in proportion.

At the exits from the galleries the same procedure was followed. Each man in turn was subjected to no perfunctory search by experienced hands, the contents of every pocket was examined, coats were scrutinised under lapels and collars, trouser turn-ups were made to yield forth their fluff, even the underside of shoes had to be offered to probing eyes. At the exit from the Ladies' Gallery two stalwart police matrons conducted a similar investigation, and Isabel Franklin herself was the first to offer herself to their efforts. Sir Hubert's plans had been thorough. They had been laid to cover the event of death itself, as well as to try to guard against it.

Long before the last person was free to go, the Colonial Secretary was dead, and his body removed from the building. He had died on his stretcher, with no one present but Sir William Greene, Lord Arthur, Sir Angus MacFerris, hastily summoned, and the Commissioner of Police. They hoped that right up till the end he did not know for certain that he must die. It was thought inadvisable to give him morphia, for fear of confusing the subsequent analysis.

Out of all the thousand-odd persons, Members, public attendants, and even Distinguished Strangers, who had undergone the ordeal by search, only one had been examined in private. That one was Mr Lloyd-Evans, and he was given no cause to suspect that the special arrangements in his case were by the express orders of the Commissioner himself. The fainting fit gave those detailed to attend to him an excellent chance to carry out their orders in the most natural way. Supporting him tenderly when he came round in a minute or two, they half led, half carried him out of the Chamber and, with soothing words, took him into one of the private rooms. Still with the same soothing words they there examined him, outside his clothes and inside them, with a thoroughness that was intended to leave nothing to chance. At the same time others were searching the floor in front of his seat, and probing down behind it where the cushions of seat and back met. The Commissioner was not sure whether he really suspected Mr Lloyd-Evans or not, but he was taking no chances.

The results of this methodical work were communicated by Sir Hubert to the Prime Minister when he reported to him personally an hour or so after Middleton's death.

The Prime Minister had insisted upon receiving all reports in person. Sir William had already been to Downing Street, and was now performing the necessary autopsy with the minimum of delay. Lord Arthur had given an account of the scene in the House, and Isabel had contributed her own story.

The Prime Minister's face, as he received Sir Hubert in his library, was drawn with anxiety. Clearly the strain and this twofold shock was telling on him badly, added to the fact that he was a sick man. A week ago he had not looked within ten years of his age. Now he looked ten years more than it.

'It's incredible,' he muttered, waving the Commissioner into a seat. 'Quite incredible. One wouldn't believe that anything like this could happen nowadays. Open assassinations, public servants shot down by fanatics in the street: God knows we've had plenty of them. But this mysterious poisoning... why, it sounds more like a page out of the history of medieval Italy.'

'There's been no analysis made yet,' hesitated the Commissioner, who liked his facts ticketed and proven. 'Sir William says he has no doubt it's curare just the same, but...'

'Oh, Sir William knows. I understand the symptoms are exactly the same as before. In any case you found more – more thorns?'

'Yes,' returned the Commissioner, bluntly. 'There was one stuck in the collar of his coat, right at the back of his neck; one actually in his hair, on the crown of the head where Middleton's hair was pretty thick; and one on the floor. Three.'

'Three,' echoed the Prime Minister, dully.

'And that settles one thing at any rate, sir. The attack must have been made in the House itself, after we'd parted with him. And in that connection...'

The door opened suddenly and Isabel came into the library. The wings of the armchair in which he was sitting hid the Commissioner from her.

'Oh, father,' she cried. 'Have you heard? Surely there must be some mistake.'

'Heard what, my dear?'

'Why, about the arrest.'

'No, what arrest? Have you been able to make an arrest, Lesley?' The Prime Minister sat up alertly.

'Oh, Sir Hubert, I didn't see you.' Isabel came further into the room. 'It's true, isn't it? You've arrested Mr Lloyd-Evans?'

The Prime Minister gasped, dumbfounded. 'Arrested Lloyd-Evans? Lesley, what induced you to take such a step?'

The Commissioner, who had intended to break his awkward news as gently as possible, took his bull by the horns.

'The fact that my men found in his coat pocket a pill-box half full of thorns, Prime Minister. And,' added the Commissioner, grimly, 'Sir Angus has identified the substance with which they were smeared as curare.'

chapter seven

Suspicion at the Board of Trade

'Lloyd-Evans!' muttered the Prime Minister. 'But it's incredible. Isabel's right. There must be some mistake.'

'There's no mistake about those thorns,' returned the Commissioner. 'And it's up to Lloyd-Evans to explain how they got there. Still, perhaps "arrested" is too strong a word. "Detained" would meet the case better.' He turned surprised eyes on Isabel. 'But how did you know, Miss Franklin? I'm keeping it a close secret for the present, naturally.'

'It seems hardly possible to keep any sort of secret these days,' sighed the Prime Minister.

Isabel explained. She had been waiting for Lord Arthur in the lobby. Sir Hubert had been talking to Mr Lloyd-Evans as they passed her; he had his arm persuasively through that of Mr Lloyd-Evans. She had heard the words 'arrest you'.

'That was unfortunate,' said the Commissioner frankly. 'I hope no one else heard. Actually, I was telling him that I had no intention of arresting him. In justice to the man I must admit he seemed quite flabbergasted when I told him what had been found in his pocket; and naturally enough he denied all knowledge of it. In fact he consented quite readily to come to Scotland Yard. I told him that obviously it was my duty to detain him, pending inquiries, and he quite agreed. Altogether,' added the Commissioner dryly, 'nothing could have been more amicable and charming. Still, Miss Franklin, you'll keep all this to yourself, of course.'

'Of course,' said Isabel, a little tartly.

'Isabel, my dear…' The Prime Minister hesitated. 'I think I'd like Arthur to hear this. You might ask Verreker to ring him up and tell him to come back. Or ring him up for me yourself.'

'Certainly, father.'

Isabel walked sedately out of the room. She knew, just as well as her father, that the Commissioner would prefer to speak to the Prime Minister alone. It was not that Sir Hubert, a bachelor of course, distrusted women, Isabel told herself with determined fairness; he was just old-fashioned.

'Now, Lesley.' The Prime Minister's voice was firm again to the point of sternness. 'Please tell me just what's in your mind. There's something more than you've said already, I'm sure.'

'Well…' The Commissioner seemed a little uneasy. 'Well, I'm afraid this will be rather a shock to you, sir; but I'm equally afraid there can't be much doubt about it. Nobody could be more alive than myself to the gravity of the step I've taken; but really, I couldn't see anything else for it. Mind you, Lloyd-Evans isn't *arrested*. He's only detained. It comes to the same thing, I know; but it sounds much better.'

There was a knock at the door.

'Isabel told me you wanted me, sir,' said Lord Arthur's voice. 'Luckily I was upstairs with Verreker.' Lord Arthur had in fact been hanging unhappily about, unable to drive himself back to his own office and half expecting that the Prime Minister would want to see him again.

'Sit down, Arthur. This concerns you as closely as anyone now you're in charge of the Department.' In a few words the Prime Minister told the other what had happened. 'Now, Lesley, if you please. We have to talk this over very closely. I must be satisfied that you had no alternative before this drastic action becomes public knowledge; for I need not tell you what serious repercussions it may have, not merely on this Government in particular, but upon the whole system of Government in this country. In a democracy such as ours the people must feel above all things that their Ministers are beyond reproach. Please tell me exactly why you have "detained" my President of the Board of Trade. I need not say that you must have other reasons beyond the finding of the poisoned thorns in his pocket. The real culprit could have slipped them in there for his own safety…"planted," I believe, is the technical word. Smoke if you want to.'

The Commissioner drew out his cigarette case and offered it mutely to the other two. Selecting one himself, he lit it with somewhat elaborate care.

'You say that someone could have "planted" the thorns on Lloyd-Evans, sir,' he began slowly. 'Well, that's true enough. But isn't it a little unfortunate that Mr Lloyd-Evans should have been chosen *again* to – er – to hold the baby, if I may put it that way? There was that matter of the impersonation, you see. Why choose Lloyd-Evans for that? Well, of course, it's all quite easy to explain away; Lloyd-Evans is easy to impersonate, Lloyd-Evans was going to be in Downing Street in any case, the presence of Lloyd-Evans on your doorstep would cause no comment, and so on. All quite feasible. But doesn't it seem to you, sir, that there's a good deal more of Lloyd-Evans in this business than there's any right to be? Who, for instance, was the most nervous man in the Cabinet? Lloyd-Evans. Who thought the Bill ought to be dropped (I'm told, even after the first apparently insignificant anonymous note)? Lloyd-Evans. Who – '

'One moment,' interrupted the Prime Minister. 'I don't think I'm betraying my Cabinet secret if I tell you that Lloyd-Evans was against the Bill from the very first, long before any threatening letters appeared. Very strongly against it. He was averse to meeting violence with stern repressive measures; he wanted to let the movement blow itself out. There were several who thought the same, but Lloyd-Evans certainly expressed himself more strongly than anyone. I'm convinced, too, that his opposition was genuine.'

'Did he try to block the Bill?'

'He certainly did his best to persuade me not to introduce such a Bill. Moreover, he converted more than one member of the Cabinet to his views.'

'Exactly,' exclaimed the Commissioner, not without triumph. 'Lloyd-Evans tried to block the Bill, even before, the first threatening letter appeared. That confirms my theory about him. I'm not concerned with his motives; they may be genuine or they may be crooked. All that matters to me is what a man does. And I've come to the conclusion that, in some way or other, Lloyd-Evans is mixed up in this business. In fact

'I'm not at all sure,' said the Commissioner boldly, 'that he isn't in it up to the neck.'

'That's a terrible accusation,' frowned the Prime Minister. 'You'd better let me have your reasons in full.'

'Well, that impersonation business. There's something decidedly fishy there. When one's carrying a letter which would lay the bearer open to a charge of murder if he were caught with it, one doesn't waste time fiddle-faddling with shoelaces and practically inviting suspicion. One shoves the thing through the letter-box and gets away as quickly as possible while the going's good.'

'You speak as if you weren't sure now that it wasn't Mr Lloyd-Evans himself, Sir Hubert,' Lord Arthur put in. 'I thought you'd quite made up your mind that it was someone impersonating him?'

'So I had,' the Commissioner replied quickly. 'But that was before I'd had a report from one of my men: one of the smartest men we've got, as a matter of fact. He thought Lloyd-Evans was behaving in a very curious manner. The fellow, either Lloyd-Evans himself or someone impersonating him, came along from the direction of Birdcage Walk, went up to the front door of this house and seemed to hesitate; he glanced all round him, and my man says if ever he saw a guilty look that fellow had one. Then he went down on one knee and did up his shoelace, right up against the door. My chap can't say whether he pushed anything under the door or not, and neither can any of the others, because this fellow had his back towards them; but they do say it would have been quite possible for him to have done so. It was an extra-small envelope, you remember, and the fellow could easily have concealed it from view.

'Now, it's a queer thing, but he was wearing gloves. And you remember there were no fingerprints on the envelope. But one doesn't keep one's gloves on to do up a shoelace, does one? After all, the fellow knew he was being watched; my men weren't concealed or anything like that. And he must have known that a little oddity like that, let alone doing up a shoelace on the Prime Minister's doorstep at all, would be quite enough to get him watched all the harder. As I said before, a fellow who wanted to do a simple job like delivering that letter under cover of impersonating Lloyd-Evans would get it done as quickly and as unobtrusively as possible.

'Anyhow, after he'd straightened up he glanced round again, seemed to hesitate once more, and then finally walked off at top speed and turned into Whitehall. And then, of course, I'm hanged if he didn't come back three minutes later, walk up to your front door again briskly enough this time, push in his letter and go off again into Birdcage Walk. That decided my man. He followed Lloyd-Evans back to Carlton House Terrace.'

'Then the second man was Lloyd-Evans all right?' Lord Arthur commented.

'Presumably,' the Commissioner replied dryly. 'Considering, that is, that he let himself in at Lloyd-Evans' front door, gave his hat and coat to Lloyd-Evans' butler, walked up Lloyd-Evans' stairs, kissed Lloyd-Evans' wife, and sat down in Lloyd-Evans' chair in Lloyd-Evans' study to do some of Lloyd-Evans' work before getting back to Lloyd-Evans' room at the Board of Trade. Anyhow, if he wasn't Lloyd-Evans, all I can say is that he deserved to be; and I can't wish anyone worse than that at the present moment.'

'How on earth do you know what he did when he got inside the house?' asked Lord Arthur.

The Commissioner looked at him quizzically. 'How on earth do we find out what goes on inside any house? But we do. It's one of the first duties of a good detective to see through stone walls.'

'Yes, yes,' broke in the Prime Minister impatiently. 'Then I take it that you now believe that the man who delivered that note under the eyes of your detectives was not someone impersonating, but Lloyd-Evans himself?'

'I wouldn't go so far as to say I believe it,' replied the Commissioner with caution. 'I only say that, on balance, the arguments for its being Lloyd-Evans seem rather better than those against.'

'Unless,' pointed out Lord Arthur, 'it was someone deliberately trying to throw suspicion on Lloyd-Evans.'

'That is a possibility,' the Commissioner agreed, 'which we mustn't overlook. But there are, I think, other significant points. Why was Lloyd-Evans in a state of abject funk in the House this afternoon? Why did he faint? Was it just a coincidence that he fainted just after I'd broken the news that everyone in the place was to be searched? Did he know what he had in his pocket, and was the idea of being searched too much for him? I may say I had my suspicions about that faint; it would have been a handy way, perhaps, of being taken out on a second stretcher with a good chance of the search being overlooked; so I asked Sir William to give him a look over. But the faint was genuine. And if so, there seems only one explanation – fright! But fright about what?

'And, then, most significant to my mind of all, who was sitting beside Wellacombe and Middleton? Frith on one side' – Mr Frith was the Chancellor of the Exchequer – 'and Lloyd-Evans on the other. I'd stake my oath on Frith, but… well, there's Lloyd-Evans again, you see.'

Lord Arthur nodded slowly. 'Yes, I see what you mean.'

The Prime Minister did not speak.

'Exactly. Well, I don't think I need elaborate the argument. In the case of Lord Wellacombe we couldn't be certain, but in Middleton's case we *know* that the poison must have been administered on the floor of the House. Apart from the attendant, who gave Middleton a quick brush down before we could stop him – '

'Grieves,' put in Lord Arthur, with a slight smile. 'I don't think you could stop Grieves giving anyone a brush who has the slightest speck of dust on his coat. He's noted for it. In fact it's become a stock joke. We tell him his name ought to have been Jeeves, not Grieves.'

'Yes. Well, apart from him, no one came within arm's length of Middleton till he passed behind the Speaker's Chair: and then he had only Frith and one or two others to pass before he was in his place. And if anyone will explain to me how those thorns could have got into him after that except by being inserted surreptitiously by someone sitting close to him, I'd like to hear it. That means either by Frith, by Lloyd-Evans, by Lord Arthur, or by Stanley or Pengelly, who were sitting on either side of Lord Arthur and against whom there's not a shadow of suspicion. So when identical thorns are actually found in the pocket of one of those persons – well, dash it, sir,' burst out the Commissioner, 'I have to do something about it.'

The Prime Minister was looking very thoughtful. 'Oh, yes, I quite see that. But Lloyd-Evans denies all knowledge of the thorns, you say?'

'He does, yes.'

'And you found the manner of his denials convincing?'

'Up to a point,' said the Commissioner slowly. 'But Lloyd-Evans can act, you know.'

'You have no idea who was in his proximity between your announcement concerning the search and the discovery of the box of thorns in his pocket?'

'You mean, who had the opportunity to put it there? Dozens of people, I'm afraid, sir. There was quite a considerable hurly-burly.'

There was a little silence.

'I suppose it's no good considering the Opposition front bench?' sighed Lord Arthur.

The Prime Minister gave him the ghost of a smile. 'It's true that they seem unusually vehement against the Bill, but I hardly think they would go to such lengths. Dickson is as great a stickler for correct procedure as anyone on our side of the House.' Mr Dickson was the Leader of the Opposition.

There was another silence.

'Well, sir,' said the Commissioner heavily, 'it's for you to say. I take it that this is hardly a matter for the Home Office to decide. Am I to hold Mr Lloyd-Evans, or am I to interrogate him and let him go?'

The Prime Minister stroked his chin. 'My dear Lesley, I fully realise your difficulty, and I admit you've made out a very good case of suspicion against my President of the Board of Trade. But, after all, it is only suspicion, isn't it? Apart from the box of thorns, you have no evidence against him at all; and that, I feel, must be capable of some other explanation. No, I'm sorry, Lesley, but I simply can't see Lloyd-Evans as a murderer. Honestly, can you? Interrogate him by all means to your heart's content. But, after that – let him go. He may know something, or he may not. If he does, no doubt you'll get it out of him. But for myself I can't believe it's possible.'

The Commissioner rose and bowed with some stiffness.

'Very well, sir. I quite understand. I'll question him myself, and that's all. You've no objection, I suppose, to my keeping him under surveillance for a day or two?'

'Of course not,' the Prime Minister replied in a weary voice. 'Keep us all under surveillance, if you're convinced that there's a member of the Cabinet mixed up in it somewhere – and I'm very much afraid there may be that.'

The Commissioner bowed again and took himself off.

'You look dead-beat, sir,' Lord Arthur said. 'Let me send Isabel in to look after you. You must rest. We rely on you, you know.'

The Prime Minister smiled at him affectionately. He had always hoped that his daughter and Lord Arthur might make a match of it; though he knew and admired the strength of the younger man's ambition, which so far had kept him from preoccupying himself with a wife. Moreover, though no one had ever guessed it, the Prime Minister was inclined to share both Lord Arthur's opinion of Mr Eric Comstock and his surprise over Isabel's choice. But the man carried the votes and even the confidence of a surprisingly large section of the public; and a man who can command both votes and confidence will usually find a seat in the Cabinet of even the most upright Prime Minister.

'Yes,' he said, 'I'd better rest, I suppose. I shall have to call another Cabinet meeting to consider this unhappy development. There'll be a great deal of opposition. Dear me, Arthur, I feel a very tired old man.'

'Nonsense, sir. You're convalescent, that's all. You've the energy of any four of us, and you know it. And you mustn't knock yourself up, especially at present, because there's literally no one to take your place. The country would be upside down in a week if anything happened to you.'

'Don't be ridiculous, my dear boy,' smiled the Prime Minister, looking nevertheless not ill-pleased at the other's tribute. 'Frith would take over, and probably manage things a great deal better than me.'

'Frith would never go on with this Bill, sir.'

'No,' said the Prime Minister thoughtfully. 'No; he's supported me over it, but I don't believe he would push it on his own responsibility.'

Lord Arthur hesitated.

'And you, sir?' he ventured. 'Do you still intend to go on with it?'

'I do, Arthur,' the Prime Minister replied quietly. The second reading will be resumed tomorrow afternoon.'

'Then let me take charge of it,' Lord Arthur pleaded. 'I doubt if you'll get another volunteer from the Cabinet, sir. Well, perhaps it isn't fair to say that. But it ought to be my job.'

'No,' said the Prime Minister, with more energy than he had yet spoken. 'In the circumstances there's only one person whose obvious job it is, and that person is myself.'

chapter eight

Assassination Is Not So Dull

The Government of Britain is not a dictatorship. A Prime Minister may have his own ideas about what should be done and he may be thoroughly determined to put them into action; but besides being responsible ultimately to Parliament, he must first convince his Cabinet that his ideas are right. Since, in the normal run of things, a Prime Minister's beliefs are fully shared by his colleagues, and he is to be regarded as little more than the executive of a concerted body of opinion, conflict rarely arises; or, when it does, is concerned with methods rather than principles.

Occasionally, however, on grave matters of policy, Ministers may disagree with their leader; and then, rather than be committed to a course of action which they cannot approve, they resign. In the present case this simple way of maintaining integrity, and incidentally of informing the country that integrity had been maintained, was virtually denied. To resign from a Cabinet threatened with piecemeal disintegration would (it was felt) only place the resigner in the position of those notorious and possibly maligned rats when confronted with a sinking ship: an invidious position, out of which no possible credit could be snatched.

It may have been due to this reflection that the Prime Minister, at his hastily-summoned Cabinet meeting on the evening of Middleton's death, found himself confronted with a determined opposition even more formidable than he had feared; for obviously, if a rat is inhibited for reasons of honour from deserting a leaking ship, the next best thing is to stop the leak. And the leak in this instance very plainly was the Prime Minister's determination to push ahead with the fatal Bill.

The First Lord of the Admiralty even went so far as to put the personal aspect of the situation in plain words.

'It's no good those of us who've been against the Bill resigning,' he told the Prime Minister. The public would only say we'd got cold feet. No good trying to explain we don't believe in coercive methods. They'd just call us funks. And that kind of thing sticks, you know, however little it's deserved. So we've got to stick together. But we can drop the Bill altogether, even if we can't drop out one by one. No question of cold feet, of course,' added the First Lord hastily. 'Just that, as I've said from the very beginning, I don't care about coercive methods.'

'It surely can't have escaped your notice that these persons, whoever they are, are employing coercive methods on us,' the Foreign Secretary remarked acidly. 'Is it your honest belief that we ought to allow such methods to be successful?'

Mr Comstock was stung. 'What's the difference? You want the coercive methods provided for in this Bill to be successful.'

'Exactly,' the Minister of Labour chimed in. 'And that's a big point. Don't you realise that force defeats its own ends? Persecution strengthens, not weakens the persecuted. Draws 'em together. Makes 'em feel they'll stick anything rather than give in. Puts backbone into 'em. Look at the bombing in China. If Japan hadn't bombed the civilian population to blazes, China would have collapsed within six months. And that's just what we'll get if we do the same kind of thing in India. I've said so all along.' It is true that the Minister of Labour had said so all along. He had also said all along that it was absolutely essential to protect the majority of peaceable Indian citizens against the terroristic methods of a militant minority. In this way he had been able happily to combine, as a member of a National Government with a strong Conservative majority, his Liberal principles with the practical needs of the moment.

'Then are we to take it that you are opposed to our continuing with the Bill?' pursued the Foreign Secretary.

'I am,' said the Minister of Labour, committing himself at last.

'I quite agree,' put in the President of the Board of Education.

'I strongly oppose,' said the Secretary of State for War.

'You oppose what?' asked the Lord Chancellor, with every appearance of polite interest. 'Continuing with the Bill?'

'No, no, no. Abandoning it. We can't possibly give in to terrorism. It's unthinkable.'

'I quite agree with you,' said the Lord Chancellor. 'It would be most unorthodox.'

'Exactly,' assented the Home Secretary. *'Most* unorthodox. Besides creating a – hum! – singularly unfortunate precedent.'

'Hear, hear,' muttered the Secretary of State for Air.

'Well, the law and the Services appear to be united,' commented the First Commissioner of Works, in a marked Scottish accent. 'Perhaps one of you gentlemen would volunteer to be the next to follow Wellacombe and Middleton?'

'There's no need to be *personal,* Fraser,' observed the Home Secretary in hurt tones.

'Gentlemen, gentlemen,' the Prime Minister put in at last, in a tired voice. 'We have now been discussing this matter for over an hour, and unanimity on either side appears impossible. I think, seeing the divergence of opinion, that one of us had better sum up the case against continuing with the Bill – perhaps Mr Robinson will do so; and then the Chancellor of the Exchequer can put the arguments in favour. After that we will take a vote. I agree that the course is unusual, but so are the circumstances.'

'Lloyd-Evans would vote against the Bill in any case, Prime Minister,' remarked the First Lord of the Admiralty, with a glance towards the vacant chair of the President of the Board of Trade. 'Will that be taken into account?'

'His vote will be added to those in opposition,' promised the Prime Minister. 'If you please, Robinson…'

'H'rrrhm! Ch'rrrhm! – I take it, Mr Prime Minister,' said the Minister of Labour with importance, 'that the five minutes' rule doesn't apply?'

'Oh, take as long as you like,' said the Prime Minister, wearily.

Mr Robinson took seventeen minutes.

Mr Pelham, in reply, took eight.

The speeches altered the opinion of no one.

The subsequent voting, the Prime Minister abstaining, showed eight in favour of continuing with the Bill and seven against.

'I take it,' said the Prime Minister, 'that the minority will loyally uphold the unity of the Cabinet outside this room. If any person is not prepared to do this, I am ready to accept his resignation here and now.'

There was a confused, and possibly somewhat reluctant, murmur of protestation.

'But I say,' remarked the Minister of Labour suddenly. 'Who's going to read Wellacombe's speech in the House?'

The Prime Minister looked at him.

'In view of the unfortunate leakage yesterday,' he said, in a tone unwontedly severe, 'I think it would be better if nothing is said about that. Let it suffice for me to tell you now that the speech undoubtedly will be made, and on Monday.'

It was a concession really to Lord Arthur.

So horrified had Lord Arthur been at the Prime Minister's decision to introduce the Second Reading himself, and so earnestly had he argued against the idea, that in the end the Prime Minister had undertaken to keep his intention secret even from the Cabinet itself by way of soothing the perturbed young man; and with this small crumb Lord Arthur had had to be content.

There was, in fact, another crumb of comfort for the Under-Secretary for India. It was a measure of the Prime Minister's own distress that he had mistaken the day. There was in any case no question of proceeding with the Bill on the morrow, for the day was Friday and the House would not meet again until Monday. This at least gave Sir Hubert and his men at Scotland Yard more than forty-eight hours to get their hands on the murderer.

'Or rather, on the assassin,' as Lord Arthur, waiting in case he might be needed in the drawing-room at No. 10 while the Cabinet meeting was in progress, remarked to Isabel Franklin. 'Our word "murderer" is far too wide. It covers everything from manslaughter to political assassination.'

'I used to think, when I read detective stories, that political assassination was dull,' Isabel said with feeling. 'It isn't. Oh, Arthur, do sit down.'

'Sorry.' Lord Arthur, who had been pacing moodily up and down the room, threw himself into a chair. 'This business is making me nervy.' In accordance with his compact with the Prime Minister, not even Isabel was to know of her father's intention to follow in Middleton's tragic wake. The secret was to be confined to Lord Arthur himself and the Commissioner of Police.

'It's terrible,' said the girl. 'You're not nervy as a rule, Arthur,' she added suddenly and with apparent irrelevance.

'No. Why?'

'Oh, nothing. I don't like nervy people, that's all. Arthur…'

'Yes?'

'I think I'd like to tell you… after all, you're one of my oldest friends… I'm going to break off my engagement to Eric.'

'To Comstock? I'm delighted to hear it.'

'Oh! Are you? Well, I'm glad you approve.'

'I'm sorry, Isabel,' Lord Arthur apologised. 'I spoke without thinking. But since I said it, I'll stick to it. I *am* delighted. He was never the man for you.'

'No,' Isabel said reflectively. 'I believe I knew that all the time, but – oh, well, women do silly things.'

'Anyhow,' Lord Arthur said a little awkwardly, 'I'm very glad indeed that you've realised it.'

'Oh, it wasn't that. At least, not altogether. It was really over this Bill. I feel so strongly that father's right in refusing to be intimidated – or rather, to allow the Government to be intimidated. But Eric…'

'Yes?'

'Well, he was trying as hard as he could before the meeting to get me to persuade father to back down. And – well, I don't like being treated as a political cat's paw, that's all.'

Lord Arthur looked grave. 'If you're no longer engaged to him, I can speak of him freely?'

'Oh, certainly. Technically I suppose I am engaged still, but I shan't be in another hour or two and we needn't stand on the letter. What's in your mind, Arthur?'

'Only this. It's been Comstock and Lloyd-Evans who have made themselves the backbone of the opposition in the Cabinet to this Bill. Without them people like Robinson and Jevons might have registered a mild protest that it offended their principles, but they wouldn't have pushed their opposition far. As it is, those two have worked on all the waverers so hard that really I'm quite doubtful whether your father will be able to keep the Cabinet behind him. And if he doesn't…'

'Yes, I know that. Eric's talked of hardly anything else for the last week. But what do you mean, particularly?'

'Well, *why* have they taken up this attitude? They've never been Liberals, or even Socialists. Dyed in the wool Conservatives, both of them. There's no question of restrictive methods being against their principles. Why have they suddenly come out as vehement as the Labour people against just the sort of Bill that one would expect them to approve?'

'It's only since the threatening letters began to appear that Eric veered round,' Isabel said, quietly. 'I don't know anything about Mr Lloyd-Evans, but Eric…'

'Yes?'

'Well, Eric's frightened out of his life. I think he believes that if the Bill goes on the whole Cabinet are marked for assassination. In fact, to put it frankly,' Isabel said, not without defiance, 'I'm afraid Eric's an arrant coward. And if you want to know, that's why I'm breaking my engagement to him. I can stand this and that, but a coward I can't and won't stand.'

'Oh!' said Lord Arthur, a little blankly. He wondered if this unexpected repercussion had occurred to the mind behind the Brown Hand.

There was a somewhat constrained silence, broken by the entrance of Dean with the final editions of the evening papers.

The staring headlines screamed the news of Middleton's death to any, if such still remained, who had not already seen the news in an earlier edition. But beyond the bare announcement, and the special correspondent's story of the dramatic scene in the House (for once this overtired adjective could be legitimately employed), there was nothing to hint at the real importance of the event. As in the case of Lord Wellacombe the word 'poison' was strictly avoided, and it was inferred that Middleton's death, too, had been the result of a sudden stroke. As a news story, the accounts were disappointing.

It was still more disappointing to the news-editors of the respective journals.

In point of fact, at the precise time while the Cabinet meeting was in progress another conference, scarcely less important, was being held in the offices (by common consent) of *The Thunderer*. It was a conference unique in the annals of journalism. The owners of all the leading newspapers in the country, eight in number, attended by their managing editors, were met to decide whether the actual facts of the situation should be revealed in the next morning's editions, or whether in deference to the Government's repeated request, the truth should continue to be hidden. The question was a thorny one. On the one side was their wish not to fall foul of the Home Office, and in no fewer than two cases a genuine desire not to embarrass the Government, though this was exactly counter-balanced by two cases of a genuine desire to embarrass it; on the other side was the knowledge, which recent history had taught them, that to preserve silence beyond a certain point merely makes a newspaper look foolish.

The conference lasted three hours, and became at times distinctly stormy. In the end, however, agreement was reached. Unless the police succeeded in catching the murderer, no mention of murder was to be made at any rate until after the weekend. It was, of course, taken for granted that the lesser fry of owners would loyally observe the decision of the Big Eight.

This decision was not reached without some heart-searching. In particular the Opposition owners considered themselves to have done a noble thing. For the Opposition newspapers had been very, very bitter against the Bill. It had indeed presented them with a simply first-class stick wherewith to beat the Government: better even than the bombing of the empty huts of unruly native villages – always so curiously truncated by the Opposition newspapers into the bombing of unruly native villagers.

Obviously, any Government which could apply force to anyone or anything or upon any excuse (except, of course, the persons or things against which the Opposition newspapers themselves wished to employ force, that is to say, any foreigner who did not happen to hold their own political opinions) must deserve the dread label Fascist. Forcibly to restrain certain misguided citizens of India from murdering, pillaging and burning the persons and property of other citizens of India was, the Opposition newspapers said (and they said it very loudly), about as Fascist a thing to do as ever Hitler or Mussolini could have conceived. The Opposition newspapers had in fact been very angry indeed, and they wanted now to be allowed to say that it would only serve such a wicked Cabinet right if it got itself murdered off man by man – and probably the whole thing was due to our policy of non-intervention in Spain.

The pro-Government newspapers, on the other hand, wanted to tell the public of the brave stand being made by their chosen rulers against the forces of anarchy and disruption. They knew that the public would love and admire such courage. They knew too that the British public, whom few things outside Association football, the University Boat Race, and the result of the 3.30 can really rouse, would get quite warm under the collar at the idea of certain persons trying to filch a piece of their Empire away from them by force (though there are certain portions of that same Empire which many would willingly give away with or without a pound of tea); and that they would in consequence insist wholeheartedly upon the Cabinet continuing to annihilate itself in the House of Commons piece by piece. This, thought the pro-Government newspaper proprietors, who of course strongly approved of the Bill, might provide a useful stiffener to those members of the Cabinet who viewed annihilation with no enthusiastic eye; for, after all, if you are hailed as a hero the least you can do in return is to behave heroically. Hence the fact that the last European war lasted four years instead of four weeks.

The Thunderer and *The Daily Telegram* took a slightly different line. In masterly leaders each had pronounced it on the whole a pity to apply force in the Government of the Empire, and at the same time a pity not to apply it when force was needed. Whatever the outcome, therefore, both *The Thunderer* and *The Daily Telegram* could point with pride to the fact that they had already prophesied that it would be (a) a pity, (b) not a pity, whichever might suit them better.

In the evening papers, however, which Lord Arthur and Isabel were scanning with somewhat abstracted eyes, there was nothing to suggest these master-wheels within the wheels open to public inspection; and Lord Arthur, who knew all that he wished and rather more about the former, threw the copy of *The Evening Wire,* through which he had been glancing, down on a table with a mild expletive.

'Isabel,' he exclaimed, suddenly, 'you may be right about Comstock, or you may not; but of one thing I'm certain. One of those two knows something – and I'm going to make it my business to find out what.'

chapter nine

A Conscience in Labour

Before going home to his flat in Whitehall Court, Lord Arthur turned, rather aimlessly, towards Westminster.

Although it was now several hours since the Speaker had adjourned the House, few members seemed to have left. Everywhere, in the lobbies and smoking-room, excited little groups were still discussing the crisis. There is no place for gossip like the lobbies of the House of Commons, and never before had such opportunity for gossip been provided. A hundred different stories, alike only in their remoteness from the truth, were born that evening, and few of them died the premature death they deserved. The lightest word of a Cabinet Minister at any time during the previous six months was a good enough peg to hang a new *canard* on, and the wilder the *canard* the better it hung.

The House of Commons is very like a public school. The Prime Minister is the Head, the Cabinet his Prefects, the Ministers without Cabinet rank and the Under-Secretaries are the Sixth, and the rank and file are the rest of the school, with here and there a bully, a promising youngster or a toady to those in High Places. (And the House of Lords is to the House of Commons much as Eton is to other schools, for reasons which it is unnecessary to particularise.) Moreover, since the average age at which intelligence ceases to develop is thirteen, the mental outlook is much the same as that of a public school too.

Only the School Prefects really know what is going on behind the scenes, and what is planned for the future. The Sixth know no more than the rest of the school, but they take care to look as if they did; and the rest of the school is inclined to lump Prefects and Sixth together, and credit the latter with as much inside knowledge as the former.

As Lord Arthur made his way through the lobby, therefore, he was greeted by more nods and becks and wreathed smiles, from friend and foe alike, than had ever come his way before. Half a dozen attempts were made to engage him in conversation, with the obvious intention of pumping him, but he was able to disengage himself from each with the ease of custom. There was indeed little that Lord Arthur did not know about Parliamentary ways, including the art of eluding awkward questions. He had been at home in the lobbies almost as long as he could remember, for when he was a small boy his father, the Marquess, had been Prime Minister. It was, in fact, Lord Arthur's father who had noted the ability of young Mr Franklin and lifted him with unusual rapidity from the oblivion of the back benches, through an Under-Secretaryship or two, to Cabinet rank. Mr Franklin, now Prime Minister, had been delighted to be able to repay the debt by encouraging the obvious abilities of his benefactor's son.

Lord Arthur, without being in any way complacent, had always taken it for granted that he would be in the Cabinet one day. He came of an old political family, he knew he was no fool, he understood the political game from A to Z, and he had a powerful patron. He knew, equally, that it was only while Mr Franklin was at the head of things that his real chance held good. The days of the old political families are passing; there is more log-rolling and worse undercurrents in politics now than ever before (and that is saying a good deal); with a Labour Government in power, of course, he stood no chance, and even with a change of Conservative leadership it would be doubtful how far he could count on the new man. Not having had an opportunity of getting into the public eye, he had no influence in the country to offer; if he were to be quietly dropped now he never would be missed.

'Old Franklin mustn't make that speech. If he goes the way of the others, it may be the end of me as well as him. I've got to stop him somehow,' he thought to himself, and then cursed himself for allowing personal politics to have any weight with him at such a time. But that was the way of it. If you were in politics, you had to be thinking of yourself the whole time. Even if your ambitions were as much for the country as for yourself, because you thought you could do real good if you had the power, you still had to keep thinking of yourself in order to obtain the power to do good.

There was a man of whom Lord Arthur was vaguely in search, a Labour member for one of the Midland industrial divisions, called Perry, a youngish man who had been making a bit of a name for himself during the last couple of years by championing on every possible and many impossible occasions the cause of the Indian Untouchables. Lord Arthur knew well enough what was in Perry's mind, just as every other Member did. To make a name for yourself in the House, according to the advice of the old hands, you can choose one of two courses: either you must single out some important member of the Government front bench and attack him in and out of season like a terrier yapping at a rat, till the great man is stung into taking notice of you and possibly placating you, or else you must specialise in some subject which is outside the range of the ordinary member, until you come to be looked upon as the House's authority on that particular topic. Cabinet rank has been won before now by each of these methods.

Perry was, of course, out to make a name for himself, and in that he differed not a jot from Lord Arthur himself. But the man did seem to know his subject, and his choice of it seemed to have been dictated as much by genuine sympathy as by practical policy. Lord Arthur thought that a chat with him would certainly be interesting, and might be helpful.

Perry was run to ground in a corner of the smoking-room, and Lord Arthur took him off to the Secretary for India's own room. A hundred envious eyes watched the exit, and at least a score of new rumours were coined on the spot.

Ensconced in an armchair, Lord Arthur opened bluntly.

'Perry, this is a bad business. I can tell you frankly, both the police and the Government are at their wits' ends. You know a great deal about India and its people – probably more than I do myself. Can you throw any light on the trouble?'

It was like a member of the Sixth, not quite a prefect yet but rumoured to be the runner-up for the next vacancy, entertaining in his study a member of the lower school.

The lower school member bridled with pleasure. It was the first time he had ever been addressed by any of the Lordly Ones of the other side. Old Pitchcroft had been right when he advised him to specialise – and, by Jove, his own instinct in choosing India had been right too!

'Well, I do know a bit,' he admitted coyly. 'But look here, Lord Arthur, is it right what everyone's been saying? That Lord Wellacombe and Mr Middleton were poisoned, right under our eyes? Curare, or some such stuff?' The lower school knew no more than the general public outside the school walls; all that could be said for it was that it heard the rumours earlier, but that was probably because it started them itself.

'Perfectly right. It's hardly a secret now. The newspapers are still holding it up, at the Cabinet's wish, but they may break away any moment.'

'Well, I think the House ought to be told a thing like that, Ministers being poisoned under our noses,' the lower school plucked up courage to say.

'I quite agree with you,' Lord Arthur returned, diplomatically. 'But unfortunately informing the House means informing the public, and the Prime Minister thinks that hardly advisable yet, for reasons which I need hardly point out to you.'

'Oh, well, of course, in that case…' The lower school subsided.

'But about the main issue,' Lord Arthur proceeded. 'I take it that the intimate knowledge you have of the lower castes isn't founded on books. You have personal contacts-correspondents perhaps?'

'Oh, lord, yes, a couple of dozen. More, probably,' said Mr Perry with pride. 'I've been at proper pains to get into touch with the real chaps themselves. No intermediaries. There's been too much of that already, and not in India alone. I could tell you some stories about that country that would make you open your eyes, Lord Arthur.' Mr Perry was no more of a snob than anyone else, but he did find it advisable to insist upon his working-class origin. It had served him well too, for he would never have reached Westminster without it. His slogan had been: 'Workers, vote for Perry! He's one of you!'

'Yes, yes, I don't doubt you could. But what I'd like you to tell me now is whether you have any information about any Indian in this country now who might be behind this horrible business. The police can't find the man, but people don't tell the police things. They might very well let drop a hint to you, though.'

'You mean, the Indian chaps I'm in touch with?'

'Yes.'

'Well, I can tell you one thing, Lord Arthur. *They* don't know anything. I'd be bound to have heard it if they did. Lord, I should think I've had something like a thousand letters since that business started out there-burning the factories and bombing the workers, you know. Real mad, my chaps are.'

'Against the terrorists, you mean?'

'That's right.'

'Your friends in India aren't opposed to the Bill, then?'

'You bet they're not. Why, I could show you cables… a dozen of 'em at least. Take it from me, Lord Arthur, there isn't a low-caste Hindu who isn't just as keen on this Bill going through as you are yourself. Why, it's their salvation.'

Lord Arthur looked at him curiously. The man was genuinely moved.

'And yet, Perry, in a division you'd vote against the Bill. Or wouldn't you?'

The Labour member wriggled unhappily. 'Well, you can't say that. Matter of fact, I haven't made up my mind yet. Ought to support the party, o' course,' he mumbled miserably, under Lord Arthur's accusing eye. 'You see, our leaders say – '

'Your leaders are trying to make political capital out of the Bill, distorting its object and raising the parrot-cry of "Fascism". Yet if they don't know as well as you do that without this Bill India's going to drop into anarchy, they're much more stupid men than I believe they are. So you have to choose between your conscience and your party, Perry. It's the old, old political choice.' Lord Arthur spoke as if he were at least a hundred and three and had been Prime Minister half a dozen times.

'Well, 's a matter of fact, I have been talking to some of our chaps, and some of us aren't too satisfied about it. I don't know but what we mightn't… anyhow,' said Mr Perry, suddenly aggressive, 'you oughtn't to talk as if the boot's all on one foot. Look at what your chaps have done in the past, voting against things they knew jolly well were right, just because it was the other side brought 'em in.'

'My dear fellow,' Lord Arthur soothed him, 'there's nothing to choose between the parties. Don't think I meant that for a minute. There have been dirty things done on both sides, and there'll be plenty more. But if you look at the lists of those voting for and against a really important measure, like this Bill, you'll find a handful of the Opposition every time among the ayes. Those are the chaps who put their conscience before their party. Mind you, it does them a lot of harm with their own party, at the time. But in the long run... it often pays.'

The Labour man looked at Lord Arthur with respect.

'What would you do about this Bill, in my place?' he asked, simply.

'I should vote for the Bill, and I should make a little speech first explaining why you intend to do so. After all, you're in a particular position. You *know*. And I don't think it will do you any harm. At all events, you'll gain the respect of the House; and that's worth having.'

'I'll do it,' said Mr Perry.

With the comforting knowledge that his time had in any case not been wasted, for a vote in the House is worth a thousand at the polls, Lord Arthur returned to the matter in hand.

Here, however, he drew a blank. The Labour man was able to give him convincing first-hand evidence, fully confirming the reports that had reached his office, that the lower castes in India were solid for the Bill, as were the higher castes; it was from the intermediates, the Babus and particularly from the new type of Nationalist business man, that the opposition came, and even these had not a majority among themselves. It was only a small, but a very determined minority, with almost isolated supporters in the Indian States, who appeared to have made up their minds to stop the Bill at all costs.

'Those chaps aren't my pigeon,' Mr Perry told Lord Arthur. 'I don't know anything about them. To tell you the truth, I haven't been much interested. But have you seen S P Mansel? There's a chap who might be able to tell you something about that lot. You know he went out there after they burned his factories down? I believe he got into touch with the actual chaps who did it, too, and talked to 'em straight. Trust Mansel to do the spectacular thing. He's much more likely than I am to be able to tell you something about that lot. You have a talk with him.'

'Thanks,' said Lord Arthur. 'I will.'

The two men rose.

'By the way,' Lord Arthur said, very casually, 'you know Dr Ghaijana pretty well…?' He paused invitingly.

It was a name which, naturally enough, had been much in his mind during the last two days. Dr Ghaijana was a Parsee, the only Indian member of the House of Commons. He had stood as an Indian Nationalist, demanding complete freedom for his country and severance from the British Empire, and he had been duly elected by one of those constituencies in the eastern half of London which seem to take a delight in returning freak Members. Dr Ghaijana was an educated man, and his reputation was of the highest; but he was a fervent patriot. The police had, of course, investigated him thoroughly, and had reached the conclusion not only that he was above reproach, but that from the place he had occupied in the House it would have been completely impossible for him to have discharged, propelled or in any other way have caused the poisoned thorns to reach the persons of the dead Ministers. So far as the police were concerned, Dr Ghaijana was out of it – but they were keeping a wary eye upon him nevertheless, and upon correspondence, his visitors and his associates still more.

'Dr Ghaijana?' repeated Perry. 'Oh, yes, I know him. In fact I know him pretty well. Not that I agree with his ideas, mind, because I know for a fact that the low-caste Hindus don't want Home Rule. They'd be a sight worse off under their own people than they are under British Raj, and they know it. But you can take it from me, Dr Ghaijana hasn't had anything to do with this business at all, Lord Arthur. They wouldn't be his methods, bombing and poisoning. Dr Ghaijana is a perfect gentleman in every sense of the word.'

'I see,' said Lord Arthur, wondering a little which sense of the word 'gentleman' indicated an inability to bomb and poison.

Parting with Perry in the lobby, Lord Arthur put *a* call through to Lloyd-Evans' home before leaving the House. The information he received was that Mr Lloyd-Evans had not returned.

Another call, however, brought the news that Mr S P Mansel would be delighted to receive him. Lord Arthur, again warding off the importunities of the seekers after knowledge, went out and called for a taxi.

The house of Mr S P Mansel was in Grosvenor Square. It had once been the town house of a ducal family. It cost Mr Mansel a great deal of money, but he considered the publicity worth it.

An envious rival had once described Mr Mansel as the impresario of finance. Whereas most financiers work under cover, burrowing their way to riches like moles, Mr Mansel had introduced glitter into the business. The floating of a new mammoth company by Mr Mansel was the financial equivalent of a C B Cochran first night. The fact that Mr Mansel was 'news' made his companies 'news' too. All that he did was on an elephantine scale which tickled the popular imagination. Moreover, his concerns paid dividends – to those lucky enough to be still holding the shares when the corner had been turned. The enormous sums which Mr Mansel was reputed to have made had been earned solely by buying up at a low figure shares in new companies of his own which had not declared a dividend during their first three or four years of existence, and holding them until the dividends began to roll in; the shares would then leap up to somewhere around twenty times their previous value, and Mr Mansel would unload. This manoeuvre he repeated with equal success over and over again, only a small proportion of the investing public ever realising that a Mansel Company was a lock-up investment for at least three years, and after that a gold mine. The small proportion who tumbled to Mr Mansel's game, and realised that a Mansel Company, so far from being over-capitalised was if anything the reverse, found themselves richly rewarded for their astuteness.

As Lord Arthur walked up the steps towards the imposing front door of the Mansel mansion, he wondered idly what had caused such a man to stand for parliament. Actually, Mr Mansel, following in the footsteps of a great rogue and always ready to learn, had thought that it might pay him to do so and had promptly bought a safe seat. He rather enjoyed the cachet it gave him.

Lord Arthur reached for the bell.

chapter ten

Inside Information

With his finger actually outstretched towards the bell, Lord Arthur paused. He knew really very little about Mansel. Would it not be advisable to obtain a little information before interviewing the man? The name of one of the Treasury officials jumped into his mind, a man whose job it was both to maintain liaison with the world of private finance and also to keep abreast of what was going on behind locked doors in the City (there are ways of doing this, as there are ways of doing most things).

Lord Arthur looked round for a public telephone. There was one on the corner, not fifty yards away. He hurried to it and put through the call.

His man was in, and provided the information promptly.

'Mansel?' he said. 'He's in pretty low water. In fact, I should say he's desperate. His bankruptcy may be announced any minute.'

'Good heavens!' The information was a complete surprise to Lord Arthur. 'What's the cause?'

'Oh, quite a few things have gone wrong with him lately. But it's chiefly the failure of his Indian ventures. He spent a colossal fortune setting 'em going – they were to have been the Sixpenny Stores of India, and he was to manufacture all the articles himself and cut out the manufacturer's profits. When they burned down his factories and bombed his work-people, the scheme went west. And if you want my personal opinion, I think Mansel will go west with the scheme.'

Lord Arthur whistled. 'If Mansel crashes, he'll bring down a good many people with him?'

'Hundreds. And there'll be a panic in all his concerns that are still sound. It'll be a very nasty affair altogether. We're hoping here that he'll still be able to stave it off somehow. And knowing Mansel, I shouldn't be surprised if he hasn't got a card or two up his sleeve yet. Well, is that all you want to know?'

'All, and more,' said Lord Arthur.

He returned to the Mansel front door. With this information up his sleeve, Lord Arthur fancied that the forthcoming interview might be an interesting one.

Mansel received him in a small room at the back of the house, round which Lord Arthur threw a quick and curious glance. It was a room which seemed to him typical of its owner. There was a workmanlike desk, for instance, in one corner; in another was a baby-grand piano. The carpet was luxuriously thick; there were a couple of good etchings on the walls; there was also a very utilitarian calendar, obviously supplied as an advertisement by some commercial firm. The colour scheme was pale yellow-green and gold.

As he seated himself Lord Arthur reflected how very different Mansel was from what the popular idea of him must be. In public Mansel cultivated the big cigar and the grey top hat, and the caricatures of him were not unlike those of Lord Lonsdale. Actually, so far from being the flamboyant figure of popular imagination, the man was a disappointment. Lord Arthur, who had met him several times outside the House as well as in it, had wondered each time to find a man who had done such remarkable things so unimpressive; yet there must be a dominant mind and a will of steel under that insignificant exterior.

Mansel this evening was plainly depressed. It was almost without a smile that he greeted his visitor, mixed him a drink from a tray on a side-table, and asked what he could do for him.

Lord Arthur murmured a preliminary apology for bothering him at all, and Mansel shook his head.

'Poor Middleton!' he sighed. 'It's upset me very much. Middleton was a good man. It was a pity to sacrifice him. I knew it would mean his death.'

'You were right, Mansel,' Lord Arthur agreed gravely. 'But he took the risk with his eyes open. He was brave.'

'The speech could have been called off, even at the last minute,' Mansel said, almost petulantly. One got the idea that he was sincerely upset over the Colonial Secretary's death, but at the same time piqued that his last-minute advice had been disregarded.

'No,' said Lord Arthur. 'That was impossible.'

'It's something in connection with Middleton's death that you want to ask me?'

'Yes. You remember when you were speaking to me in the House just before Middleton rose, you said something about having your own sources of information concerning affairs in India. I want to ask you to put those sources at the disposal of the India Office.'

Mansel shook his head. 'They wouldn't help you,' he said frankly. 'Besides, if my informants found out that I was doing anything like that, the stream would dry up at once.'

'They're "agin the Government," then?' Lord, Arthur suggested.

'Well…' Mansel looked as if he had said a word too much. 'Well, they're not in favour, certainly.'

'Terrorists?' Lord Arthur pursued.

'Oh, no. Nothing like that. But… well, it's possible they may be in touch with some of the Terrorists.'

'Has their information given you any inkling at all who is responsible for these murders, and how they're being committed?' Lord Arthur asked, bluntly.

'Good heavens, no.' Mansel sounded shocked. 'If it had, of course I'd have passed it on to you at once. Believe me, my dear fellow, no one is more upset about these terrible deaths than I am.'

Lord Arthur believed him. He remembered, too, the note of desperate urgency in Mansel's voice as he urged him to stop Middleton from speaking that afternoon.

'Well, does the information reach you in the shape of written reports, or by word of mouth?'

'Sometimes one, sometimes the other. Mind you,' Mansel said, with an effect of defensiveness, 'you mustn't make too much out of what I told you. I only said I had my own sources of information. So I have. But I don't get such a great deal of information from them. Nothing like regular reports, or anything of that sort. It's just an occasional message, often no more than a dozen words; but valuable, because absolutely reliable.'

'Would you let me see such written messages as you have had?' Lord Arthur persisted.

'No, I couldn't do that.' Mansel spoke gently, but this time the effect he conveyed was that of inflexibility. 'You must believe me when I say they wouldn't help you. For one thing, they're almost entirely concerned with commercial matters. For another,' said Mansel, with a slight smile, 'you might find a few items of which as a Government official you would have to disapprove. And in any case I destroy nearly all the written messages the moment I've read them.'

'But there must be some political information in them, or how could you have said with such certainty that these people mean business? You spoke as if you knew.'

'I do know,' Mansel returned, quietly. 'That's one thing I do know, with complete certainty: that any Minister who gets up in the House to introduce that Bill will die as surely as I'm talking to you now.'

Lord Arthur felt chilled. Mansel's conviction was infectious.

'But *how* do you know?'

'That doesn't really matter, does it?' Mansel parried. 'The facts on which I base my knowledge might not even seem compelling to you. But I know – and I passed my knowledge on. Why do you think I headed that deputation to the PM? I of all people would welcome this Bill, you'd say. I don't know if you've heard what the brutes have done to me out there, but believe me it's pretty serious.'

'It's put you in an awkward position, I believe?' Lord Arthur ventured.

'Yes, it has. Damned serious. In fact, about as awkward as any business position could be. There's no harm in my telling you. The City's summed it up all right.'

'Well, I hope you'll pull round.'

'Oh, I'm not quite lost in the wood yet,' Mansel said, with another small smile. 'In fact, I don't mind telling you in confidence that I'm even considering opening negotiations with the other side. That's just one iron I've still got in the fire.'

'The other side?' Lord Arthur was puzzled.

'Yes. The chaps who'll be running India if they pull this Nationalist business off.'

'Oh! You mean the Terrorists?' Lord Arthur's tone was properly disapproving.

'No, no,' Mansel said testily. 'The Terrorists are only cats' paws. They'll win the game for someone else to scoop the prizes. That's always the way. No, the men I mean are the men who are waiting till the Terrorists have won the game for them – lying low, not encouraging the factory-burners and the bomb-throwers (or not so that anyone would notice it), outwardly absolutely loyal to Emperor and Empire. Those are the fellows for whom it's "Heads I win, tails you lose." And if you want to know, it's from among that lot that my information – such as it is – has been coming.'

'I see,' Lord Arthur said, thoughtfully. 'And you're opening negotiations with them. I suppose you'd hardly tell me on what lines?'

Mansel frankly grinned. 'Would you tell me if I asked you whether the Cabinet intends to go on with the Bill or not?'

'Perhaps not,' Lord Arthur smiled. 'I shouldn't have asked.'

'Oh, I don't mind telling you,' Mansel said, carelessly. 'You don't seem to me like a man who talks too much. And in any case it's pretty obvious. I want to get my foot in on the right side of the line, just so that if India ever becomes a self-governing country again – or rather, I suppose, a loose collection of self-governing States – there'll be Mansel factories running and Mansel stores operating with the full consent and benevolence of the new Authorities. That's all.'

'I see. Well, that seems reasonable enough. But really, Mansel, you almost sound as if you believed in India's forthcoming independence.'

'Of course I do,' Mansel retorted. 'In any case, it's only a question of time, and in my opinion it'll be sooner rather than later. I believe this Terrorism is going to *win*. The Cabinet can't go on putting up Ministers like Aunt Sallies one after the other. Of course, they could make special provision to introduce the Bill without a speech, I know, but that would be such a confession of weakness that it would be worse than quietly dropping the thing altogether. Besides, this Cabinet's got no guts. They're just a lot of silly old women, not three of them fit for the jobs they're holding. That's why I'm so upset about Middleton: he was worth all the rest put together, barring the PM. The PM's got spirit, I grant you. But what will happen? Why, it's obvious. He'll call for volunteers to introduce the Bill, and there'll be no volunteers. So he'll get the idea that it's his duty to do the job himself. Then he'll get wiped out like the other two, and that will be the end. There's no man, on either front bench, who could keep a Cabinet solid for the Bill, once the PM's gone.'

Lord Arthur said nothing.

'Ah,' said Mansel, in a different tone. 'I see. That's what's happened. The PM's already announced that he's going to introduce the Bill, has he? No, I'm not asking you. I saw it in your face. You should learn to control your features better, Lord Arthur. They give you away too much. A mobile face may be all right for a politician, but it's a rotten depository for secrets. Well, if that's the case, let's hope no one else is giving the game away. Not that it matters, in my opinion. Whether the secret is kept or whether it isn't, if the Prime Minister once gets up to speak on this Bill it'll be like a dead man talking. For God's sake, can't you stop him, Lord Arthur? You're supposed to have influence with him. He's the best man in the country, for all that the Opposition say about him: and in their hearts they know it, too. He mustn't be allowed to throw himself away.'

Lord Arthur rose. 'I've already asked for permission to introduce the Bill myself,' he said, admitting by default the truth of Mansel's forecast and more than a little annoyed with himself for having given that truth so easily away.

Mansel seized his arm. 'Don't do it, don't do it, my dear chap,' he urged. 'I promise you, it's death.'

'Oh, I shouldn't say that,' remarked Lord Arthur, more easily than he felt.

'But I do,' Mansel returned.

He did not ring for the butler, but saw his guest to the front door himself.

As Lord Arthur was putting on his coat he remembered another point on which he had intended to question Mansel.

'By the way,' he said, 'I think I can give you one piece of information in return for all you've told me, though it's confidential for the present.' He explained to Mansel how curare-smeared thorns had been found in Middleton's coat collar and hair, and added the news, which had come through to Downing Street just before dinner, that Sir William Greene had discovered two or three small scratches across the inside of the dead man's fingers on the left hand, though it had not been possible yet to say whether these bore traces of curare or not.

'You remember when we picked the poor fellow up,' he said, 'you had hold of his shoulders, I think. Did you notice the thorns at all then?'

'No, that I certainly didn't.' Mansel sounded alarmed. 'If I had, I'm afraid I should have dropped him like a red-hot brick. Good heavens, this is getting too much. Why, any of us might have got a dose of the stuff too.'

'Yes, that's true.' Lord Arthur passed through the door which the other had opened for him, and pulled his black hat down well over his right eye in his usual way. He paused on the top step. 'But not a fatal dose, I fancy. That is, unless the stuff's of a quite remarkable strength.'

'Strength? Isn't curare all the same strength?'

'No, apparently it isn't.' Lord Arthur explained in a couple of sentences something of the vagaries of the poison, and added: 'As a matter of fact, the Home Office experts are a bit puzzled. It's been generally understood that even an arrow tipped in curare doesn't necessarily kill a man, and here only two or three thorns are causing death. They say that's all wrong. Apparently the theory is that it was mixed with some still more powerful poison, but they can't discover what. Snake venom was the first choice, but now they say that isn't good enough.'

'Oh, experts,' Mansel said, contemptuously. 'It's my opinion that an expert opinion isn't worth the paper it's written on. Still, if they do discover what this second stuff is, that may give you a better pointer to the man who's using it than the curare.'

'We hope so. Well, I mustn't keep you shivering out here any longer. Good night.'

'Good night,' Mansel returned. 'And for God's sake use every ounce of influence you've got over – well, you know what.'

'I will,' promised Lord Arthur.

As he walked rapidly through the square he wondered whether he had said too much. But there was something almost childlike about Mansel which seemed to encourage confidences. Or rather, not so much childlike as simple: the simplicity of a man who has never quite grown up. That no doubt was how he got things done: he would believe in simple, even in crude methods. And crudity often achieves results which not all the tortuous cleverness of the sophisticated ones can obtain. Anyhow, the man should be safe.

Moreover, Lord Arthur reflected, if anything did leak out now about the Prime Minister's intentions, the source would be obvious.

He turned into Brook Street and stopped a passing taxi.

It was too late now to try Lloyd-Evans again. Besides, the man would probably be exhausted after his gruelling at Scotland Yard. There had been a glint in Sir Hubert's eye which indicated that he was not going to let the President of the Board of Trade off lightly.

Lord Arthur's conviction that Lloyd-Evans knew something had grown. The box of thorns in his pocket could be dismissed as unimportant; the chances were a hundred to one that it had been planted there by someone anxious to get rid of it. But Sir Hubert's other arguments against Lloyd-Evans had been convincing, not so much that he was the actual murderer but that he had some kind of guilty knowledge. Lord Arthur was more than ever determined, if Scotland Yard had failed, to prise that knowledge out of Lloyd-Evans himself.

His thoughts switched to the box of thorns. Who had slipped it, in the confusion and turmoil, into Lloyd-Evans' pocket? The fact alone was an invaluable clue, for it showed that the murderer had been some person who had been close to Lloyd-Evans during those feverish five minutes – and that probably meant close to Middleton before them. The galleries were definitely out of it now.

Lord Arthur knew he was far too restless to sleep. He would spend half the night in compiling a list of everyone so far as he could remember within a dozen seats of Middleton – a circular plan radiating out from Middleton's seat on the front bench. Such a plan would almost certainly include the murderer. And after that he would ponder over each separate name on the list, to see if some hint, however slight, might not indicate that here could be the man.

chapter eleven

Introducing Our Mr Lacy

Saturday morning found the people of England still laudably cool.

A few of the curious had wandered down the evening before to Downing Street, but since there was nothing in the least degree unusual to be seen, they had had to content themselves with staring at each other. The Fascists, as usual, had thoughtfully supplied a much-needed note of comedy, by providing a van to drive slowly up and down Whitehall intoning at measured intervals, through a loudspeaker, 'Stand by the King,' which sounded good but a trifle out of date. There was also a Communist meeting in Trafalgar Square, to advocate Home Rule for India, with vigorous interruptions from certain Indians who did not want Home Rule, but did look to the Communists to carry out their expressed policy of supporting minorities against their oppressors. The difficulty of agreeing on the oppressor in this particular instance led eventually to the meeting being dispersed by the police. Otherwise there was nothing to report.

Not that the Saturday papers intended to report anything. So far as they were concerned there was no crisis, no danger, and no threat to democratic government. Everything in the garden of England was lovely, and several weighty articles were devoted to the prospects of the team of cricketers then on the point of embarking for the Antipodes to engage the Australians in a series of Test Matches. The general opinion was that the odds were pretty tough, but England ought to pull it off.

Lord Arthur wandered restlessly over to the India Office immediately after breakfast, but finding nothing at all to do there and few of the permanent staff in attendance, wandered back again.

He felt fagged out. The seating plan on which he had been engaged had kept him busy until nearly three o'clock in the morning, and even then was far from complete. His memory left many gaps, which would have to be filled up with the help of the police, but there were nearly four dozen names on his chart so far as he had been able to carry it. Pore over these as he might, however, no glimmer of light had reached him. The persons represented seemed all either of an eminence or a respectability too great to be suspect, or else of an insignificance so obvious as to be a passport to innocence.

Only one telephone call had come through to him at the Office. It was from the same financial expert whom he had consulted the previous evening, to say that he had been looking up the dossier of Lord-Arthur-knew-whom and was sending a special messenger over from the Treasury that moment with a report which might prove of interest.

The report arrived within five minutes. The new information was to the effect that it had been learned from reliable sources that Mr S P Mansel had been in negotiation with the Maharajah of Barghiala. The nature of the negotiations, which were very secret, was not known, but it was believed that they were concerned with concessions of so far-reaching a nature as would put Mr Mansel, if they were successful, in practical commercial control of the whole of Barghiala, from its mineral resources to a new chain of electric power stations up the whole length of the River Khoum. These concessions were far in excess of anything the British Government could possibly allow, and amounted to not much less than the floating of the whole State of Barghiala as a limited company, with the Maharajah as Chairman of the Board and Mr Mansel as its Managing Director.

Lord Arthur knew all about Barghiala and its Maharajah. Of all the Indian native rulers, he was possibly the only one who would be unmitigatedly glad to see the end of the British sovereignty. He was a backward, lazy man, with medieval ideas about divine rights, and he had several times to be pulled up with varying degrees of sharpness of overstepping the bounds of what Britain considered correct in the matter of good government. He was, indeed, just the sort of man who would be delighted to strike a bargain of the kind indicated, and the information bore out exactly what Mr Mansel had hinted on the previous evening when he had referred, frankly enough, to the foothold which he was trying to obtain in the other camp.

Lord Arthur rang up the Treasury and thanked his informant, adding that the details were news to him, but the general idea had already been divulged by Mr Mansel himself.

'I suppose it would be a pretty big thing, if it came off?' he added.

'Big? It'd be tremendous. I told you SP probably had an arrow or two in his quiver yet. This would put him right on his feet again, bigger and better than ever.'

'And what are the chances of it coming off?'

'Well, we've no information about that. We don't even know how far negotiations have gone. But, of course, as he told you, it would only be in the event of this separatist agitation being successful – or at any rate, successful enough to get this Bill shelved.'

'Oh, yes, of course,' Lord Arthur concurred. 'I quite understand that.'

Arrived back in his flat, Lord Arthur found the Leader of the Opposition waiting for him.

Mr Dickson was long and lean and cadaverous, and he uncoiled a sinuous length from an armchair in the sitting-room as Lord Arthur entered. He was an academic Socialist, with a brilliant University career behind him, and was credited with little initiative. Certainly it had seemed as much of a surprise to Mr Dickson as to everyone else when the Labour Party, unable to decide between two Trade Union bosses, had suddenly cut the knot by offering its leadership to a semi-obscure Professor of Economics at a northern university, the author of several pugnacious books, it was true, but with small experience of the Machiavellian powers needed to hold a heterogeneous political party together.

'I – um – have just been seeing the Prime Minister,' he began. 'I wanted to give him my personal assurance, if indeed it were needed, that the Opposition will do nothing to embarrass the Government at the present unhappy juncture – um – nothing at all of course. We reserve the right to criticise, of course, but anything else…'

'That's very good of you,' said Lord Arthur, as the other showed signs of tailing off. The Prime Minister will be grateful.' His voice conveyed a question as to what Mr Dickson could want with a mere Under-Secretary.

'Yes, yes. I further intimated that the whole Opposition front bench puts itself unreservedly at the command of the – um – the police, and so forth. I did in fact spend an hour last night with one of the Scotland Yard Superintendents, giving such information as I could: which was, I am afraid, very little. However, the Prime Minister suggested that I might have a further talk with you. And I am here for – um – that purpose.'

Lord Arthur was a little nonplussed. He gathered that the Prime Minister's suggestion might have been somewhat in the nature of a hint to speed a long-winded guest; and though he appreciated the other's obvious wish to help, there seemed nothing specific to ask him.

'Well,' he hesitated, 'I've already had a talk with your man Perry, but nothing very much emerged. I don't know whether… oh, yes, we discussed Dr Ghaijana. It's a beastly thing, but every Indian must be suspect to some extent, especially those with strong Nationalist views. I should be very much obliged if you'd tell me quite frankly whether you think there's any possibility of Dr Ghaijana being mixed up in the business.'

'The police asked me that, too,' replied Mr Dickson, a little stiffly. 'I told them, as I can only tell you, that so far as my own personal opinion goes, such a thing is impossible. Im-possible!'

'Ah!' said Lord Arthur. 'That's my own opinion, too. Thank you.' The conversation seemed to have reached a dead end.

A sudden thought occurred to Lord Arthur. 'Tell me, if you were called upon to form a Government in the very near future, Mr Dickson (and the possibility's not so remote), who would be your Secretary for India?'

It was the other's turn to be taken aback, but he answered without hesitation. 'Lacy.'

'Lacy?' Lord Arthur turned over the name. 'Yes… well, I should imagine he'd make a very good one. But does he know a great deal about India?'

'Yes, he does. A great deal more than one would think. He feels – um – quite strongly about India, too. One might almost say, passionately.'

'Really? I had no idea.' Lord Arthur was interested. 'Let's see, is he a separatist?'

Mr Dickson smiled. 'It's a little difficult to pin him down on that point, but I should say… yes, Lacy and Dr Ghaijana undoubtedly have many views in common. But the man is well informed. Perhaps you didn't know he spent several months in India last year? And that was not his first visit by any means. But he doesn't advertise them. I'm sure I don't know why. But, yes, if you were thinking of having a word with him, I'm sure you'd find him as helpful as anyone. Not that he approves of this terrorist campaign, of course, any more than Dr Ghaijana does. But it's quite possible that he may have his ideas, better than anyone else, who may be responsible for the London end of it.'

'I'd like to have a talk with him.'

'Of course. He'd be delighted. I'll ring him up at once, and ask him to come round here, shall I?'

While Mr Dickson was telephoning, Lord Arthur wondered why he should be regarded as running a kind of inquiry more or less supplementary to the official police investigations; but it seemed that he was being edged somehow or other into doing so. He did not mind, though he entertained not the faintest hope of success. Any action, even of the most futile description, was preferable to waiting with folded hands for the next tragedy, as most other people appeared content to do.

Mr Dickson obtained from the telephone the information that Mr Reginald Lacy would be enchanted to help in any way, and might be expected within half an hour at the most. Mr Dickson then, with many expressions of civility and helpful noises, took his leave.

Lord Arthur took advantage of the interval to ring up Scotland Yard. Sir Hubert was out on the job; the Assistant Commissioner to whom Lord Arthur spoke intimated in guarded terms that there was as yet no news, but developments could be expected at almost any moment. To an equally guarded inquiry as to whether anything useful had been extracted from Mr Lloyd-Evans, the reply was that Sir Hubert, after an interrogation extending until past midnight, was finally satisfied that nothing could be expected from that quarter.

Lord Arthur's expression, however, as he hung up the receiver was anything but satisfied. He even wondered, for an insane moment, whether some species of third-degree method could not be employed on the President of the Board of Trade. For that Mr Lloyd-Evans knew something, Lord Arthur was still convinced.

He glanced at his watch. It was just past twelve o'clock. He rang for the sherry to be brought in. Lacy would expect a drink. A drink would make things easier, too.

Lord Arthur did not like Reginald Lacy. Indeed, he privately considered him as one of the major blots on the political landscape. Not that there was any doubt about his ability. To reach a seat on a front bench, even the Opposition front bench, at the age of twenty-eight, was an achievement which could not be denied.

It may have been his complete inability to understand Mr Lacy which accounted for some of Lord Arthur's dislike. Lord Arthur knew himself to be a simple man, with simple ideals; sometimes he wondered uneasily whether he might not be a bit of a prig. Reginald Lacy was anything but simple. He also belonged to that disconcerting type which is able to conceal its likes and dislikes as well as its thoughts. No one was ever quite sure whether Lacy liked or disliked him, just as no one was ever quite sure whether Lacy was really a bit of an obsequious time-server or a man of truculence and pugnacity, with as rough an edge to his tongue as could be heard in a twelve-month; for one day Mr Lacy would be the one to the life, and the next day he would switch to the other. A disconcerting man, considered Lord Arthur, who did not like being disconcerted.

In point of fact, Lacy had an interesting history. He came of an excellent family, and his father, Colonel Lacy, had held an important administrative post in India at the time of his son's birth. Neither he nor the mother, however, survived that birth by many months for both were killed in a railway accident while on a journey in connection with the Colonel's official duties. Curiously enough, these two had been the only persons on the train to lose their lives. The ayah, travelling in another carriage, had escaped unhurt; and so had the infant Reginald.

Conveyed back to India, Reginald had been brought up first by his paternal grandparents and, after their deaths, by a sister of his father's. The family traditions were strong, and one might have expected Reginald to have imbibed them in the usual satisfactory manner. This, however, had not been the case. Up till the age of twenty-one or thereabouts Reginald had appeared the perfectly conventional Lacy, if a good deal more intelligent and rather more good-looking. Both his brain and his swarthy good looks, in such contrast to the normal bleak blondness of the Lacys, were debited by his paternal relatives to the account of his mother, who was known to have some rather dubious Italian blood in her; they deplored this break away from tradition, particularly in the matter of intelligence, but they could not justly condemn Reginald.

In other respects, too, the boy showed great promise. In the important matter of games, for instance, he was really brilliant, with a cricket blue in his first year at Cambridge and a golf blue before he went down. Up till this time it had been taken for granted by all concerned, and apparently by Reginald himself, that he would follow in his father's footsteps and enter the Army, *via* the University. Round about his twenty-first birthday, however, some very odd change came over the young man. As others get religion, Reginald suddenly got politics. He took to addressing uninterested wayfarers in public streets from the summit of a soapbox, and joined the Fascists.

The relatives could survive that; but when a year or two later Reginald, treading in his Leader's footsteps, but as it were backwards, left the Fascists and joined the Communists, his outraged family washed their hands of him. Reginald did not seem to mind. He had plenty of money in his own right (to be a successful Communist one must have plenty of money) and all he did by way of mourning for his lost shepherds was to give up all games as too bourgeois to contemplate, and grow definitely stout.

The Communist fit seldom lasts long with the modern young intelligentsia. By the age of twenty-five Reginald had gently detached himself from the party. In three more years, by methods which no one could quite determine, he had reached the Opposition front bench, a thoroughly respectable and now almost portly Socialist and representing a constituency that was neither quite East London nor West Essex, but combined the most unfortunate features of both.

It was news to Lord Arthur that Lacy had specialised in Indian affairs. He knew that the man was vaguely interested in India, but the interest had never been obtrusive in the House. As he was shown in, sleek and well-groomed almost to the point of foppishness in spite of his girth, Lord Arthur needed all his training to offer his guest a glass of sherry with just the right amount of friendly welcome.

The contrast between the two men was certainly an interesting one. So far as birth was concerned there was little to choose between them; in appearance and manner they might have come from different hemispheres. Lord Arthur, after all, in spite of his attributes, belonged at heart to the type of Simple Britisher, as good a type as any in the world when at its best. As for Lacy...

'Damn it all,' thought the Simple Britisher, with the Simple Britisher's instant reaction which he could not quell, 'the fellow looks like a Dago. Might almost be an Indian himself, with that sallow skin and black hair.' (The reaction is worth noting, since for real Indians who looked like Indians Lord Arthur had nothing but respect and liking; it was only Englishmen who looked like Indians that lifted his hackles.)

There were indeed other regrettable things about young Mr Lacy which upset Lord Arthur's strictly British soul, and confirmed his secret despair of the generation immediately below his own. For one thing, the man undoubtedly used scent; another equally heinous crime was that he wore side-whiskers. Lord Arthur had been brought up to believe that side-whiskers were unmanly, and he could not help believing it still. While finally...

'Hang it all,' Lord Arthur groaned in spirit, 'the fellow actually paints his fingernails.'

It was true. Mr Lacy's beautifully-shaped, oval nails were enamelled prettily with a mother-of-pearl finish. It seemed impossible that such a person could play any effective part in the grim affair of life and death which had brought these two opposites into contact.

But it was so.

'You want to know if I can be of any help, Lord Arthur?' he said, with a smile which matched the obsequiousness of his tone. It seemed that Lacy had deliberately elected to turn on his obsequious tap, and of all things Lord Arthur detested obsequiousness. 'Well, I think I can.'

'You can? Good man,' Lord Arthur returned, with heartiness.

'Yes. As a matter of fact, I've been working on the affair myself, so far as I could in a humble, extra-official way. I've had luck of course, but – well, I think I'm in a position now to tell you actually who murdered Wellacombe and Middleton.'

'Eh? What's that? Who was it, then?'

Lacy showed his white teeth in another smile. 'It was Dr Ghaijana,' he said.

'Can you prove that?'

'I think I can.'

'Sit down,' said Lord Arthur briefly. 'We've got to go into this.'

chapter twelve

Thorny Problem

Lacy's story was brief, and, privately, Lord Arthur did not find it very convincing.

'It was none of my business, I know,' Lacy began, 'but for some reason or other I took this murderous business very much to heart – I might almost say, personally.'

Lord Arthur could understand that. The murder of the Secretary of State for India would naturally perturb anyone who might be called upon to take over that office himself one day. Lacy could hardly explain that he had every reason to take a personal interest in the matter, but Mr Dickson's remarks had already made that interest clear, Lord Arthur nodded.

'Even on our side of the House,' Lacy went on with a slight smile, 'we're agreed that things must not be done that way. And as I was convinced from the beginning who was responsible, and the police seemed so stupid about it, I took it on myself to see what I could do.'

'You mean – Ghaijana?' Lord Arthur put in.

'Of course. Why look elsewhere when the obvious is staring you in the face? Ghaijana is a fervent Separatist. Not only that, but he's the only Separatist in or anywhere near the House of Commons.'

'I thought you were rather by way of being a Separatist yourself?' Lord Arthur interrupted again.

Lacy waved this rather obvious feeler away with a smile.

'Oh, we all know that India will revert to the Indians one day. Some of us think that the sooner the Hindus, the Buddhists and the Mahometans get it fought out between themselves, the better. As for me, if you were to say that I think India's already become rather more of a liability than an asset to the Empire, you'd represent my own personal feeling fairly well. But all that's beside the point. Let's stick to Ghaijana.'

'By all means,' Lord Arthur murmured.

'Well, to begin with, the man's technically a traitor. He preaches high treason in and out of the House itself. In any other country but this he'd have been arrested long ago, and probably executed by now. Mind you, the fellow's absolutely sincere. I know him pretty well, and he's one of the most upright of men. And to anyone who says, "Oh, but Dr Ghaijana would never do a thing like that," I'd answer, "My dear sir, you don't know fanatics; where their own particular pet prejudice is concerned a fanatic would stick at nothing."' Young Mr Lacy flicked his enamelled fingernails in the air with a gesture so un-English as to make Lord Arthur blink. That's what I'd say to 'em, Lord Arthur. And I'd be right.'

'Oh, undoubtedly. But all this is very theoretical…'

'Wait!' Mr Lacy stood the fingernails upright under Lord Arthur's fascinated gaze. 'I told you I know Ghaijana pretty well. I know him well enough at any rate to be sure that if Ghaijana didn't want the police to find a certain article, they wouldn't find it. And they didn't. Did they?'

'What article?'

Mr Lacy's eyebrows expressed, with the utmost respect, his surprise at Lord Arthur's obtuseness. 'The box of thorns. Remember, his flat was searched before Middleton's death. If I'm right, the box of thorns was there then. Mind you, it *might* have been in the possession of one of his subordinates, a man quite possibly unknown to the police. But I doubt it. Ghaijana's a man of strong character; he has to trust others, of course; but he'd keep all the main threads in his own hands. I think that box of thorns was in his flat when the police searched it. Or wait!' The enamelled fingernails waved excitedly in the air. 'He's clever, you know. Infernally clever. I wonder if he had it concealed somewhere in the House itself. Yes, that's more likely. Well, no wonder the police didn't find it.'

'You think this man – if you're right in assuming him responsible – has subordinates?' Lord Arthur liked to get one point clear at a time.

'Undoubtedly. This isn't the work of a single man. There's a big and powerful organisation at work.' Mr Lacy looked reflective. 'Yes, they couldn't have picked a better man for the job. You know his history, of course?' Lord Arthur nodded, but the other went on. 'He was associated with Gandhi in the original non-violence campaign, but as Gandhi's views became less extreme, Ghaijana's grew more so. But he kept up the non-violence front. That was clever. He took most people in.'

'Except you,' said Lord Arthur, with a slight smile.

'Except me,' Lacy agreed complacently.

'If what you say is right, Ghaijana must be one of the moving forces behind the Terrorist campaign.'

'He is.'

'Yes, yes. But have you any proof of all this?'

'If we can bring these two murders home to him, surely that will be proof enough?'

'That's so. But you haven't produced any evidence of that yet.'

'I've only theory,' Lacy said slowly. 'It's for the police to find the evidence. This is my theory. Assuming that Ghaijana is the London executive of the Terrorists, he must think he's safe now. The intelligence service of the organisation is remarkable; you know that. They even seem to know what has been decided at Cabinet meetings. So they're sure to have accurate information about Scotland Yard. I understand that Scotland Yard is satisfied that Ghaijana is innocent. In that case Ghaijana must feel quite safe – so safe that *if* there are any thorns left and that box-full didn't represent the entire supply, they're probably back in his flat. I suggest that the police pay a surprise visit there and search the place again. And I should like to go with them. I have some knowledge of the workings of the Indian mind, and it's possible I could be helpful.'

'Well, it should be easy enough to arrange that,' Lord Arthur concurred. 'I'll ring up Sir Hubert at once, and perhaps you'd go over and see him. But there seem a terrible lot of "ifs" about your theory.'

A smile creased the round face of the portly young man. 'Well, here's a fact. Did you know that Ghaijana comes from Barghiala?'

'The devil he does!' The information interested Lord Arthur more than anything else Lacy had said.

'Exactly.' The other's smile deepened. 'You've heard no doubt that the ruler of Barghiala would welcome the disappearance of the restraints which a motherly British Raj imposes on him, and that doesn't mean merely freedom to impale the more unruly of his subjects in the palace courtyard in the good old-fashioned way. With the help of our friend S P Mansel he hopes to become a very rich ruler indeed. And at present he's a very poor one. That's what Separation would do for the Maharajah of Barghiala. Yes, I rather fancy there may be something more than patriotism behind the activities of our worthy doctor. No wonder he keeps his origin secret.'

'Ah, he does, does he?'

'It's not difficult,' Lacy returned carelessly. 'I believe his parents left Barghiala when he was quite an infant. They settled in Calcutta, you know, where the father built up a big business as a carpet merchant. He's dead now, but you can be sure that the Maharajah kept the tapes on the family. Once a native of an Indian State, always a native, you know. They're still distressingly feudal,' said Mr Lacy cynically, 'in spite of all we've tried to teach them.'

Lord Arthur rose to telephone.

'But wait a minute,' he said suddenly. 'If you're right about this man, how on earth do you imagine he managed the thorns? He's on the other side of the House, right down below the gangway. He couldn't possibly do anything from there. Besides, the thorns were at the back of Middleton's head, and Middleton was facing him.'

Lacy smiled again, in a superior way which Lord Arthur found peculiarly irritating.

'My dear Linton, why assume that the thorns were "managed" on the floor of the House? I know that's the theory that the police have been working on, but one expects the police to be rather foolish. Of course, it's manifestly impossible.'

'Then when in your opinion was it done?' Lord Arthur asked, nettled. 'And how?'

'Obviously, on his way to his seat. There were plenty of people about in the lobbies when both Wellacombe and Middleton passed through, with their escorts. Ah, those singularly ineffective escorts! Really, do you think that the greatest conjuring nation in the world couldn't manage a simple job like passing a small thorn or two under the noses of a few stalwart but so obtuse English policemen? Of course that's when it was done, and how.

'And here's a final fact,' added Mr Lacy, with the air of one offering a titbit to a Pekinese, that is to say with courtesy and respect, but at the same time with a superiority which must be highly offensive to any Pekinese, a sensitive and intelligent race. 'On both occasions Dr Ghaijana took his seat *after* the others were already in their places.'

'You're sure of that?'

'Perfectly,' returned Mr Lacy, suavely. 'For on the first occasion I followed on his heels, and on the second he followed on mine.'

Lord Arthur took up the telephone receiver.

After his guest had gone, with an immediate interview with Sir Hubert satisfactorily arranged, Lord Arthur helped himself to another glass of sherry. He felt he needed it. Without wishing to do young Mr Lacy any injustice, and sure that he was trying to be nothing but helpful, Lord Arthur could not bring himself to feel any affection for the fellow. In fact, and not to put any fine point upon it, Lord Arthur would have felt it a considerable pleasure to kick Mr Lacy sharply on the hinder parts. He was not alone in that desire. Mr Lacy often affected Simple Britishers in that way. The fact that he did so gave him in his turn a good deal of pleasure.

Lord Arthur ate a meditative as well as a solitary lunch. The more he thought about it, the less likely it seemed that Lacy's intervention would lead to any useful results. Even if his theory about Dr Ghaijana were anywhere near the mark there was really no evidence to support it. Lord Arthur determined to treat Lacy's visit as if it had never been made, and pursue his own lines of action as before.

Not that there was very much choice. The only line that Lord Arthur could see was the one that led to Lloyd-Evans. Having allowed a decent interval for digestion, he therefore called for his hat and set out for Carlton House Terrace.

It was in a somewhat grim mood that he arrived there, to learn with satisfaction that Mr Lloyd-Evans was at home. The police, using correct methods, had failed to obtain any information from the President of the Board of Trade. There were only two inferences to be drawn. Either no such information existed, or else correct methods were not adequate. Lord Arthur, convinced that the information was there, had made up his mind to take a risk; for a man in his position, a big risk.

Shown into the Lloyd-Evans study therefore, and greeted with a certain wariness which, if anything, increased his suspicions, Lord Arthur came to the point with deliberately brutal directness.

'Mr Lloyd-Evans,' he said, coldly and firmly, 'I'm conducting a quite unofficial, investigation of my own into the murders of my Chief and his successor, and I must warn you that I've already made considerable progress. You are implicated, at present only you and I know how deeply. Do you wish me to go to the police with the information at my disposal, or would you rather discuss the matter privately with me?'

For a moment Lord Arthur thought he had missed the mark. Mr Lloyd-Evans drew himself up and seemed to bristle all over.

'Will you kindly explain what you mean by that remarkable speech, Lord Arthur?' he demanded.

'Certainly.' Lord Arthur drew a quick breath. 'I know you have been divulging Cabinet secrets to the Terrorists; I know it was you yourself and not anyone masquerading as you who delivered the anonymous letter naming Middleton at 10, Downing Street, and finally I know the details of the discreditable business about which they have been blackmailing you.'

This time there was no mistaking that the mark had been hit. The President of the Board of Trade seemed to shrink in his chair; his face became pasty, his forehead moist; he looked as if he were going to collapse at Lord Arthur's feet.

Lord Arthur almost gasped with relief. It had been a terrific shot in the dark, but his reasoning had not been at fault. Certain that Lloyd-Evans was the cause of the Cabinet leakage, and equally certain that the man would not be risking his whole career and almost his freedom for material gain, Lord Arthur had come to the conclusion that the other side must have some kind of hold over him and had been using it to the limit. The shot had in reality not been so wild. Cabinet Ministers, after all, were human once. There are incidents in the lives of most of them that they would not care for the public to know; there are episodes buried in the past of more than a few which, if brought to light, would write *finis* to the most brilliant career. It does not need such a very large scandal to wreck a Minister's reputation. And once reputation was gone, office has gone with it.

Lord Arthur gazed unrelentingly at the wretched hulk before him. Mr Lloyd-Evans reminded him of the skin of a squeezed orange, a minute before bulging with pompous rectitude, now a shapeless mass of pulp.

'Well?' he said.

Mr Lloyd-Evans made an effort to retrieve his voice, but only a dry whisper resulted.

'You know about… about what happened at…?'

'Yes,' Lord Arthur said stoutly, wondering what on earth had happened, and where.

'Oh, God!' whimpered Mr Lloyd-Evans.

Lord Arthur felt uncomfortable. 'Oh, that's all right,' he said awkwardly. 'I won't divulge it, of course…'

'You *won't?*' repeated Lloyd-Evans, incredulously.

Lord Arthur began to feel that the hidden misdeed must be a formidable one. 'In the circumstances,' he said, not without a touch of pomposity of his own, 'no. Provided, of course, that you talk freely to me now.'

'Oh, I'll talk,' agreed Lloyd-Evans, miserably. 'It doesn't matter what I say now. I'm finished, anyway.'

'Oh, surely not,' Lord Arthur tried to comfort him.

'What do you think *they'll* do, when they know I've talked?' asked the dreary voice. 'Well, never mind. I knew it could only be a question of time. You want to know everything, I suppose? I'm afraid I can't tell you such a very great deal. But first I'd like to say that I… I'd have faced it out if I'd been alone. At least, I think I would. It was just that I couldn't bear to bring the disgrace on my wife and daughter. I… oh, well, never mind. What is it you want to know?'

Lord Arthur, reminding himself that in the national interests he must not spare the unfortunate creature before him, began to put his questions.

By the end of an hour he was in possession of a fairly connected story.

Lloyd-Evans had been blackmailed from the beginning. How the other side had learned of the unnamed incident in his past, he could not imagine; but they had. One evening, just five months ago, he had had a telephone conversation with a person of unknown identity. Lloyd-Evans had the idea that his voice sounded vaguely familiar, but could not place it. The unknown had referred in guarded tones to the past, sufficiently clearly at any rate to send Lloyd-Evans scurrying out into the summer night to keep an appointment with the speaker.

There he saw that he must have been mistaken, for the man, though speaking perfect English, was an Indian and quite unknown to him; his voice still sounded faintly familiar, but this was evidently some trick of memory, for Mr Lloyd-Evans could not remember ever having spoken with an Indian in his life.

To cut a long story short, the man had laid down his terms, and Lloyd-Evans had accepted them.

At first the coils had not been drawn very tightly. Lloyd-Evans had been required to use all his influence to prevent the Government from introducing restrictive measures in India, and to furnish reports concerning the Cabinet's deliberations on the subject. These reports were always made by word of mouth, and nearly always to a different person. A code had been arranged, and Lloyd-Evans was informed by telephone where he was to go and at what time. He never knew whom he was to meet, but the other party always seemed to know him. The places chosen varied from West End restaurants, through cinemas, to Underground stations, but always within a mile or two of Westminster. Sometimes the contacts were made by night in a quiet street.

Gradually he had found himself more and more enmeshed, until Wellacombe's murder. Lloyd-Evans was never given any information himself; he had known of the anonymous letters and the threats only in the same way as the rest of the Cabinet, and in spite of his position he had never seriously believed that murder was intended. Even when he had received orders to make sure of sitting beside Lord Wellacombe on the front bench he had attached no importance to the injunction. The actual death of the Secretary of State for India had been a ghastly shock to him. Then had come the decision to appoint Middleton. Half-dead with panic, Lloyd-Evans had passed on the news, wondering as he did so whether he might not be signing the Colonial Secretary's death-warrant. The same inexplicable order had followed. Lloyd-Evans had obeyed it... and Middleton had died. This time the shock had nearly killed Lloyd-Evans, too; he almost wished it had.

As to the box of thorns...

A knock at the door interrupted the story. It was the butler with a note addressed to Lord Arthur.

Dear Linton, ran the note, I think you may like to hear at once that your friend delivered the goods all right. We raided the flat in question, and found a supply of thorns right under our noses, forming part of the pattern of a bit of native embroidery hanging on the wall. The ingenious owner is now under lock and key. — Yours, Hubert J Lesley.

Lord Arthur looked up.

'Well, cheer up,' he said exultantly. 'At all events they've nabbed the man at the top.'

chapter thirteen

Scent and Sensibility

Mr Lloyd-Evans jumped in his chair.

'What?' he almost shouted.

Lord Arthur explained Lacy's visit to him, and its sequel.

Mr Lloyd-Evans ran a bewildered hand through his rather sparse hair. 'Ghaijana! I should never have thought… well, it's possible… good heavens!'

Lord Arthur vanquished a wish to rush round at once to Scotland Yard, and proceeded with his questioning. Lloyd-Evans would talk even more freely now, and it was best to get all the information possible out of him while he was in the mood to talk.

'These men you met,' he said. 'They were all Indians, I suppose. Could you identify them?'

'Oh, but they weren't all Indians,' Lloyd-Evans explained. 'There were only two Indians, the man I met first of all in the restaurant, and one other later. The others were all nationalities. There were at least three Germans, two or three Italians, even a Japanese. The others were English.'

'English?' Lord Arthur was startled. 'Oh, yes. I think,' said Mr Lloyd-Evans, cautiously, 'that they were probably Communists. At least, they looked like Communists.'

'How do you mean?'

'Well, you know. They were young, and their hair was rather long, and they mostly wore red ties. They *looked* like Communists.'

Lord Arthur pondered this rather vague explanation.

'It almost seems as if it was some kind of international plot,' he said, a little incredulously.

'I've thought that myself,' Lloyd-Evans admitted.

'The Anti-Comintern pact joining hands with our own Communists to separate India from the Empire.' Lord Arthur meditated anxiously for a moment. 'That doesn't sound as if Ghaijana is at the head of it after all, though he may be one of the principals. Mr Lloyd-Evans, you must come and see Sir Hubert at once.'

Lloyd-Evans demurred vigorously. Lord Arthur insisted giving a promise that Sir Hubert should give an undertaking that the matter should go no further than himself personally. Mr Lloyd-Evans gave in.

'By the way, how did you manage to hold out against their questioning yesterday?' Lord Arthur asked, curiously.

'I don't know. It wasn't difficult. I just maintained that I knew nothing, and continued to maintain it.'

Lord Arthur, looking at the weakly obstinate face opposite, felt satisfied that he had taken the right course.

It was a much chastened Cabinet Minister who accompanied the Under-Secretary for India to Scotland Yard. Not a trace of Mr Lloyd-Evans' self-important manner remained. Even the butler looked after the pair with surprise and wondered what had come over the old bloke all of a sudden, he looked that queer.

The two spoke little. Once Lord Arthur asked: 'And that box of thorns? You really had no knowledge of it?'

'None at all,' Mr Lloyd-Evans assured him earnestly.

At Scotland Yard Lord Arthur left Mr Lloyd-Evans downstairs in the waiting-room and himself hurried up to explain the situation briefly to the Commissioner. Sir Hubert was so elated over the capture he had just made that Lord Arthur saw with relief that Mr Lloyd-Evans would be let off lightly.

'Most useful, most useful,' was Sir Hubert's comment, after he had expressed himself with the necessary force over the way in which Mr Lloyd-Evans had held out on the previous evening. 'We've got the man at the top; this will give us a chance to round up the small fry.'

Lord Arthur mentioned his fears based on the employment of certain foreigners by the Separatist organisation, but Sir Hubert did not consider this important.

'Of course certain Continental nations have been giving 'em a hand,' he commented. 'I've been half expecting that all along. In the East, too. And of course these chaps had the backing of their own Governments. But that would all have been under the nose. The minute they hear the game's up, they'll fade out. We may be able to get one or two at the ports, but I doubt it.'

'Yes, I suppose that's the way of it,' Lord Arthur agreed. 'Germany would go out of her way to help make us so busy in India that we'd have no time to interfere with her schemes in Europe; Italy wants to hurry on the break-up of the Empire; and no doubt Japan thinks that with an independent India she could help herself to a slice or two. But, of course, none of them can come out in the open. Yes, I think you're right. The foreign element will fade out now: always supposing, of course, that we really have got the man at the top.'

'Oh, we've got him all right,' returned Sir Hubert, confidently.

'Has he anything to say?'

Sir Hubert smiled. 'A great deal. Denies the whole thing, of course. Says someone must have planted the thorns on him, just like they did on our friend downstairs. In fact, I believe in another minute or two he'd have been saying that Lacy planted them himself, just so as to be able to find them for us. There's not much love lost there, I gather.'

'No,' Lord Arthur laughed. 'I can imagine that.'

He did not stay for Sir Hubert's interview with Mr Lloyd-Evans, but having obtained the former's undertaking that the discreditable part played by the latter should remain concealed took himself off to No. 10 Downing Street.

In answer to his tentative inquiry, Dean told him that the Prime Minister was engaged; Miss Isabel, however, was in the drawing-room, and tea was about to be served. Lord Arthur agreed that a cup of tea was just what he needed.

To his disappointment, however, Isabel was not alone. Of all unexpected people Lord Arthur was surprised to find Lacy with her. To add to his chagrin it was evident that his entrance had interrupted what must have been a serious conversation, for Isabel greeted him in an absent manner and Lacy made it plain that his arrival was unfortunate.

Not that anything could disconcert that young man for long; for no sooner was Lord Arthur seated and had uttered, with a stiffness he could not help, a few congratulatory remarks about his part in the capture of Dr Ghaijana, than Lacy divulged the subject of his discussion with Isabel.

'Yes, yes,' he said, waving Lord Arthur's congratulations aside with one of those too-expansive gestures of his. 'Yes that's all very well, and I'm glad to have been of use. But what is the next move? As I've just been telling Miss Franklin, that's what is worrying me.'

'In what way?' Lord Arthur asked, adjusting with some care the crease of his striped trousers.

'Why, you don't imagine these people will allow Ghaijana's arrest to stop them, do you? I tell you, Linton, I know them. It's a dangerous type, and a cunning one. They'll have allowed for any ordinary emergency like that.'

'But if Ghaijana was directing them...?'

'How do we know he was?' Lacy countered swiftly. 'He may have been only a subordinate himself.'

'I thought it was your own theory that Ghaijana was the executive head in this country?'

'Oh, theories...!' The swarthy young man settled himself more comfortably in the corner of the couch on which he was sprawling, in an attitude which Lord Arthur would have found scarcely admissible in a club smoking-room and certainly not in a lady's drawing-room. Theories are all very well, so long as they don't take possession of one. The thing to do is not to lose sight of alternatives. I think it quite possible that Ghaijana was the executive head of the movement in this country, but I'm still more sure that there has been someone else waiting to take over the job the instant anything happened to Ghaijana.'

'Then you don't think the danger's over?'

'Of course it isn't,' Lacy said, with a contempt that was positively rude. That's my whole point. That's what I'm here for.'

'Mr Lacy thinks father ought to give up the Bill,' Isabel put in. 'He seems to think that I could persuade him. I've told him there isn't a chance.'

Mr Lacy waved a deprecatory hand. 'Now, now, Miss Franklin, I didn't say "give up the Bill". I said that it ought to be postponed, until this organisation has been really and truly smashed. And I maintain that's only common sense. Your father, if you'll allow me to say so, is in danger of mistaking obstinacy for firmness. It isn't firmness to set up one Minister after another as a target for assassins. It's merely obstinacy. Don't you agree?'

'No,' Isabel replied flatly, flushed with annoyance.

Lord Arthur, who had been keeping his own temper with difficulty, came to the rescue.

'If you were Secretary for India yourself, Lacy,' he said, mildly, 'would you advise your own Prime Minister to shelve the Bill?'

'After I'd been killed myself, or before?' queried Mr Lacy with asperity.

'If you saw a danger of being killed,' Lord Arthur suggested.

Mr Lacy showed his white teeth in a slightly mocking smile. 'But of course I should. What good could I do by getting killed? What good could I do dead? Still, the question hasn't very much point, because no Government of the Left would introduce a repressive, vindictive Bill like this one.'

'Well, we won't discuss the merits or demerits of the Bill here. You and I are at one, I know, in agreeing that a threat of this kind against organised Government has to be countered with all possible energy. So what in your view ought the next move to be?'

'I've told you my opinion. The Bill ought to be held up while proper inquiries are made, based on what the police can get out of Ghaijana.'

'But if Ghaijana won't talk?'

'There are ways of making any man talk. I should have thought,' sneered young Mr Lacy, 'that with the safety of the Empire at stake even you would have thought such methods permissible.'

'I'm not sure I don't agree,' Lord Arthur returned, equably. 'But I'm afraid others won't. In the meantime it would be interesting to hear your views on the state of India in general. Did you know,' Lord Arthur added to Isabel, as Dean appeared with the tea-tray, 'that Lacy spent several months out there last year?'

'Really?' Isabel's attention was obviously more on the tray than on the question. 'No, I didn't know. How interesting.'

'And what were your conclusions?' Lord Arthur asked Lacy.

For some reason Lacy suddenly flushed: a dull, dusky red.

'Oh, that India's a good enough subject for tea-table prattle, but not much more,' he said, with an intensity of bitterness which astonished Lord Arthur as much as it disconcerted him.

He was about to make some noncommittal reply when Isabel, looking at the younger man with more interest than she had yet shown, said:

'You feel strongly about India.'

'I was born there,' Lacy returned, in a sullen voice.

'Were you? I didn't know. Oh, yes, of course I did. Your father had some official post, of course. Yes, naturally you have almost an inherited interest. Do tell us what you saw out there, and what you thought about it. I'm quite sure you didn't do the usual political round.'

Lacy's mood suddenly changed. He grinned at Isabel almost boyishly.

'You bet I didn't. No, I did the thing properly. I took the trouble to learn Hindustani before I went out there, and I talked to everyone – made all the contacts I could. It was illuminating, I promise you. There are so many sides, you know. India's like a gigantic jewel, with a million facets; and each facet represents some different point of view, or some different personal little axe to grind.'

Isabel showed her interest. 'Did you meet any of the extremists?' she asked, her hand resting on the handle of the teapot.

'I certainly did. As a matter of fact, I brought round a copy of their newspaper. I thought you'd like to see it; it represents a point of view you've probably never even heard.' Lacy felt in his pockets. 'I must have left it in my overcoat. I'll get it.' He rose with an agility surprising in one of his bulk and hurried out of the room.

Lord Arthur made a comical grimace at his hostess, who replied in kind.

'Get rid of him,' he whispered. 'I want to be alone with you.'

Isabel nodded, but could not reply before Lacy was back in the room, offering her the newspaper in question.

'Read that leading article,' he said. 'It may give you something to think about.'

'I'll just pour out the tea first.'

Isabel applied herself to the tea-tray and the usual queries about milk and sugar.

Lord Arthur looked at Lacy with a little more sympathy. After all, it seemed that the man had one genuine feature; his anger over the perfunctoriness of the questions about India had been beyond his power to control. Lord Arthur, who hated treading on other people's corns almost worse than he hated having his own trodden upon, felt that some implied apology was needed.

'I'm afraid,' he said, 'that people in this country don't take the Indian question as seriously as they should.' 'Well, you're in a position to know,' Lacy smiled. 'And, of course, you're right. But does the British public take any of its own responsibilities seriously? It gets all worked up when a big nation bullies a small one, but can you see a wave of sentimental anger sweeping over the British nation about anything that really concerns themselves? The deadly, dull, complacent indifference of the British public! That's what we politicians are up against all the time. It's like battering one's head against a feather bed. The Irish problem… Irishmen murdering Englishmen, Irishmen murdering each other, Irishmen trying to cut themselves out of the Empire, Irishmen terribly excited and truly believing that they're kicking up the deuce of a shemozzle… and the British public spends its evenings filling in football coupons. The British public just isn't interested in Ireland. The Indian problem… Indians assassinating English officials, Indians assassinating each other, Indians truly believing that they're the centre of the world's attention. And the British public only thinks of India as a place that sells us tea and buys our cotton goods – or used to, before Japan unfairly stepped in and sold 'em cotton goods at half the price. The British public just isn't interested in India, you see. And what's more, you can't make 'em. In fact, as a matter of flat truth, the British public just isn't interested in the British Empire. It sings "Land of Hope and Glory" and makes itself feel all good inside, but does it really care? It does not. Would it put itself out by half a step to keep the Empire intact? It would not. Good old British public.' As if to atone for his tirade, Mr Lacy burst into hearty laughter.

'Oh, come,' said Lord Arthur, smiling. 'I don't think it's really as bad as that.'

'No,' Isabel said, not smiling. 'Mr Lacy's perfectly right. British indifference to almost everything that really matters is simply monumental. You mustn't delude yourself, Arthur. And we need people like you, Mr Lacy, not only who will prick the British hide but who realise that there is a hide to prick. By the way, if you feel like that I wonder what your reactions were to the British Civil Servant in India. I've always wanted an unbiased opinion as to whether Forster exaggerated the type in "A Passage to India" or not. It's a book that makes me go hot with shame every time I read it.'

'Of course he exaggerated,' Lord Arthur put in. 'He was so prejudiced that he just couldn't help it. Why, the whole plot's impossible, with that absurd court-case brought without any evidence at all. It could never have happened.'

'What do you think, Mr Lacy?'

'Forster did exaggerate, I think, in the incidents he used to prove his case against the Service,' Lacy replied seriously, 'and possibly in some of his characters, but not in the general effect. I attended a few mixed functions of the kind he describes, that's to say out in the districts and lacking the *savoir faire* you get in the big cities, and honestly, Miss Franklin, if the book made you feel hot the actual thing would make you want to sink through the ground. The rudeness of the official British to the high-class Indian is something quite incredible. No wonder any Indian of spirit feels he can't put up with that kind of treatment much longer. And in his own country at that. If there ever is another mutiny, it'll be the Civil Service who are responsible. The Civil Service and their wives. Above all their wives. Stupid female morons, blown out with self-importance.'

'Is it really so bad?' Lord Arthur murmured. Lacy was obviously working himself up again, and Lord Arthur did not very much want to hear another lecture.

'It's worse,' Lacy retorted. 'And the funny thing is that if it's plain blank rudeness on the part of the ruling race that causes the next mutiny, it's the last mutiny that is the cause of the rudeness. At least, that's my view of it. Of course, the English are a stupid unimaginative race at best, with a knack of trampling quite unconsciously on other people's toes, and when you put the class from which most Civil Servants are drawn in authority you're bound to get the most appalling bumptiousness and snobbery – in this case race – snobbery. But I think it's more than instinctive bad manners. It's a deliberate policy, based on fear – the ever-present fear of another mutiny. Keep the blighters down – tread on their faces – rub their noses in the dirt – we'll show the swine who's master here...'

To the relief of Lord Arthur the entrance of Dean cut this harangue short. Lacy's face had become suffused again, and his manner had become almost that of the platform. In a way Lord Arthur admired the man. He understood now Lacy's success. He had the twin gifts of feeling and ability to work himself up in half a minute to express that feeling. It might be a superficial feeling or it might not, but at any rate it was genuine. Today it was India, tomorrow (thought Lord Arthur) it might be Empire Preference, or any other darned subject you liked; but while it was there it was good.

Dean had approached Lord Arthur and was murmuring respectfully in his ear.

'If you would follow me, my lord...'

Lord Arthur jumped up. 'The Prime Minister? Yes, of course, Dean.'

He hurried out of the room. Dean, following, closed the door behind them.

'It isn't the Prime Minister, my lord.' The butler seemed oddly nervous.

'No? Well, what is it, Dean?'

'I thought it best to speak to you alone, my lord,' Dean said, in a lowered voice. 'I really don't know what to do for the best. I thought I'd put it to you first, my lord.'

'Put what?' Lord Arthur was beginning to catch something of the butler's nervousness. 'Don't beat about the bush, man. You're looking deuced queer. What's the matter?'

'Yes, my lord.' The butler gulped. 'I'm afraid it's another of those anonymous letters, my lord. The Brown Hand, my lord. I don't like to take it in to the master, not without a word of warning; but he said I wasn't to let one of his secretaries have it, like in the ordinary way. I thought perhaps you'd tell me what I'd better do with it, my lord.'

chapter fourteen

Danger in Downing Street

Lord Arthur thought quickly.

'Where is the letter?' he asked.

'It's down in the hall, my lord. I slipped it under the salver as soon as I realised what it was.'

'It was in the letter-box?'

'Yes, my lord. I just happened to be passing through the hall and glanced into the letter-box, as I usually do. The front-door bell hadn't rung or anything. I don't know how long it had been there.'

'When was the box cleared last?'

'Well, I couldn't say exactly, my lord. I looked into it myself about half an hour ago and took out a few things; the letter wasn't there then. But someone may have looked since.'

'I see. Well, Dean, you mount guard in the hall. I'm going to ring up Scotland Yard at once. I think perhaps it might be better not to upset the Prime Minister with the thing until Sir Hubert has seen it.'

The butler's face expressed relief and agreement.

Lord Arthur was able to get Sir Hubert himself on the telephone, and arranged for him to come over immediately. Within four minutes the Commissioner and three other officials were in Downing Street. Lord Arthur met them at the door, and took them into the morning-room.

No time was wasted. Having learned the brief fact of the letter's arrival, one superintendent slipped out of the house to question the men on guard outside, while the other carefully dusted the envelope for fingerprints before it was opened. Except for Dean's, which the superintendent evidently knew by heart, none were found.

Sir Hubert slit the letter open, and drew the sheet of cheap notepaper out with infinite care. Holding it by its edges, he read the contents out in a low voice.

> *To the Prime Minister and Members of the Cabinet.*
> *Gentlemen,* – *Ghaijana's arrest means nothing. There are a hundred ready to take his place. The loss of our thorns means nothing. We have a hundred alternative means ready. If the Prime Minister persists in his decision to speak on Monday, he will die just as surely as Wellacombe and Middleton did. But this time his death will be still more mysterious. There will be no curare. The doctors will call it heart failure, but it will not be heart failure. Why let him lose his life so uselessly? Abandon the Bill before it is too late. You will have to do so in the end.*
>   *The Brown Hand.*

'Persistent devils,' commented the Commissioner laconically.

The Assistant Commissioner for the CID raised his eyebrows. 'Is this right, Linton? Did the Prime Minister intend to speak himself on Monday?'

'Yes, damn it,' said Lord Arthur, almost in despair. 'But no one knew. Only the Prime Minister and myself. No one else at all.'

'I knew,' the Commissioner remarked shortly.

'Oh, yes, you, Sir Hubert. But one hardly counts the police.'

'Seems as if we've got to count everyone on this job,' remarked the Superintendent in gloomy tones. 'I want a word with that butler.' He oozed unobtrusively out of the room.

Sir Hubert, the Assistant Commissioner and Lord Arthur looked at each other.

'Well?' said the first. 'Has no one got an idea? How did these blighters get hold of that news about the Prime Minister?' He caught Lord Arthur's anxious eye and shook his head slightly. 'No, I asked our friend, in a roundabout way, but he didn't even know himself, so that's out.'

The Assistant Commissioner was frowning in a concentration of thought. 'It might be a try-on, you know,' he said slowly. 'A guess in the dark. After all, it's not so unlikely.'

'Almost obvious, in fact,' the Commissioner agreed, not without relief. 'Yes, I shouldn't be surprised if you're right.'

Lord Arthur, having cause to remember a similar guess the accuracy of which had startled him more than it need have done, nodded his assent too.

'But if they don't know for certain...?' he said tentatively. 'I mean, if there's anything in the theory that it's done during the passage through the lobby, how could they make sure of getting the right man?'

'Humph!' The Commissioner seated himself on the edge of a table and stared at his toes. 'I'm not satisfied with that theory. I still believe it's done somehow on the floor of the House. But how? That's the devil. I don't believe this chap Ghaijana did it himself – fact is, I don't see how he could. He must have had someone working under him.'

'And that someone's still at large,' muttered the Assistant Commissioner.

The Superintendent, who had been to interrogate the men outside, edged gently into the room. The Commissioner looked up.

'Well?' he demanded.

'They're all agreed, sir. Except Lord Arthur, no one's been near the front door since Mr Comstock left, about three-quarters of an hour ago.'

'Mr Comstock, eh? Did he come to see the Prime Minister?'

'No, sir. I believe he came to see Miss Franklin.'

'Call that butler in, Keat, there's a good fellow. We must get these times as pat as we can.'

Dean, summoned from his interview with the second Superintendent and attended by both those great men, was as helpful as he could be. The times of Lacy's arrival, at 4.09 p.m., and Comstock's departure, at 4.13, were fixed by the plain-clothes men, as was Lord Arthur's own arrival at 4.34. Dean was almost sure that there had been no letter in the box at 4.34, but was not prepared to swear that he had looked after opening the door to Lord Arthur. He could and did swear, however, that he had cleared the box when he let Mr Comstock out, at 4.13. He remembered quite well, because Mr Comstock, having been helped on with his coat and handed his hat, had delayed two or three minutes to adjust his tie in the looking-glass, and Dean, not wishing to hold the door open on a cold day, had occupied the time in clearing the box and laying the letters on the hall table.

Mr Comstock, moreover, Dean explained, had not seen the Prime Minister. He had arrived at a few minutes after three o'clock, and had spent all the time with Miss Isabel, in the drawing-room. Lord Arthur, who had more than an idea as to the purport of the interview, wondered intensely whether Isabel had carried out her intention of breaking the engagement or whether she had allowed herself to be persuaded to continue it. He felt more than ever annoyed with Lacy, still sprawling tactlessly on the sofa upstairs.

'Well, perhaps I'd better see the Prime Minister,' observed Sir Hubert, not altogether happily. 'Dean, will you find out if he's available? You can say it's important.'

The butler withdrew, and Sir Hubert gave orders for further inquiries to be made during his absence concerning the delivery of the letter, suggesting that one of the Private Secretaries might have information.

Through the half-open door of the morning-room Lord Arthur saw Lacy descending the stairs alone. He waited a few moments for the coast to clear, and then hurried upstairs.

As he entered the drawing-room, Isabel jumped up.

'Arthur, what's happened?' she demanded in an anxious voice.

'How do you know anything's happened?' Lord Arthur countered.

'I feel it. Besides: I've rung twice for Dean and he hasn't come. Arthur… what is it?'

Lord Arthur scarcely hesitated. 'Another anonymous letter.' He briefly explained the facts, without however mentioning the naming of the Prime Minister in the note. Isabel was still in ignorance of her father's intentions in that respect.

To Lord Arthur's pleasure Isabel seized on the vital point at once.

'But who delivered the note?' she demanded.

'That,' said Lord Arthur, 'is precisely the question.' He hesitated. 'I suppose Dean's above suspicion?'

'Absolutely,' Isabel answered with conviction.

Lord Arthur sighed. 'I'm glad to hear you say so. And yet it's a pity, you know. We've only his word for the times of the clearing of the box. If only he'd been bribed to produce the letter at a certain moment…'

'Yes, I see that,' Isabel said sensibly. 'And I suppose really everyone in the house must be more or less under suspicion.' She laughed, without mirth. 'It's really rather an amusing situation, isn't it? Everyone at No. 10, Downing Street, under suspicion. Of all houses in England, that ought to be above suspicion!'

'Sir Hubert suggested one of your father's secretaries might know something.' Lord Arthur stiffened as a sudden rather vague memory came to him. 'Isabel, what do you know about young Verreker?'

'Tommy? Not very much. He's a bit too good-looking to be good for him. That's all. Why?'

Lord Arthur frowned. 'I seem to have heard something about him. Goes to nightclubs rather a bit, doesn't he? Or used to?'

'I don't know. I dare say. I should imagine he's the type that's always careful to be seen at the right places. He goes to Ascot and all that, of course. But father says he's not by any means such a fool as you might think. He works hard, and he's determined to get on. Of course he's hard up at present, and will be till his father dies, but…'

'I wonder,' said Lord Arthur.

'What do you wonder?'

'Oh, nothing. In any case, the police will see to it. But, Isabel!'

'Yes?'

'Is one allowed to ask? About Comstock…?'

'Oh, I've broken the engagement,' Isabel replied in a matter-of-fact voice. 'It would never have done, you know.'

'I'm sure of it.' Lord Arthur answered sincerely. 'And I'm only too glad you realised in time. Comstock's a good fellow, no doubt, but he's not your sort. You ought to marry…'

'Whom?' Isabel asked with amusement.

Lord Arthur looked at her. In her dark frock, with her brown hair parted in the middle and the slightly quizzical expression on her face, she was (he thought) deucedly attractive. Yes, Isabel would make some man a very charming as well as a very capable wife. No, on second thoughts 'charm' was not quite the word for Isabel. But she had a quality just as valuable, perhaps even more so: companionability. Isabel would make a real friend to her husband, as well as a wife; and that, Lord Arthur surmised, was rare. But what sort of man ought she to marry?

'I'm blessed if I know, my dear,' he said with a little laugh.

'Well,' said Isabel, 'if you ever find out, you'll tell me, won't you?'

'As your oldest male friend,' promised Lord Arthur, 'and almost brother, I'll do just that.'

Isabel looked as if she were about to add something. Instead, she changed her mind with disconcerting swiftness.

'Anyhow, this is no time for fooling,' she said, almost tartly. 'Tell me, Arthur. Father won't give me an answer. Has he decided to speak himself on Monday?'

'I... what makes you think that?' Lord Arthur stammered, for the moment taken aback.

'He said something about it the other day. It would be just like him, too.' Isabel searched his face. 'Arthur, he does mean to! I can see you know. Oh, Arthur, what are we going to do? I can't try to stop him. It's his plain duty. But... do you think they'll kill him too?'

'No, no, of course not,' Lord Arthur tried to comfort her. 'We've got the head of the bunch under lock and key, you know. They may go on threatening, but they'll be helpless without him. No one else in the House, you see. There'll be no more deaths, I'm sure.'

'You think he ought to speak, then?' Isabel asked piteously.

'My dear,' returned Lord Arthur gently, 'if even you think so, how could I think otherwise?'

Isabel brushed away her gathering tears with an impatient gesture.

'Yes, of course he must. And I mustn't hinder him in any way. This is no time for personal feelings. But, Arthur, are you quite sure Mr Lacy wasn't right? It must obviously be a big conspiracy. Don't you think someone will take Dr Ghaijana's place? And even now we don't know how Dr Ghaijana managed to kill those two in the House itself. Do you think it was really done in the lobby, as Mr Lacy says it must have been?'

'Frankly,' Lord Arthur confessed, 'I don't know how far to trust Lacy's conclusions. He argues very plausibly, but he's very much prejudiced. What on earth did the fellow want to come and bother you for, Isabel? Has he ever been here before?'

'Never. I don't even know him well. Of course I've met him often enough, at receptions and so on. But I don't think I like him very much,

Arthur. He has such a queer manner. You never know what he's going to do or say next.'

'He uses scent and paints his fingernails,' said Lord Arthur with disgust. 'Can't understand it at all. Very decent family, too. Oh, well, modern generation, I suppose.'

'You talk as if you were at least sixty, Arthur,' Isabel smiled. 'After all, I'm of the modern generation, too, you know. At least, I think I can still count myself in it – just.'

'But you don't behave like 'em,' Lord Arthur told her earnestly. 'You're just right. You don't go about with a bare, shiny face, but on the other hand you don't plaster it an inch deep in make-up. And thank heaven you don't paint your nails.'

Isabel contemplated her delicately coral-pink nails with a smile.

'I hate to shatter an illusion, Arthur, but I do. The colour comes out of a bottle.'

'I mean, blood-red. Any woman who paints her nails blood-red,' pronounced Lord Arthur, with complete conviction, 'is not only bad form, but a fool.'

Isabel laughed. 'I think that's perhaps a little sweeping, though I certainly don't care for blood-red nails myself. But you were asking about Mr Lacy. I think he came to suggest that I ought to try to persuade father to drop the Bill. I can't imagine why everyone should think that I have the slightest influence in a matter of real importance. They simply can't understand father if they do. Under that benevolent, elder-statesman appearance of his he's got a will like a steel bar.'

Lord Arthur was meditating. 'Lacy seemed in earnest?'

'Very much so. I got the impression that he knows something, or at any rate can make a very shrewd guess. He-he frightened me in a way. He seemed so absolutely sure that the Terrorists weren't finished yet. In fact I don't think he attached really very much importance to the arrest of Dr Ghaijana.'

'You know how he helped us in that? He pretended to me that it was just a logical deduction, but I think you're right, Isabel. If he doesn't actually know something, he has a very shrewd inkling. He told me that he made contact with the Separatists when he was in India. You say he frightened you. Was it a case of fright communicating itself? I mean, did he seem alarmed himself?'

'It's difficult to say. You know what an odd manner he has; one can never tell quite what he's thinking. But he certainly got very much worked up, and...yes, I shouldn't be surprised if he was a bit frightened himself. At any rate he was a good deal more vehement than I should expect anyone on the Opposition front bench to be. I'm explaining very badly. What I mean is, it was almost as if he had something personal at stake.'

Lord Arthur nodded. 'He does know something. I'm sure of it. He won't tell us, probably out of some misplaced loyalty or other; but he'll co-operate when he sees the chance, as over Ghaijana. I wonder... couldn't we possibly get some kind of a pointer to his knowledge? What about a cable, asking for full information on his trip to India? They're sure to have kept some sort of tabs on him over there. In fact there may even be a report in the files at the India Office.'

'It's worth trying,' Isabel agreed. 'Anything's worth trying.'

'I'll rout out some of the staff and get them on the job at once,' Lord Arthur promised, and made for the door.

'And... and come back here some time,' Isabel asked him. 'You're about the only person I can talk freely to, and I am really terribly worried about father. You're not going away this weekend, I suppose? Could you come to dinner?'

'Of course,' Lord Arthur said warmly. 'There's nothing I'd like better.' He hurried downstairs.

Dean was hovering in the hall, and Lord Arthur noticed that the old man was looking distressed.

As the butler held his coat with hands that were palpably shaking, Lord Arthur paused to rally him, but the other cut short his words.

'Oh, my lord, haven't you heard? I don't know what things are coming to, I don't indeed. They've arrested Mr Verreker.'

chapter fifteen

Bombshell in Whitehall

'That will do, Dean.' The voice of the Assistant Commissioner behind him made the old man start. 'You're in a position of great confidence here, and you must learn to keep a shut mouth. In any case, Mr Verreker has not been arrested. He has merely consented to go back to the Superintendent's office to answer a few questions. You may go.'

Dean withdrew, looking much abashed, and Lord Arthur followed the other back into the morning-room. Sir Hubert had not yet returned from his interview with the Prime Minister.

'Do you really think Verreker's implicated?' Lord Arthur asked as soon as the door was shut behind himself and the Assistant Commissioner.

The latter shrugged his shoulders. He was a lawyer, with a distinguished career at the bar behind him, but he retained little of the legal manner.

'Heaven knows,' he said. 'Someone in this house is implicated, that seems clear enough; and at present young Verreker looks the most likely candidate. I hope it's not so, for the sake of his people.' Tommy Verreker's father came of a family of soldiers; his grandfather had commanded an army in the last European War, and still survived to enjoy the peerage and grant which his services had won him; his father would probably command an army in the next European war. His elder brother might even command an army in the European war after that.

'How do you mean, he's the most likely candidate?'

'He's broke.' The Assistant Commissioner took a cigarette from the case Lord Arthur offered him and struck a match. 'We've had the tabs on him, of course, since this business began, and everyone else too. He went to the Jews about a year ago and borrowed pretty heavily on his expectations. He's been having difficulty in making the payments. He's a spender. That's all.'

Lord Arthur was shocked. 'But you can't think that one of the Prime Minister's own Private Secretaries would…'

'I'm prepared to think anything, my dear fellow. Aren't you? Someone's implicated all right. Let's hope it's no one worse than a Private Secretary. Good heavens, man, don't you realise that when the full story of this comes out it's going to make the biggest scandal in the history of this country? The Dreyfus affair will be nothing to it. There's treason in high places all right. I've got to such a state now that I'm ready to suspect the Prime Minister himself if anyone gave me a ha'porth of evidence.'

'It's a pretty bad show,' Lord Arthur muttered. The other's words had upset him more than he cared to show. Treason is an ugly word.

'Pretty bad show, chaps; pretty bad show,' quoted the Assistant Commissioner with savage mockery. His nerves were obviously on edge.

Lord Arthur looked up. 'Have you had tabs on me too?'

'Of course we have. What do you think? You were the first.'

The entry of Sir Hubert cut short any reply Lord Arthur might have made. He nodded to Lord Arthur and spoke curtly to his assistant.

'Come on, let's get back. There's nothing more we can do here. Keat's staying here.'

Lord Arthur ventured a question. 'The Prime Minister, Lesley…?'

'He took it very well. But he's a bit rattled, naturally. You might go up. He's alone.'

Lord Arthur nodded, and rang for Dean.

He had a plan, which he wished to lay before the Prime Minister.

When Dean took him upstairs a few minutes later he found the Prime Minister, fully dressed now, but still by the doctor's orders confined to the house, apparently quite composed. His greeting was as friendly as ever, but Lord Arthur's delicate conscience suspected a question behind it. He answered it at once.

'I can't imagine how they knew, sir. Lesley, of course, won't have mentioned it; not even his staff knew. You must be thinking that I let it out somehow.'

'Of course I don't think anything of the sort, Arthur,' the Prime Minister assured him smoothly. 'Lesley suggested that it was just a guess in the dark, and I quite agree.' He waved the younger man into a chair.

'Well, I did let it out in a way,' Lord Arthur confessed, from the depths of a big leather armchair. He explained how Mansel had twitted him on the way in which his face had given him away.

'And I'm afraid I haven't learnt my lesson,' he admitted, ruefully. 'I gave it away to Isabel in just the same way. She guessed, and my denials weren't convincing.'

'Well, there you are, you see,' said the Prime Minister. 'Where two people can guess, two thousand can.' He paused. 'So Isabel knows, does she?'

'I'm afraid she does, sir.'

'And what did she say about it?'

'She... was upset, naturally.'

The Prime Minister laughed. 'Mansel was right, Arthur. You've still to learn how to dissemble successfully. Isabel was upset, but she approved. Isn't that so?'

'You must find that out from Isabel herself, sir,' Lord Arthur smiled back. 'I'm not saying anything that might weaken my entreaty that you'll give up the idea and let me do the job.'

The Prime Minister shook his head. 'Don't waste your time, Arthur. My mind's quite made up.'

'Well, don't be in too much of a hurry, sir,' Lord Arthur urged. 'If I may suggest it, there's one course which I think you might follow without any loss of prestige to the Government. A most reasonable course, in fact.'

'And what is that?'

Lord Arthur thought for a moment. 'You probably know, sir, that Dickson is thinking of moving an adjournment on Monday, for the purpose of discussing the deaths of Lord Wellacombe and Middleton. It's certainly a definite matter of urgent public importance, and I think there's a good deal to be-said for the view that it would be right for the House to discuss it before the Bill is proceeded with. Well, sir, why not postpone your speech until after the discussion? I'm sure Dickson would like a division, and you could treat it as a vote of confidence. You'd get the opinion of the House, at any rate.'

The Prime Minister smiled more broadly. 'Arthur, I have an idea you're being rather subtle. Let's see what might happen. First of all I don't doubt that Dickson would get his quorum. The discussion would then be shelved till half-past seven, and would probably last the whole evening. That, of course, would mean postponing the Bill until Tuesday. Well, there's no particular harm in that, *but*... what about the division? I'm really very doubtful as to how we should come off, in a vote of confidence on this particular issue. A great many of our own people would vote against us, of that I'm sure; some out of the highest motives, such as saving my valuable life (for which I hope I should be grateful), and some out of sheer cold feet.

'And supposing the vote went against us? I should have to resign. But I'm quite certain that Dickson wouldn't care about forming a Government at the present juncture. In fact I should say that he'd care about it so little that he'd be quite willing for a certain proportion of his own men to vote against him and for us, just to ensure that he didn't carry his own motion. However, if a win was forced on him and he found himself compelled to form a Government, of course he'd drop this bill like a red-hot coal; and that, I imagine, is the last thing he'd want to take the responsibility for doing. He knows as well as I do that without this Bill it's just a toss-up whether India remains in the Empire another fortnight. If she walked out, the responsibility would be his and his party's. They wouldn't live it down for a generation. It would be the biggest set-back the Labour Party has ever had: far worse than the General Strike. No, it's one thing for Dickson and his friends to use their thunder against the Bill so long as we're bringing it in, but quite another matter to live up to their own words when the responsibility's their own. Their front bench know all this as well as we do; so I think we can safely say that if it came to a vote of confidence, we should get it, *malgré* our own discontents.

'But what about the discussion itself? Do you really consider it advisable? I'm afraid I don't agree. Some very unfortunate things would certainly be said. A still more unfortunate impression would be left, not only in India itself but on the Continent: that over a matter of being masters in our own house, we are divided amongst ourselves. In point of fact that is exactly the impression I am so anxious to avoid. We must at any rate present to the world the appearance of being firmly determined to stand no nonsense. Terroristic methods must not even seem to perturb us. If we let it be seen that we are rattled, then goodbye to everything that this country has ever stood for in the councils of the world.

'And that, my dear Arthur,' concluded the Prime Minister, with another smile, 'is why I've already given Dickson quite plainly to understand that if he insists on moving the adjournment after questions on Monday, I shall do all I can to prevent it. And between ourselves, Arthur, I rather fancy that the adjournment will *not* be moved.'

'Oh,' said Lord Arthur, a little blankly. 'I see.'

The Prime Minister continued to regard him for a few moments with benevolence. Then he said mildly:

'Well, if that's all you wanted to see me about, Arthur...?'

Lord Arthur took the hint.

As he closed the door of the library behind him he glanced at his watch. The time was twenty-five minutes past six. He had better get back to his flat and see about changing for dinner, early though it was. There was nothing more he could do here, and the idea of a Club, and the anxious questioning of men whom he either knew too well or did not want to know at all, was repugnant. Perhaps half an hour's rest would not be amiss. Now he came to realise it, he felt all in. There was that seating-plan of the House yesterday afternoon to pore over too, and a few more blanks to fill in.

In the street, however, he remembered the cable he had promised to send off about Lacy. There did not seem quite so much point in it now, but it had better be done. Wearily Lord Arthur turned his steps in the direction of the India Office.

There were signs of activity about it, he was glad to see. For one thing the porter was on duty, which was unusual at that time on a Saturday in any Government office. Refusing the man's offer of the lift, Lord Arthur walked up the stairs to his own office on the first floor. Scarcely had he sat down at his desk when the door burst open and a young man tumbled in.

'Who the hell...?' began the young man, and then blushed vividly. 'Oh, it's you, sir. I'm awfully sorry, sir. I'm on duty, you see, and hearing someone come into your room...'

Lord Arthur smiled. The young man's face was vaguely familiar, and his youthful exuberance was refreshing. During his term at the India Office Lord Arthur had been brought into contact with few but the more elderly of the permanent officials; and an elderly Civil Servant is a dull stick. It seemed sad that this bouncing, tow-haired young man would one day be an elderly stick himself. But he would. Bureaucracy would get him down, as it got down all the rest.

'That was very alert of you,' Lord Arthur said. 'No, come in. I want to learn what arrangements have been made. Let's see... I've forgotten your name for the minute.'

'Farly, sir,' replied the young man, blushing again, but this time with pleasure. He went on to explain that orders had been given for one junior member of the First Division staff to be permanently on duty; a camp-bed had been set up in the Secretary of State's own room for him to sleep on at night. He was to take all incoming telephone calls and deal with all matters as they arose; he was to keep in touch with Sir Everard Johns, and if possible with Lord Arthur himself.

'Just as well you told me, because no one else has,' Lord Arthur commented, dryly. It was, he thought, fairly typical that he, the nominally responsible head of the Office, should be the last person to be informed of the emergency arrangements. Sir Everard Johns, the Permanent Under-Secretary, had always made it plain that he considered any Secretary of State a bit of a nuisance and the Parliamentary Under-Secretary little more than a cypher.

Lord Arthur questioned the young man further. Farly told him that the police were not only guarding the place strongly outside, but had men posted throughout the building as well.

'I had a talk with one of them just now. They're expecting an attempt to blow us up,' said the young man, hopefully. 'Do you think there's any chance of it, sir?'

'I don't know,' Lord Arthur said. The idea seemed ridiculous. But why? The Terrorists had blown up plenty of buildings in India. It was quite right of the police to take precautions, but... 'I shouldn't think it was very likely,' he added, with a smile.

'Oh, don't you think so, sir?' Farly said, in a disappointed voice. He seemed to have welcomed the idea of being blown up.

There were one or two papers lying on the desk, and Lord Arthur took them up.

'No, don't go, Farly,' he said, as the young man turned towards the door. 'I've got a job of work for you in a minute, but I'll just see whether there's anything to deal with here first.'

He glanced rapidly through the papers. One contained statistics concerning the sterility of oxen in the province of Genkhan; the other was a report of the dismissal from his post of the ticket-clerk at Baipoul station for getting drunk and assaulting the station-master with an automatic machine.

'No,' he said. 'There's nothing here.'

'Sir,' burst out young Farly, 'is it true that the Prime Minister is going to speak on the Bill on Monday?'

Lord Arthur looked at him sharply. 'Where did you hear that?'

'I don't know, sir.' Farly looked taken aback. 'It's all round the Office. Everyone was saying so this morning.'

'I see. Well, there's no truth in it. It isn't decided yet who is to speak, or when. So you can put that all round the Office too.'

The young man mumbled something contrite and looked at Lord Arthur like a puppy that has been whipped for another puppy's misdemeanour.

'That's all right, Farly,' Lord Arthur said, more kindly. 'I'm glad to have known. These silly rumours cause a lot of harm. You can make it your special duty to report any others you hear to me personally, at once.'

Farly brightened, and Lord Arthur went on to give him instructions concerning the cable.

As he was doing so, the telephone bell rang. Lord Arthur answered the call himself, and the voice of the porter informed him that a messenger from Scotland Yard was waiting with a document and instructions to put it in the hands of Lord Arthur himself.

'Send him up.' Lord Arthur turned to Farly. 'There's a man coming up with a report of some sort from Scotland Yard for me. You can sign for it. I want to go up to the registry. I suppose there's someone on duty there?'

Young Farly thought that there would probably be a clerk on duty, and offered to go himself.

'No,' said Lord Arthur. 'You get that cable off right away.'

They left the room together, Farly to turn into the Secretary's room next door, Lord Arthur to walk a few steps down the corridor and push the button for the electric lift; for the registry containing the files of all the Office's documents was on the top floor. As he stepped into the lift he heard the porter conducting Scotland Yard's messenger up the stairs below and just caught a glimpse of two men in the blue and gilt of the State service. The lift shot up.

There was a clerk on duty in the registry, and he was very anxious to oblige Lord Arthur; but ten minutes' search of the files could produce no such thing as a report on the journey of Mr Reginald Lacy to India during the previous summer. Leaving the clerk to investigate further, Lord Arthur made his way downstairs.

As he was walking along the corridor of the floor on which the registry was located, he heard what sounded like a faint pop far down the stairs. Instantly a man jumped out of a doorway just ahead and hurried down the stairs. Somewhat surprised, Lord Arthur hurried after him. It was, he surmised, one of Lesley's men and the pop had obviously alarmed him.

There was the sound of other feet on the stairs, and Lord Arthur's alarm grew. It was to be justified. Scarcely had he descended a couple of flights, with the broad back of the Scotland Yard man a flight ahead, when a dull boom sounded three or four floors below and the concrete step under Lord Arthur's feet perceptibly trembled.

'By Heaven!' he thought. 'They've done it.'

They had.

When at last Lord Arthur reached the floor that he had left only a bare twelve minutes earlier, it was to find his room a mass of splintered wreckage and half a dozen plain-clothes men already busy about the body of young Farly who lay, a bullet through his head, across the threshold of the door.

chapter sixteen

Agitation of a Home Secretary

'Well, we've got the man at all events.' Sir Hubert Lesley spoke with grim satisfaction. He seemed to attach much more importance to that fact than to the dead body of young Farly.

Lord Arthur had taken it for granted that the man would have escaped and had been far too much occupied during the last ten minutes in seeing to the disposal of the body and examining the wreckage of his room to bestow more than a passing thought on the perpetrator. He looked round eagerly.

'You've got him?'

Sir Hubert nodded. 'My men outside caught him making off. He must have mistimed his bomb. Another three minutes, and he'd have been clear away.'

'I doubt if he mistimed it, sir,' respectfully suggested the Superintendent who had arrived with Sir Hubert. 'Our men were on to him as soon as he fired at Mr Farly. He must have set the fuse for almost instantaneous explosion and then run for it, hoping for the best.'

'It was the fellow who said he was a messenger from Scotland Yard?' Lord Arthur asked.

The grimness of the Commissioner's expression deepened. 'It was. He walked right past the noses of my prize idiots outside. There'll be a word or two coming to them later. As if anyone couldn't get hold of a Government porter's uniform!'

'He's English?'

'Not he. He's an Indian. Light enough to deceive anyone at a few yards, I grant you, but the porter downstairs should have spotted him. Young Farly probably did, and that's why he got shot. Well, it'll be like old times to me. And if,' added the Commissioner, ominously, 'I don't get something out of him, I shall be very much disappointed.'

Lord Arthur forbore to inquire into the methods by which the Commissioner proposed to obtain his information. After all, it was the Prime Minister's life, in a way, against this man's silence; and squeamish though we are in our treatment of the unconvicted thug, squeamishness would be out of place now.

'What do you think happened, Lesley?' he asked.

The Commissioner pulled at his chin. 'Well, I think it's fairly clear. This fellow told the porter downstairs that he had an important message from me to you, to be delivered to you personally. You tell me that you gave Farly instructions to sign for it. The man probably told Farly that he would wait for you; that would account for the ten minutes' delay. Then Farly must have got restive, or spotted him, and may have been about to give the alarm; so the fellow shot him, chucked his bomb into your room, and legged it.

'Curiously enough,' added the Commissioner, 'we had a warning a couple of hours ago that there might be some sort of an attempt to blow this place up. I've had it under guard, naturally, after what's been happening in India; I rather suspected they might try the same sort of thing here. But it was funny we should get a warning.'

'Whom from?'

'God knows. Anonymous call, from a telephone box in Ludgate Circus. Asked for one of the Detective Chief Inspectors – not me or any of the Superintendents. My man says he's pretty sure it was an English voice, but speaking as if he had a hot potato in his mouth; meaning that he was trying to disguise it. Cultured, but so low he could hardly hear it. All he said was that there was going to be an attempt this evening to blow up the India Office and this fellow thought we ought to know about it. Then he rang off. Curious, very.'

'Ludgate Circus?' Lord Arthur repeated, thoughtfully. 'That doesn't help you at all?'

'Not much, would it? We had a man at the call-box within three minutes, but there was nothing to be seen. After all, Ludgate Circus is one of the busiest spots in London. No doubt that's why it was chosen. Well, so far as their main object was concerned, they drew a blank. I suppose from Farly's manner the fellow guessed you were in your room, and Farly wouldn't let him in to you. Obviously they followed you here.'

'But I only came round by chance,' Lord Arthur objected.

'Suited their book all right. Two birds with one stone. By the way, I've detailed a couple of men to escort you out of here wherever you want to go; and they'll wait outside while you're there. Keat will tell you who they are. Give them a list of your movements. Where are you dining?'

'At No. 10.'

'Good. You'll come under the ordinary guard there. That will set you two free for a couple of hours for something else.

'We're short-handed enough as it is,' grumbled the Commissioner.

An uneasy, cold feeling began to make itself felt in the region of Lord Arthur's spine. 'But why all this?' he protested.

The Commissioner looked at him pityingly. 'Well, my dear fellow, what do you imagine that fellow who shot Farly was really after?'

'I've no idea.'

'Why, you,' said the Commissioner, and turned on his heel.

Lord Arthur stared at the little knot of detectives clustered in his room, at the doctor busy with Farly's body on the couch, at the detective-constables who passed him with brisk tread on their various errands bent. It seemed to him that all returned his gaze with looks of pity and apprehension. Did they really think that he was next on the assassins' list?

'Good God!' muttered Lord Arthur with feeling.

It was in a curious mood that he returned to Whitehall Court with the two plain-clothes men on his heels: part uneasiness, part bravado, and part exhilaration. The feeling of danger was bracing; the sensation that the danger might take the form of a shot in the back was not so pleasant. Lord Arthur did not try to hide his relief as the friendly portal of Whitehall Court received him safe and sound. The bravado had forbidden him to take a taxi – but he was glad when the walk was over.

Near the entrance to the Court a newsman was bawling his wares.

'Attempt to blow up the India Office,' he intoned, amplifying the more laconic wording of the placard, 'Bomb Explosion in Whitehall.'

Lord Arthur's wonderment found expression in a question to the man as he stopped to buy a copy of the newspaper.

'How long have these papers been on sale?'

"Bout five minutes after the bomb bust, guv'nor,' the man grinned. 'Tuppence, it is.'

Lord Arthur glanced at the paper in his hand and saw that it was not an evening newspaper, but a copy of *The Sunday Record*.

'Speshul edishon,' amplified the man.

Lord Arthur's wonderment increased. 'But they can't have got a special edition out in this time. Why, it's barely a quarter of an hour since it happened.' He glanced at the paper. A short notice in the stop-press stated baldly that an attempt had been made to blow up the India Office shortly after six o'clock; the damage had been slight, and since the building was empty at the time there had been no casualties. So apparently the police had seen fit to censor the news of young Farly's death.

One of the plain-clothes men, who had looked at the paper over Lord Arthur's shoulder, suggested an explanation. 'I should say this would probably be the provincial edition, my lord. That would have gone to press at about three o'clock this afternoon. They diverted it when the news came through, and got it on the streets at once. I should say they've got a scoop too,' he added, listening. 'I can't hear any other man shouting it.'

'That's right,' grinned the newsman. 'Fust with the noos, that's *The Sunday Record*. An' I orter know. I've bin 'awking it nah fer twelve years. Thank *you,* guv'nor,' he added, as Lord Arthur supplemented his inadequate penny with a sixpence.

On his way up in the lift Lord Arthur unfolded the paper and looked at the headlines on the front page. What he saw startled him. Splashed right across the page, in huge type, was the banner:

MURDERED MINISTERS

Below, supplementary headings made public the information which had hitherto been so rigorously suppressed: that the Secretary of State for India and his Successor, the Colonial Secretary, had been murdered by means of poisoned thorns by Indian Terrorists in the House of Commons as a result of disregarding threats against the Indian Restriction Bill. *The Sunday Record* had broken faith-and landed the biggest scoop of modern times.

Before he went into his bedroom to dress Lord Arthur hurriedly ran through the rest of the paper. The whole story was there, even down to the wording of the anonymous letters: while under the heading, 'Sacrifice No More Lives,' the leading article contained an impassioned appeal to the Government to postpone the Bill until the Terrorist organisation had been broken up and its leaders were in prison. Dr Ghaijana, it was suggested, was a very minor cog in the wheel; and doubts were even thrown upon the fact of his being a cog at all.

Well, the milk was spilled with a vengeance. As he submitted to the silently sympathetic ministrations of his valet, Lord Arthur was not sure that he was sorry. A genuine democrat in his views, he was never in favour of concealing from the people the true facts of a bad situation. The British, after all, were not given to panic. It was only right that they should know what had been happening. The censorship of Farly's death seemed not only unnecessary but stupid, and he determined to suggest as much to the Prime Minister that evening.

The thought occurred to him: who owned *The Sunday Record?* It had changed hands frequently during the last few years, descending with rapidity from old-fashioned dignity and sobriety to the worst kind of yellow vulgarity. Lord Arthur could not remember if he had heard who was its last purchaser, but it was obviously a lone wolf in the domain of newspaper ownership. There would be some fat frying in that camp tonight, reflected Lord Arthur, not without amusement.

Downstairs his two attendants were waiting.

'We'll have a taxi, I think,' Lord Arthur told them solemnly.

He was not quite sure what was the correct etiquette, but the plain-clothes men took the matter into their own hands. One got in beside the driver, the other followed Lord Arthur inside. He had noticed that as the three of them crossed the pavement, the men had unobtrusively ranged themselves on either side of him, although the pavement was quite empty. It all seemed rather absurd and quite unreal. Hadn't someone written a novel once called *It Can't Happen Here?* But it could happen. Young Farly's death showed as much. Perhaps the Jews had said that in Germany a few years ago. And after all, what was there more improbable in the Indian malcontents bringing their methods of bomb and murder to London than that a whole nation, which the world had once thought civilised, should revert to the savagery and tortures of the Middle Ages? No, it could happen here.

'There was an interesting point in that paper I bought,' Lord Arthur made conversation to his escort. 'You saw that they've made the whole affair public, no doubt? The leading article was very emphatic that if we continue to disregard the Terrorists, we may expect bombs and arson in London as well as Calcutta. It's interesting that the man who wrote that should have been proved right before the paper was even on sale.'

'Ah, there's not much that gets past the newspapermen,' opined the detective, with resignation.

The Prime Minister did not appear before dinner, and Lord Arthur was given his glass of sherry by Isabel. He was unreasonably annoyed to find that there was again to be no *tête-à-tête*. The Home Secretary, Mr Beamish, was already installed; and a much perturbed Mr Beamish at that.

'It's not safe,' he was saying fussily as Lord Arthur was shown in, and immediately turned to the latter for confirmation. 'Eh, Linton? Isn't that right? The Prime Minister ought to have gone to Chequers as usual. We could have guarded him there easily enough. I could have come down to him. But here in London…'

Lord Arthur tasted his sherry and exchanged a small smile with Isabel.

'Surely you can guard him more easily still in Downing Street?' he suggested.

Mr Beamish snorted. 'Against what? That's the trouble. We don't know what we're up against. They're using bombs now, you know? Oh, of course, you know; you were there. Yes, well, imagine the effect of a bomb in Downing Street now. You saw the crowds? The slaughter would be horrible. There'd be a panic. It's only a step from bombs to aeroplanes, you see. We don't know what resources these people have. Imagine a bomb dropped on Downing Street from an aeroplane now! Why, it's war in a way – war!' Evidently Mr Beamish was very badly rattled.

'They could drop bombs on us at Chequers, just as easily,' Isabel said, brightly.

'Yes, yes. But they might not hit it. And there wouldn't be anything like the same moral effect,' Mr Beamish retorted, testily. 'You don't grasp my point at all.'

To Lord Arthur the conversation seemed to be verging on the fantastic. He changed it abruptly.

'You think it a good thing to hide up Farly's death from public knowledge?'

Mr Beamish blinked. 'Hide it up?' he was beginning, when Isabel interrupted him with a little cry.

'Oh, Arthur, it's terrible. Poor young man! If they're going to do that sort of thing...'

Lord Arthur glanced at her in surprise. Isabel looked quite white and shaken. It was unlike her, he thought. Somehow he had never thought of Isabel as... well, for want of a better word, womanly.

'Come, Isabel,' he rallied her. 'It's not like you to lose your nerve.'

'No, I mustn't, of course,' she muttered, turning away.

'But... it might have been you.'

Mr Beamish was impatient of these exchanges. 'Hide up Farly's death?' he repeated. 'I don't understand what you mean.'

'Didn't your department give orders to the Press that Farly's death was not to be mentioned?'

'Certainly not. And that's another thing!' Mr Beamish's shirt-front gaped with agitated indignation, showing a glimpse of grey wool inside. 'Have you seen *The Sunday Record?* It's outrageous. The plainest flouting of instructions. Positively, I wish sometimes that we had a Press censorship here. There are some things that the Dictator countries manage better. Now, of course, they'll all follow suit. One of the evening papers is out with it already. They must have had it set up in type in advance. It's – it's scandalous.'

'Personally, I think it's a very good thing,' Lord Arthur said, a little shortly. 'The public ought to know.'

'Nonsense! The public ought to know what's good for 'em to know, and no more.'

'But this is sheer Fascism, Mr Beamish,' Isabel smiled. She had recovered herself already, Lord Arthur was glad to see.

'Fascism? Certainly not. It's government.' Mr Beamish took a gulp of sherry. It seemed to do him good. 'But that no doubt will be Mansel's excuse,' he added in a milder tone.

'Mansel?' Lord Arthur pricked up his ears. 'Does Mansel own *The Sunday Record?*'

'He does. And I hope to have a word personally with him concerning his action with it this evening.'

Lord Arthur was thinking. It was like Mansel to do the spectacular thing. It was like him, too, to seize the chance of a magnificent scoop, and let the ethical question slide. But there were queer points about the story.

'I wonder why it was specifically stated that there were no casualties?' he said aloud.

Mr Beamish snorted. 'Typical inaccuracy. One of their men happened to be on the spot no doubt, heard the explosion, just stopped to ask whether anyone was hurt and got the stereotyped answer from someone that the building was empty, and rushed off to print false information.'

'I wonder.' Lord Arthur did not like to say that according to the official police view, which perhaps Mr Beamish had not heard, it was he himself who had been the intended object of the attack. It sounded rather important; and, besides, it might upset Isabel; Lord Arthur secretly hoped it would – and then wondered why he should hope such a thing. But surely any reporter worth his salt would have nosed that out, to say nothing of Farly's death, before rushing off as Mr Beamish supposed. And there were other things, too.

'And that false information was on sale in the streets within ten minutes or so,' he went on slowly. 'Well, I suppose that's possible. I don't know much about newspaper offices. But the contents bill was properly printed. No smudgy, stop-press effect: clear lettering. Isn't that a bit odd?'

'Oh!' Isabel stared at him. 'But, Arthur, you can't possibly think…?'

'I'm just saying it's odd,' Lord Arthur repeated.

Mr Beamish had taken the point more slowly, but it had penetrated at last. He looked at Lord Arthur with a new respect.

'That's a most interesting observation, Linton. Most interesting.'

'I think an interview with Mr S P Mansel is indicated?'

'Undoubtedly. And without delay. I'll ring up Lesley at once.'

'Would you mind letting me see him?' Lord Arthur hesitated. It sounded presumptuous to say so, but he felt sure that he could get more out of Mansel than the police could.

'I don't know why you should,' Mr Beamish fussed. 'This may be very serious. We must...'

'The idea was mine, and I want to follow it up,' Lord Arthur interrupted, with an authority which obviously surprised the Home Secretary.

The entrance of the butler saved the latter from a reply.

'Mr Lacy is asking for you on the telephone, my lord,' Dean said to Lord Arthur. 'Do you wish to speak to him?'

'I'll go,' Lord Arthur nodded.

Behind him he could hear Dean add to Isabel:

'The Prime Minister wishes dinner not to be kept waiting for him. He may be detained some time.'

Over the telephone came Lacy's indolent, rather high-pitched voice:

'That you, Linton? I say, have you seen *The Sunday Record?* You have? Good. Oh, congratulations on your escape, by the way – Yes, well, no doubt certain queernesses made themselves evident to you? Eh? I mean, you can put two and two together as well as I can. Explanations are rather called for from a certain quarter, don't you think? I just thought I'd ring up in case you hadn't seen it.'

'Many thanks. Yes, I had done the sum. And I'm just about to call for the explanation,' Lord Arthur replied, grimly.

'Then I've wasted my penny,' sighed Mr Lacy. 'Goodbye.'

Dean was waiting about as he hung up, and Lord Arthur asked him to summon Mr Verreker.

'Mr Verreker has not returned from Scotland Yard yet, my lord,' the butler said, unhappily.

'Oh, no, of course not. Well, anyone who is on duty.'

'Mr Jeans is upstairs, my lord. Shall I ask him to come down?'

'Yes, No, don't bother. I'll run up myself.'

Lord Arthur felt he needed the physical action. As he took the stairs two at a time he was thinking that young Mr Lacy might enamel his fingernails, but his head was screwed on shrewdly enough. He wondered if the police had done that sum in addition, too.

Upstairs he took authority into his own hands without excuse or even justification.

'Find out if Mr S P Mansel is in London,' he told the Secretary, 'and ask him if it would be convenient for him to call at 10, Downing Street at half-past nine this evening.'

chapter seventeen

Financial Fade-out

'But, of course, I had advance information, my dear fellow,' said Mr Mansel, equably. He applied a match to the cigar which he had already asked permission to light, and looked benevolently over the smoke at Lord Arthur.

The two were closeted in the little morning-room. Lord Arthur, who was conducting the interview entirely on his own responsibility, had opened it by bluntly asking Mr Mansel to account for the fact that the contents-bill of his newspaper, announcing a bomb explosion in Whitehall, must have been printed before ever the bomb burst. Mr Mansel, plainly concealing his disappointment that the summons should not have brought him into the presence of the Prime Minister but only into that of a lowly Under-Secretary of State, was nevertheless prepared to divulge information.

'I told you I had my sources,' he added.

'Yes, but…' Lord Arthur found himself somewhat nonplussed, not only by Mr Mansel's frankness but by his equanimity. Somehow Lord Arthur could not get rid of the impression that Mr Mansel had been conniving at a criminal outrage. Mr Mansel himself, however, evidently did not think so. 'You *knew* these people intended to blow up the India Office?' he said, reprovingly.

'Not as one knows that twice two are four,' replied Mr Mansel, in his gentle, rather melancholy voice. 'All I knew was that it had been reported to me that there was going to be an attempt to blow up the India Office. That's very different.'

'But didn't you take any steps to stop it?' Lord Arthur was still out of his depth.

Mr Mansel stopped adjusting the faultless crease of his black trousers in order to spread out his hands, palms upwards.

'What could I do to stop it? I didn't even know who was instigating the attempt.'

'You could have at least passed the information on to the police.'

Mr Mansel gave his deprecating smile. 'I did.'

'You did. Oh! It was you who rang up from Ludgate Circus?'

'Ludgate Circus is so near Fleet Street,' explained Mr Mansel.

'But why didn't you give your name? Why didn't you interview them personally and let them question you?' Lord Arthur could not help feeling there was still something wrong somewhere.

'Because I didn't want them to know my name, and I didn't want to answer their questions,' Mr Mansel replied, mildly. 'I couldn't have helped them any further, and they'd simply have spoilt my scoop.'

Lord Arthur was taken aback by this point of view. In his simplicity he had assumed that there was only one possible attitude towards the outrages: that of helping to get them cleared up, and their perpetrators under lock and key, at the earliest possible moment. Mr Mansel's attitude was equally simple: that whatever happened in the world, however deplorable, must be made if possible to turn to the advantage of S P Mansel.

'Oh, well,' Lord Arthur murmured, with the usual contempt for the other person's point of view. 'You had the whole story ready set up in type?' he added, curiously.

'More or less,' Mr Mansel admitted.

'And that's why your stop-press announced that there had been no casualties?'

'Exactly. An unfortunate error. But I was specifically assured that there were to be no casualties.'

Lord Arthur pounced upon what looked to him like a slip. 'Then you were in touch with the instigators?'

'Oh, no.' If it had been a slip Mr Mansel remained outwardly unperturbed. 'My informant may be in touch with some members of the organisation; in fact, he must be. But not I personally.'

'Who is your informant?'

'I'm sorry. I can't tell you that.'

'I shall have to report this conversation to the police, you know,' Lord Arthur frowned.

Mr Mansel shrugged his shoulders. 'By all means. But I shall equally withhold the name of my informant from them. It would mean the man's death if I divulged it, and I shall certainly not cause that. He's far too useful to me,' added Mr Mansel, simply.

There was a pause.

'I'll give you my own view of this bombing, if it's of any interest to you,' Mr Mansel said, mildly.

'Certainly it's of interest.'

'Well, I don't think they were after you at all. No doubt it suited them to make it look as if they had been, and perhaps they wanted to give you a good scare; but the death of that poor young man was certainly fortuitous. I should say the emissary lost his head. What they really wanted was to provoke publicity.'

'Publicity?'

'Certainly. Rightly or wrongly the Home Office have asked the newspapers to hush the whole business up as much as possible. I think wrongly: in fact, I think so very strongly. I feel the public should know what is happening.'

'I'm inclined to agree with you.'

'Exactly. It's for the public to decide, after all. And rightly or wrongly again the Terrorists think that the public would… well, I don't say panic, but at any rate insist on the postponement of the Bill. As it is, the public officially knows nothing. Therefore it's not terrified. Well, it's not much use being a Terrorist if you don't succeed in terrifying, is it?'

'The public wouldn't panic,' Lord Arthur said, staunchly. 'You of all people ought to understand popular reactions. Don't you agree that the country would take the truth quite calmly?'

'I'm sure of it. But I'm equally sure that it would require the Bill to be postponed until this organisation has been broken up.'

'In the Cabinet's view, to postpone the Bill means to abandon it.'

'You mean, surely, in the Prime Minister's view?' corrected Mr Mansel, gently. 'My own opinion is that the Prime Minister is wrong, just as he's wrong to insist on pushing on with the Bill at all costs, and against all opposition. And that,' added Mr Mansel with a smile, 'is why my newspaper has broken out of the ring of silence and, incidentally, is giving the Terrorists the publicity they want.'

'Yes, I see your point,' Lord Arthur said slowly. 'Ministers may collapse in the House of Commons, but the cause of death can be hushed up; whereas it's impossible to hush up a bomb explosion in Whitehall. That seems quite reasonable.' He looked sharply at the other. 'But you're quite sure you're not playing into their hands by publishing the full story?'

'I have my own hand to play,' Mr Mansel returned, with a deprecating little smile. 'To say nothing of the hands of all the investors who have come into my Indian ventures on my recommendation. I feel my responsibility towards them very keenly, I can assure you. There are literally millions of pounds involved. No! No one can be more interested in restoring law and order to India than I am.'

'Ye-es.' Lord Arthur thought for a moment, then decided to try a venture. 'But according to reports in my Office you might be in an even better position if the Separatists carry the issue. I understand in that event you would be a kind of commercial dictator of Barghiala?'

Mr Mansel laughed. 'It's impossible to keep the whole of a secret, isn't it? But unfortunately the bit that gets out only distorts the rest. It's quite true that I'm trying hard to strike a bargain with the Maharajah of Barghiala – and a man who wanted more *quid* for his *quo* I've frankly never met; and if it comes off I shall still manage to save a little from the wreck. But my dear fellow, you know Barghiala. It's one of the poorest States; it's certainly the most backward. Even if I did succeed in becoming its commercial dictator (which, let me assure you, is not likely to be the case so long as the present Maharajah is alive), what possible comparison is there between that and being the most formidable commercial proposition – I won't say "dictator" – of the whole of that exceedingly rich conglomeration of peoples and territories which we lump together under the name of India? For that, in confidence, is the end to which I've been working for the last few years.'

'Commercial dictator of the whole of India?' Lord Arthur was staggered by the immensity of such an ambition.

Mr Mansel waved a deprecating hand. 'No, no. Not "dictator," I said. Just a colossal system of inter-linked commercial ventures, from an Indian

"Woolworth's" to an Indian Morris Motors and Rolls-Royce combined. It's possible. And I,' added Mr Mansel with simplicity, 'am the man to do it. So you can see that I'm more interested than anyone in keeping India within the Empire for just so long as she'll stick – with British protection for British capital ventures. The very first thing the Indians would do if they ever get control,' Mr Mansel added with feeling, 'would be to expropriate all British interests – just like Mexico.'

'Yes,' Lord Arthur agreed. 'I quite see that.'

'And yet,' Mr Mansel pointed out, 'with all that at stake, I think this Bill, which is designed to protect property like mine, ought to be postponed.'

'Why?' Lord Arthur's question was blunt.

Mr Mansel thought for a moment.

'Well, for a multiplicity of reasons. The deaths of Wellacombe and Middleton upset me very much, but frankly I wouldn't let that deter me if I thought the Bill ought to be pushed on. Nor your death, if you take the job on next. The Prime Minister is rather different; he's the best man we have in politics today, on either side, and if he insists on getting himself killed the results may be very bad. But apart from all that, I feel the Bill is unnecessary. Not even martial law is going to stop these Terrorists if their organisation is really formidable, and the Bill doesn't go so far as that. But in my opinion it actually defeats its own object. By appearing to persecute the Separatists in the interests of the Empire, it's much more likely to bring more and more recruits into their ranks. Whereas if it's left to itself, the thing is likely to blow itself out in a few more months, just as non-co-operation and all the other campaigns have done. Leave well alone is the best policy, in my opinion.'

'Then you think the Bill ought to be not merely postponed but abandoned?'

'I do.'

'You feel that strongly?'

'Oh, no,' said Mr Mansel, carelessly. 'I don't think it would do much active harm. It's just my opinion that, on balance, it would be better not to take the risk of stirring up another mutiny. That's all.'

'I see.'

'But I do feel strongly,' Mr Mansel added, 'that the Bill should be postponed, to be taken up again later if advisable. I feel that very strongly indeed, and in my opinion the very small amount of prestige that might be lost would be far outweighed by the Prime Minister's life – which he will certainly lose if he speaks on the Bill next Monday.'

'You really still think that?' Lord Arthur asked, almost incredulously.

'Make no mistake, Linton.' Mr Mansel's tone was deadly earnest. 'Make no mistake, if the Prime Minister speaks on Monday, he'll die. I know. The police think they cut off the head of the conspiracy when they arrested Ghaijana this afternoon.' Mr Mansel paused for a full minute. 'My information is that Ghaijana isn't even a member of the Terrorist gang.'

'Good heavens! Are you sure of that?'

'No, I'm not sure. How can I be? I merely pass on the information to you,' said Mr Mansel, sombrely, 'for what it's worth. But my information,' he added, 'is usually accurate.'

The two men looked at each other.

'The Government – and that means the Prime Minister – should be very, very sure that they're not repeating the Irish mistake in India,' said Mr Mansel slowly. 'I'm no statesman, but I know that separation is coming to India very soon now. I knew in 1919 that it was coming to Ireland. The policy of repression didn't pay this country then. Is there any reason to suppose that it's going to pay now?'

It was somewhat thoughtfully that Lord Arthur, without ringing for Dean, showed his visitor out into Downing Street. The last few sentences had impressed him. Mansel, referring to the Prime Minister's danger, had spoken as a man who knew. And it had been clear, too, that he believed Dr Ghaijana innocent. If that were the case, they were no nearer to coping with the Terrorist threat than they had been yesterday, when Middleton was murdered – unless, of course, the Commissioner succeeded in getting anything out of the captured bomb-thrower, which seemed a thin hope.

As for the Irish parallel, Lord Arthur was not inclined to attach too much importance to that. The cases were not the same. In Ireland practically the whole population had joined in the struggle to throw off British domination. But this Bill, as the Prime Minister had always insisted, was designed primarily to protect peaceable Indians themselves against the Nazi-like attacks of their own countrymen. No, there was no parallel.

The Prime Minister, who had put in a belated appearance at dinner, was still closeted with Mr Beamish in the library; Lord Arthur had understood that the Home Office plans for dealing with any possible extension of the bombing incident, and allaying any possible panic on the part of the public in consequence, were receiving the close scrutiny of the Prime Minister himself. A number of different officials were coming and going for purposes of consultation and arrangement. Lord Arthur turned his steps towards the drawing-room. At last he could reckon on having Isabel to himself. It surprised him to realise how much he wanted to hear her cool brain analysing and dissecting the situation and the results of his own enquiries. There was much that she did not know, and for nearly half an hour Lord Arthur was occupied in detailing his own experiences to her and answering her questions upon matters of fact. She was, naturally, interested most of all in the bombing outrage of which Lord Arthur himself had so nearly been the victim.

When the recital was finished Isabel leaned back in her chair and stared into the fire. She was wearing an informal little evening coat and frock of pale-green figured taffeta, and the lamp just behind her left shoulder lit up her dark hair and softened the somewhat austere lines of her face. She did not look like a girl who had taken a first in Greats at Oxford. Lord Arthur, who had aspired to no more than a pass degree, had a respect for Isabel's brains; but at the moment he was more occupied with her appearance. The thought occurred to him that she might have sat thus, on the opposite side of a fireplace, for the rest of her life with Comstock. Thank goodness at any rate that she had had the courage to put right that mistake.

'Isabel,' he said, suddenly, 'how did Comstock take his... dismissal?'

Isabel glanced at him. 'Rather badly. Why, Arthur?'

'I just wondered.'

'He's ambitious,' Isabel went on slowly. 'I'd never realised how ambitious he is. He seemed to think that the fact of my being the daughter of one Prime Minister ought to be a good reason for my wanting to be the wife of another.'

'Meaning himself?' Lord Arthur asked in surprise.

Isabel smiled. 'Just that. It may be news to you, but Eric expects to be forming a Government of his own quite shortly.

I think he genuinely believes it.'

'But it's absurd.' Lord Arthur felt quite annoyed.

'Is it? He has a big following in the country, you know. If anything happened to father, whom do you suppose the party would choose as leader?'

'Frith, without a doubt,' Lord Arthur replied, promptly.

'According to Eric, there's every doubt. Mr Frith is a safe man, but one can't deny that he's unenterprising. Eric's theory is that someone rather more spectacular will be needed to pull the party together after this affair is over. He's his own choice.'

'I know he's been doing a good deal of lobbying lately, but…'

'Eric's a cunning man,' Isabel said, equably. 'And a born wire-puller.'

'Well, thank goodness you were one wire he couldn't pull,' Lord Arthur grinned.

'Oh, yes,' Isabel agreed. 'He looked on me as a wire.'

There was a pause.

'He was one of the prime movers against the Bill in the Cabinet,' Lord Arthur said, slowly. 'Right from the beginning. I wonder what his game was.'

'I don't know. But knowing Eric as I do now, I'm sure he had one. Still, Eric's intrigues are rather small beer compared with the other matter. Arthur… there's one thing that strikes me.'

'Yes?'

'Do you think Mr Mansel told you all he knows?'

Lord Arthur considered. 'No, I should think it very probable that he didn't. Why, Isabel?'

'Well,' Isabel said, slowly, 'it's that point about the stop-press in the newspaper. Mr Mansel told you that he had advance information about the bomb attack, but his informant assured him that there were to be no casualties; it was only intended as a demonstration to gain publicity. But surely in an organisation like that there would be no leakages. Doesn't that mean that Mr Mansel's informant must be a member of the organisation, a Terrorist himself?'

'Of course it does. Stupid of me not to have seen it.' Lord Arthur jumped to his feet.

'What are you going to do, Arthur?'

'Ring him up. He'll be home by now, easily. Mansel must talk. I had the feeling all the time that he was concealing something. It may be my imagination, but I believe he was in two minds whether to tell me or not. He may know a great deal. At the very least he can put us on to one member of the Terrorist executive. I'm going to put it to him straight that he mustn't hold up vital information any longer, just to serve his own interests.'

'I should think not,' Isabel concurred, warmly. 'It's abominable.'

It was some few minutes before Lord Arthur was able to establish telephone contact with Mansel. When he did so, he put his demand with cogency, carefully veiled against possible eavesdroppers though his words were.

At the other end of the telephone Mansel sighed.

'I was half expecting you to ring me,' he said. 'I can't give you an answer now, I must think it over. You don't know what it is you're asking of me. But… well, I'll think it over. Do you think you could come and see me here at eleven o'clock tomorrow morning?'

'With pleasure. And I'm sure you'll do the right thing. Good night, then, Mansel.'

Lord Arthur hung up the receiver not without elation. From Mansel's tone there was much to be hoped from the appointment that he had conceded.

The hope was not to be realised, for the appointment was never kept. Before eleven o'clock the next morning the spectacular Mr S P Mansel was dead.

chapter eighteen

Chat in the Chamber

Mr S P Mansel's death was as spectacular as his life. He was killed in his study, the same small room in which he had received Lord Arthur, at twenty-seven minutes before midnight on the Saturday evening, two days after the death of Lord Wellacombe; and it appeared that he had been killed in the same way. He was found lying sprawled over his desk, and sticking in the side of his rather thick neck were two thorns which subsequent analysis proved to be smeared with curare. Pinned on his coat was a white card, on which was written, in a neat, copperplate hand:

> *Positively the last thorns. But there are other means.*
> *Let all enemies of India beware.*
>
> The Brown Hand.

It was possible to fix the exact time of death by a coincidence. The police, with the thoroughness characteristic of Scotland Yard, were neglecting no possible line of inquiry which seemed to point in any way to India. Mr Mansel was known to have Indian connections; and Mr Mansel had therefore been under observation. A discreet watch had been kept on all comings and goings to his house, and his telephone had been tapped. It was in the middle of a telephone conversation, as it happened, that the attack on him was made.

The call, an incoming one, had been promptly traced to Mr Reginald Lacy, and the shorthand record in the possession of the police ran as follows:

Mansel *(after the butler, having first obtained permission from his master, had put the call through)*: S P Mansel speaking. Yes, Lacy?

Lacy: Hullo! Good of you to let a comparative stranger bother you at this hour, but there are one or two things I should rather like to ask you.

Mansel: What the devil do you mean?

Lacy: Oh, just trifles light as air, you know. But a shade odd. Yes, decidedly a shade odd.

Mansel: If you've anything to say, say it. I'm busy.

Lacy: You mean, you're engaged?

Mansel: Of course I'm engaged.

Lacy: No matter, no matter. I don't want to disturb you now. I just want to ask whether we could arrange an appointment, perhaps, for tomorrow?

Mansel: You know quite well – *(loudly)* here, what the devil are you doing? *(The receiver was then apparently dropped and there were confused noises, as if a struggle was taking place.)*

Lacy: Hullo! Hullo! What's the matter? What's happening? (No *answer was received to this, and about half a minute later Mansel's receiver was replaced, breaking the connection.)*

Lacy, it was ascertained, had then rung up his exchange, and about ten minutes later, Scotland Yard. Within a further ten minutes the body of Mr Mansel was found. The police surgeon put the time of death at approximately a quarter of an hour to twenty minutes earlier, which tallied nicely.

Lord Arthur did not learn of Mansel's death until Sunday morning. The news, of course, was not in the papers, and it was a personal visit of the Assistant Commissioner for the Criminal Investigation Department, Mr Willis-Carter, which apprised Lord Arthur of this unexpected development.

The former nodded understandingly as Lord Arthur, still in his dressing-gown and slippers, mentioned the appointment which he had arranged with Mansel for that same morning.

'The man knew too much,' said the Assistant Commissioner. 'That's obvious. We've had our suspicions all along that he might know something.'

'But why didn't he tell what he knew before?' Lord Arthur asked, with the helpless irritation with which one contemplates lost chances.

'Scared, I expect,' the Assistant Commissioner answered laconically. 'The way he impressed on you the Prime Minister's danger seems to show that. Danger means danger, from this crowd.'

A thought struck Lord Arthur. 'If the mere possibility that he might be going to reveal secrets brought Mansel his death,' he said slowly, 'what about Lloyd-Evans, who has actually told all he knows?'

'The man's scared stiff, naturally. Not so much of a rough and tumble – I believe he'd half welcome that; he used to be quite a tidy amateur boxer in his youth, you know – but of a thorn in the back of his neck. Well, it's a nasty prospect. We're doing our best for him, of course; strong guard on the house; couple of men with him whenever he puts his nose out of doors – which, by the way, he hasn't done yet.'

'That reminds me. You can take my two sleuths off. Mansel told me that he didn't think they were after me at all yesterday; my presence was just a bit of extra luck.' Lord Arthur gave an account of Mansel's theory.

The Assistant Commissioner smiled. 'Yes, that may be so. Still, I'll keep the men on if you don't mind.'

'Is Mansel's death going to help you at all?' Lord Arthur demanded. 'You haven't got the man?'

'No, we haven't. And no idea who it was. The butler never saw him. He must have come in through a side-door which opens into the passage close to Mansel's study. He used to let confidential callers in himself that way, I gather.'

'It was someone known to him,' Lord Arthur pointed out.

'Oh, obviously. It's a pity Mansel didn't mention his name when he shouted at him,' sighed the Assistant Commissioner.

'That must have been the actual attack. Curious that your listener-in should have heard it, to say nothing of Lacy. In fact, it's curious that it should have been made at all during a telephone conversation.'

'Oh, I don't know,' Mr Willis-Carter demurred. 'Very good opportunity, while Mansel's back was turned and his attention engaged. And perhaps he was afraid Mansel might give something away over the telephone about his identity. That would have made it impossible for him to carry out the murder, you see.'

'You think the visit was made with the deliberate intention of murder, then?'

'Oh, I think so. That seems plain.'

'I wonder,' Lord Arthur said suddenly, 'whether my own telephone conversation with Mansel had anything to do with his death. It followed so closely, and Mansel had almost promised me to talk a bit more freely when I was to see him this morning. Is there any possibility of that conversation having been overheard by these people–wires tapped, or something?'

'That's an idea,' the Assistant Commissioner admitted. 'I'll have it followed up. We ought to be able to find out if the wires have been tapped by anyone besides ourselves. Yes, that's certainly an idea. Well, I must be getting along. I just called in to give you the news. I'm meeting one of the Superintendents in a minute or two to pay a call on Lacy. He hasn't told us yet why he wanted to see Mansel, and what it was that had struck him as queer.'

'I think I can give you some idea of that,' Lord Arthur said. 'Lacy rang me up at No. 10 yesterday evening, and said much the same sort of thing. I told him I was just about to take it up with Mansel, but I suppose he thought I might have bungled it and wanted to have a try himself. I think you'll find that it was the fact of the contents bill of Mansel's Sunday paper having been printed before the explosion took place. I've told you Mansel's explanation.'

'And that it was he who rang us up. Yes, well… queer chap. The City won't be the same without him. And I shouldn't be surprised,' opined the Assistant Commissioner, 'if a sigh of relief doesn't go up from a few of the orthodox offices, too. Well, I must be off.'

As he rang for his man to show Willis-Carter out, Lord Arthur said:

'And young Verreker?'

'Returned to No. 10 without a stain – thank goodness!'

'Then you're as far off as ever from knowing who delivered the last letter?'

'Farther,' said the Assistant Commissioner dismally.

Before the door opened Lord Arthur just had time to ask: 'And that fellow you caught? Got anything out of him yet?'

'Nothing. They've been working on him all night, and they'll go on all the weekend; but if you ask me, short of lighting a fire on his chest, I doubt if they'll get anything – and I'm afraid our Beamish wouldn't stand for that. He'll hang all right, but he'll hang mum.'

When his visitor had gone, Lord Arthur completed his dressing. He felt restless, and more disturbed than ever. The murder of Mansel, while not affecting him personally, seemed to him sinister in the extreme. It was obvious that the Terrorist organisation was prepared to observe no limits. How far would that realisation affect the weaker spirits in the Cabinet, only stiffened as they had been by the Prime Minister's inflexibility? And if the Prime Minister himself should go the way of Wellacombe and Middleton…?

Lord Arthur found a resolve, which had gradually been forming in his mind for the last twenty-four hours, suddenly harden and become fixed. Somehow the Prime Minister must be prevented from speaking and he, Lord Arthur, must take his place. It might mean death, but there was still more than twenty-four hours in which to save the situation – and himself.

But what could he do that the police were not already doing better?

Restlessly Lord Arthur took his hat and stick and went downstairs. His two attendants were there, chatting with the porter. They came towards him at once, and one inquired respectfully where he proposed to go.

'I don't know,' Lord Arthur confessed. He looked at them, two Scotland Yard men at his disposal: only detective constables, it was true, but keen and eager. Could he not make better use of them than this barren duty of guarding his own person?

An idea came to him. 'We'll go over to the House. We shall have it to ourselves, and it's a good opportunity to study the possibilities. Perhaps we could make out how Dr Ghaijana manipulated the thorns – if he did manipulate them at all.'

The two men expressed approval and interest, and the trio set out. On the short walk Lord Arthur encouraged the detectives to talk and soon found that neither entertained any doubt that Dr Ghaijana had been the actual executive of the murders, though they admitted that he must have a powerful organisation behind him. Lord Arthur wished he could share their certainty.

All the approaches to the Parliamentary buildings were closely guarded, but no difficulty was made in passing Lord Arthur inside. Still accompanied by his guardians, he walked quickly through the lobby, where scattered knots of plain-clothes men were lingering, ready for a call to any part of the building.

The great hall of the House of Commons was empty. Lord Arthur paused for a moment beside the Speaker's chair, populating the empty benches in his imagination with the persons who had occupied them on the two fatal afternoons. There Wellacombe had sat, and from the same place Middleton had risen; there he himself had been, just behind them, and there S P Mansel; and over there, away down below the gangway had sat Dr Ghaijana.

'Sit there, Curtis,' Lord Arthur said abruptly, pointing to the Government front bench. 'You're Mr Middleton.'

'Here, my lord?' One of the detectives seated himself in the position indicated.

Lord Arthur frowned. It was difficult to fix the exact place when the benches were empty. He scrutinised the rather shabby upholstery. 'No, a foot or two to your right; where that button's missing; that's right.'

'Time they did the place up a bit,' ventured the other man.

'This is an economical Government,' Lord Arthur smiled, a little absently. He walked down to the gangway and seated himself as nearly as he could judge where Dr Ghaijana had been. Curtis looked a long way away.

Lord Arthur called the other detective to him. 'Could you, however skilful you were, somehow propel three or four poisoned thorns at Curtis from here, and make sure of hitting him every time?'

'It doesn't look much like it, my lord, does it?' admitted the man.

'I should say it was out of the question. Besides,' Lord Arthur remembered, 'in Mr Middleton's case there was a thorn at the back of his head. He might have turned towards the Speaker, of course, but even so... no, I think it's impossible from here.'

'Couldn't it have been done from behind, my lord?'

'I was sitting just behind, on the look-out for the slightest move. Still, we'll see.'

They circled about the sitting man, but from no point did it seem that the thorns could possibly have been despatched, even by a mechanical contrivance, without attracting attention. From the galleries, too, it appeared to be an impossible feat.

'I don't know,' Lord Arthur had to confess, after half an hour's effort. 'I suppose it must have been done somehow in the lobby, or behind the Chair.'

'I fancy that's what our people think,' one of the detectives agreed.

Lord Arthur shrugged his shoulders. 'Goodness knows. There are plenty of objections to that, too, apart from the actual difficulty. For instance – Oh, hullo, Sir Angus!'

The elderly Scotsman who held the responsible post of Senior Official Analyst to the Home Office did not remove his hands from the baggy pockets of his greatcoat as he nodded curtly in response to the other's greeting. The detectives withdrew discreetly.

'Ah, Linton! On the same quest as myself, no doubt.'

'I was trying to see a glimmer of light somewhere. But surely your part of the business is simple enough, Sir Angus? Once you've established the poison, your job's finished.'

'Indeed and that it's not,' retorted Sir Angus MacFerris. 'That's only the beginning. There's the very important question of quantity, ye see.'

'Quantity?'

'Aye.' Sir Angus pulled at his short grey beard and looked at Sir Arthur from under shaggy brows. 'There's no exact quantitative test for an elusive alkaloid substance like curare. In fact, we can't say much more than that it's there or it isn't there. And that makes things a wee bit difficult.'

'Why difficult?'

'Well, well… now you wouldn't know what's reckoned as the fatal dose of curare?'

'Thirty milligrams,' Lord Arthur replied glibly.

'That's so. Thirty milligrams. Well now, I've heard of wee birds not much larger than a pigeon being shot in flight by an arrow dipped in curare, and it didn't kill them. Will you tell me, if that's the case, how one thorn could kill a man like Wellacombe? No, no; you couldn't get thirty milligrams on a thorn, and that's a fact.'

'But Middleton had three or four thorns in him.'

'Maybe. But Wellacombe had but the one.'

'They only *found* one,' Lord Arthur corrected. 'But wasn't there another wound on the ball of his thumb that showed traces of the stuff?'

'Aye, there was. But wouldn't you say that if only one thorn was found, only one was used? Or do you think Lesley's men overlooked two-three more lying about under their noses?'

'No, I don't think that,' Lord Arthur said slowly. 'But I can think of at least one good explanation of why only one should have been found.'

'You mean, the murderer picked the others up in the confusion. Well, maybe, maybe. But even three-four thorns...' Sir Angus shook his shaggy old head in a dissatisfied way.

'How much is thirty milligrams?' Lord Arthur demanded. 'About as big as a small pea, I suppose?'

'Gosh, man, no!' Sir Angus sounded quite shocked at such ignorance. 'Thirty milligrams is approximately half a grain, and a grain is – well, an ordinary pin weighs about a grain and a half.'

'About a third of the weight of an ordinary pin,' Lord Arthur meditated. 'Not much bigger than a large pin's head. You could get that amount on two or three thorns, surely?'

'Maybe you could. Maybe. But I shouldn't have said so. And then it would all have to be absorbed, ye see. No, I'm not satisfied.'

'But isn't it the theory that some other substance was mixed with the curare?'

'I can find traces of no other substance,' admitted Sir Angus gloomily. 'Not a trace. But, mind you, that doesn't say no other substance was employed. Some poisons are extremely volatile. In fact, I can think of two-three that are well-nigh untraceable. But they act quicker. There's the time factor, ye see.'

'But we don't know when the thorns were inserted,' Lord Arthur pointed out. 'No one seems to have noticed them – not even the victims.'

'Oh, they wouldn't feel a wee prick like that. It's surprising what a big prick will pass unnoticed if you don't see it happening. But we have one point to fix the time by: the moment the victims entered this building. For it's very sure the attacks weren't made beforehand. That's important, ye see, because the collapse in each case followed less than a quarter of an hour later. That means a fair-sized dose – more than thirty milligrams if anything. So I thought,' concluded Sir Angus, 'that I'd just take a walk round here this morning, to clear my brain a bit and see if I could make out how it was done.'

'I thought the same. In fact, those two detectives and I have been trying to reconstruct the crime. But – '

'Ye haven't seen the light?'

'Not to say seen it. But I'm not at all sure,' Lord Arthur said slowly, 'that a sentence in this conversation of ours hasn't given me an idea.'

'Something I said to you?' asked Sir Angus with interest.

Lord Arthur smiled.

'No. Curiously enough, something I said to you.'

chapter nineteen

A Minister Shows His Mettle

Lord Arthur ate a solitary lunch, and thought a good deal.

As he was sipping his coffee afterwards a diffident visitor arrived to see him. It was the clerk from the registry in the India Office who had searched vainly on the previous afternoon for any record of Lacy's recent visit to India, and he brought with him the answer to Lord Arthur's cablegram. The message was not in cypher; and having bade the young man be seated and ordered another cup to be brought for him-a proceeding which caused his visitor to alternate rapidly between a deep pink and a pale puce – Lord Arthur set himself to study the laconic wording.

The result was disappointing. No particularly close watch had been kept on Lacy, and only a few of his more important interviews had been recorded. These were more or less what might have been expected of any politician of the Left visiting India, and the only name which caused Lord Arthur the least interest was that of the Maharajah of Barghiala.

'So that's where he got his information about Mansel's activities,' Lord Arthur thought to himself. 'But not from the Maharajah himself, I'll be bound. The old boy's too foxy for that. Some underling must have given the game away.'

'Humph!' he said aloud. 'Not much here, I'm afraid.'

The young man, now almost mauve, produced a couple of folders from under his arm, nearly upsetting his coffee-cup in the process.

'I th-thought you might like to see these,' he stammered.

'I had another look round this morning and came across them.'

'Thank you. I'm afraid our activities were rather abruptly interrupted yesterday evening,' Lord Arthur said, taking the folders. 'Did you know that poor young fellow – Farly?'

'No, I didn't know him, not to speak to. Is it – is it true they were after you, my lord?' asked the young man in a rush.

Lord Arthur smiled. 'I wish I could think I was so much in their way. No, I fancy that was just a coincidence. Let's see, what are these?'

'One's a report on the railway accident, when Colonel and Mrs Lacy were killed in 1912. The other's a file on Dr Ghaijana. I thought you might like…'

'Yes, very thoughtful of you,' said Lord Arthur courteously.

In order not to disappoint the young man he ran quickly through the contents of each folder, little though he saw how they could help him.

The first contained only information which in a general way he knew already. The accident had taken place in a deserted part of the country; the subsequent inquiry showed definitely that a deliberate attempt had been made to wreck the train, but fortunately the attempt had been half-hearted and the result had not been so serious as it might have been; by an unhappy chance there had in any case been a bare half-dozen passengers aboard in addition to the Lacy party, against whom the attempt had obviously been made; unhappily, a telegraph pole, which apparently had been intended to fall in the path of the engine, must have proved tougher than the wreckers expected, for it had fallen instead by an unhappy chance across the compartment occupied by Colonel and Mrs Lacy, killing them both. There was a coldly gruesome description of the head injuries which had caused their deaths, and accounts of various witnesses who had seen men running away from the scene of the accident. Needless to say, these men were never caught, though there was some suspicion that the engine-driver might have been privy to the attempt, since it seemed clear that the train must have slowed down as it approached the fatal place; this, however, the driver strongly denied, and his denials were corroborated by the fireman. The report hinted that both men were probably lying.

The ayah had finished the journey with the baby alone, handed the infant Reginald over to the first Government official she could find, indulged in a fit of hysterics, apparently under the impression that she was to be blamed for the whole thing, and then incontinently vanished.

Lord Arthur wondered idly what Freud or Adler or any other Continental psychologist might have found to say about the possible effect of all this on the infant mind, and whether they would have traced a direct line from the telegraph pole in 1912 to the enamel on young Lacy's fingernails today. Lord Arthur thought they probably would.

The other file had even less news to impart. Lord Arthur, already tolerably conversant with the details of Dr Ghaijana's restless career, skimmed hastily through the tale of his activities almost from the time of his birth, in Benares, of obscure and respectable middle-class parents, to his election to Parliament two years ago.

He handed the folders back with a word of thanks.

The young man, having no further excuse for remaining, hastily gulped the dregs of his coffee and departed.

Lord Arthur wondered what to do next: for do something he felt he must.

The question was answered for him. A ring on the telephone was followed by the appearance of his man with the information that Mr Lloyd-Evans was on the line.

Mr Lloyd-Evans was brief. Could Lord Arthur come round to Carlton House Terrace and see him, at once? Lord Arthur promised to be there in ten minutes, sleuths and all.

He was there in nine.

Lloyd-Evans was pale but calm.

'It's come, Linton,' he said, as soon as they were alone. 'I knew it would, and it has.'

'What has?' Lord Arthur asked patiently. He disliked drama in the home, but could not deny that Mr Lloyd-Evans had every excuse.

Lloyd-Evans spread his hands. 'Exposure. Ruin.'

'Oh?' Lord Arthur felt he was being inadequate. 'You mean, you've heard something?'

'I have. I was rung up half an hour ago. I don't know by whom. It was a man, and he simply said that my… my secret would be made public in two days' time. They know I've talked, already. I've written out my resignation.'

'That's bad.' Again Lord Arthur felt inadequate. 'Did you ring up Scotland Yard and ask them to trace the call?'

'No need. At my own request Scotland Yard have been listening in on my telephone ever since I… came clean.' Mr Lloyd-Evans smiled wanly. 'I've already heard that the call had been made from a public call-box. When the police got there it was of course empty. By the way, I've released Lesley from his promise of secrecy. I thought it would be more helpful if other police officials could know that I was at any rate involved.'

'That was good of you, in the circumstances.'

'It can't make any difference now,' said Lloyd-Evans, drearily. 'I'm finished anyhow.'

'Oh, I shouldn't give up yet,' Lord Arthur returned, with a heartiness that to his own ears rang dismally false. 'Er – at all events they haven't dealt with you as they did with Mansel.'

'No, they haven't,' agreed Mr Lloyd-Evans with sudden energy. 'But why not? That's been puzzling me. As soon as I heard about Mansel of course I expected the same. But there's been no attempt. I know I'm guarded – well guarded; but upon my word I'm beginning to believe these people can get past any guards if they've the mind. Why did they kill Mansel, but not me?'

'Mansel must have known more. And they got him before he had a chance to talk. You've done so already.'

'Yes, I suppose that must be it. And after all, I don't know very much. Just the faces of a few of the smaller fry. No, I suppose I'm of no real importance to them. They'll just break me, and make me a present of my life,' Lloyd-Evans said bitterly.

Lord Arthur broke an uncomfortable silence.

'You haven't seen the man they caught, I suppose? The fellow who blew up my office?'

'Yes, indeed I have. I was taken to Scotland Yard yesterday evening, and was able to identify him as one of the men who had once given me instructions. Not the man I met in the restaurant; another Indian. At least I've been able to give the authorities that much help.'

'Well, that's something,' Lord Arthur rallied him.

'Not a great deal, I fear,' Lloyd-Evans sighed. 'Well, you'll be wanting to know why I asked you to come here. It's for this reason. I told you I have written out my resignation; but I haven't sent it to the Prime Minister yet. I propose in fact to postpone doing so for twenty-four hours: by which time,' added Mr Lloyd-Evans with a ghastly smile, 'there may be no need.'

'What exactly do you mean?' Lord Arthur asked uneasily. Mr Lloyd-Evans reminded him in a grotesque way of a schoolmaster. It seemed somehow indecent to be present when a schoolmaster was baring his soul. Schoolmasters ought not to bare their own souls. Their job is to bare other people's.

'Quite simple,' said Mr Lloyd-Evans. 'I'd like to do a useful job before I go. I want to make that speech in the House tomorrow, instead of... well, I don't know who is to make it, but he can't fail to be of more use than I can ever be, now.'

'You know the risk?' Lord Arthur asked mechanically. He was wondering if this was a clever plan to elicit the name of the speaker: information to be passed on to the Terrorists in a final bid for their silence. It seemed cruel to suspect the unhappy man before him of such a piece of treachery, but Lord Arthur was in the mood to trust no one. And after all, Lloyd-Evans had already shown his base metal.

'The risk? You mean, the certainty. Oh, yes, I know. But in a way I welcome it. My life's over. I can't face disgrace, and possible public prosecution... and yet I know I should never have the courage to kill myself. If these persons would be kind enough to do it for me...'

'Come, don't let's be melodramatic,' Lord Arthur said sharply. 'If your offer's genuine, it's a brave one whatever may be prompting it. But you should make it to the Prime Minister, not to me.'

'I know that; I know that,' returned Mr Lloyd-Evans, testily. 'And of course I shall do so, in due course. I merely wished to consult you, as Under-Secretary for the Department, to learn if you approved.'

'Why should I disapprove? Except that in my opinion the job is properly my own. In fact I've already offered to do it, but my offer has not been accepted.'

'That means... yes, I feared as much... the Prime Minister is going...' Mr Lloyd-Evans threw an interrogative glance, perhaps an involuntary one, at his visitor.

'I have no information concerning the proposed speaker,' Lord Arthur answered it stiffly.

'Of course not. After all, it is the Cabinet's privilege… and duty… exactly. In any case, Linton, we won't beat about the bush. You are understood to be in the Prime Minister's confidence over this matter. I should be obliged if you would use all your powers of persuasion on him to allow me to speak on the Bill on Monday. There is no need to mention my forthcoming resignation. As I said, if I am privileged to speak I anticipate that matter will not arise. I am under no illusions. To speak on Monday, I'm convinced, will be certain death… for anyone. I am the only person to whom death would be a relief, and the easiest way out. Therefore I ask you earnestly to further my cause with the Prime Minister.'

Lord Arthur was moved. In contrast to the touch of the dramatic in his earlier manner, Lloyd-Evans had spoken simply and quietly. If ever a man was sincere, thought Lord Arthur, this one was. And what he said was plain sense too. If this wretched secret was really as bad as he seemed to think, if it really involved a possible criminal prosecution, then he would be much better dead than exposed, for his own sake as well as that of his wife and daughter.

'Write your offer to the Prime Minister,' Lord Arthur said. 'I'll take it round myself, at once; and I give you my word that I'll use every effort to persuade him to accept it.'

'Thank you, Linton; that's very good of you.'

Without a further word Mr Lloyd-Evans drew a piece of notepaper out of the drawer beside his hand and began to write.

No sooner had the silence settled than Lord Arthur began to fret. Uneasy doubts presented themselves. Was Lloyd-Evans really to be trusted? He had the reputation of a clever, almost too clever man. Was he really throwing in his hand like this? It did not seem like him. But if there was anything wrong, what was his object in wanting to speak? How could he help the Terrorists by doing so… assuming that this was one last tremendous bid to rehabilitate himself with them and, even at the last, almost impossible moment, buy off exposure and disgrace? It was true that the man had sounded pathetically genuine, but… he had been an actor, and…

Lord Arthur caught his breath. Supposing that Lloyd-Evans wanted to gain the floor not to speak for the Bill at all but to move its abandonment?

The Government benches would be taken completely by surprise. The Prime Minister might not even be in the House at all. Only three or four minutes would be needed, and...

Why, in three or four minutes the whole game might be deliberately lost. It was touch and go as things were. There would be no lack of supporters from the Opposition. The whole thing might even be prearranged, with Lacy or someone, or even Dickson himself, ready to jump up the moment the Government benches tumbled to what was happening, second the motion and force a snap division. And if the proposal actually came from the Government side of the House, the result of a division would almost certainly be against the Bill.

Lord Arthur's mind raced.

'Here you are, then,' said Mr Lloyd-Evans, sealing the envelope. 'I really am most grateful to you, Linton.'

'That's all right,' Lord Arthur muttered. He took the letter and put it in his breast pocket, but did not rise to go. Somehow, he felt, he must clarify his ideas before trying to see the Prime Minister. What could he usefully ask Lloyd-Evans?

'And just in case, perhaps you'd let me have a copy of poor Wellacombe's speech,' he heard Lloyd-Evans saying, in an almost cheerful voice. 'No need for you to waste your time going through it with me. I'll just read it off.'

'I'll send a copy round,' said Lord Arthur, mechanically. He added the first question that came into his head: 'Who gave you that anonymous letter to deliver to No. 10?'

Lloyd-Evans looked surprised. 'That letter from the... Brown Hand? No one. I told Lesley. It wasn't I who delivered it.'

'Not you?' It was Lord Arthur's turn to look surprised. 'But I thought...'

'Oh, you had every reason for thinking so, no doubt,' said Mr Lloyd-Evans with acridity. 'I remember now that it was among the accusations you hurled at me in our previous conversation. I was too taken aback by the large number that were true to collect my wits sufficiently to deny the false.'

'Then... it was someone impersonating you all the time?'

'Undoubtedly.'

Lord Arthur considered this new development: or rather, this return to the old *status quo ante*.

'It's queer. Very queer, taken in conjunction with that box of thorns. They seem to have been deliberately trying to throw suspicion on you, in spite of the fact that you were helping them – and very usefully. I don't understand it at all.

You haven't any personal enemy who could be mixed up with them, have you? It would be a valuable pointer if you had.'

'The police asked me that. I can't think of anyone.'

Lord Arthur reflected. Mr Lloyd-Evans was a rich man: or rather, he had been prudent enough to marry an extremely rich wife, the young widow of an elderly shipping magnate. Rich men always have enemies; but unfortunately the majority are hidden enemies, from the obscure employee nursing some grudge to a jealous rival of equal standing. No, there was not likely to be much help there.

He stood up abruptly.

'Well, I'll be off. I may not be able to see the Prime Minister, and even if I do it's very doubtful whether he'll listen to me. I have no more influence with him than you have yourself. In either case I'll notify you as soon as possible.'

Mr Lloyd-Evans went with him to get his hat and coat. Passing through the hall as Lord Arthur came out of the cloakroom was Mrs Lloyd-Evans, and he stopped for a word with her. The young widow of the shipping magnate was now a handsome matron and the mother of a remarkably pretty daughter. Most people, Lord Arthur knew, were a little afraid of her, for she had a biting wit, inspired by a penetrating intelligence, and she seldom hesitated to use it; but he found her refreshing and honest. Her husband's disgrace would be a terrible shock to her, for his career had been largely her work.

Feeling uncommonly depressed, Lord Arthur waited for his sleuths to disentangle themselves from the still more numerous sleuths guarding the Lloyd-Evans house and then, deep in uneasy thought, turned into the Mall and walked rapidly towards Whitehall.

It was a quarter to four when he reached No. 10. By four o'clock he was ringing up Lloyd-Evans in accordance with his promise. Five minutes the Prime Minister had been able to spare him, but five minutes had been more than enough.

Glancing quickly through Lloyd-Evans' note, the Prime Minister had said:

'Yes? And what have you to say about this, Arthur?'

'I strongly urge you to accept the offer, sir.' Lord Arthur had decided in the end to back Lloyd-Evans against his own doubts.

'It's very handsome of Lloyd-Evans. Frankly, I shouldn't have thought he had it in him. Ring him up for me and thank him, Arthur, and say I much regret that other arrangements have already been concluded. He doesn't know what arrangements, of course?'

'No, sir.' Lord Arthur hesitated. 'You still intend…? Honestly, sir, it's madness. The country can't afford to lose you. It's your duty to keep alive. You *must* let me make that speech-or Lloyd-Evans, of course, if you prefer.'

The Prime Minister smiled. 'The Opposition newspapers call me an obstinate old man, Arthur. I am. Now run along. By the way, Isabel knows, so you can discuss my obstinacy with her. But I rather fancy you'll find she shares the same brand.'

Lord Arthur went. He knew it was no use to persist further.

Isabel was in the morning-room, filing some press cuttings.

'Isabel, I want you to come back to Whitehall Court with me,' Lord Arthur said, abruptly. 'I've just seen your father, and he's quite determined. If I can't persuade him to change his mind, at least I can still try to save him. I've got an idea. It sounds quite fantastic and it's probably all wrong, but it's the only idea I've got. It involves rehearsing that speech of Wellacombe's, perhaps a dozen times over. Could you bear it?'

Isabel asked no questions.

'I'll get my hat,' she said.

chapter twenty

The Bill Is Presented

On Monday morning the newspapers were in full cry.

Smarting under the uncricketerlike march stolen on them, they had let themselves go. Banner headlines, leaded type, all the attributes of the modern goddess of Publicitas Stridens were employed to the full. Threats of murder, murder as threatened, terrorism at Westminster, extermination of the Cabinet... there was plenty of scope. The only wonder was that the newspapers of the Left, faced with this menace to all they professed to hold most dear, namely democratic government, were yet loudest in the denunciation not of the threateners but of those whose determination it was to repress such threats. Logic, however, never has marched with politics. (It is, after all, not so long since politicians of a certain complexion found themselves in a most irksome dilemma by realising that they were morally bound to clamour for force to be applied to a particularly undemocratic aggressor State and, in the same breath, denounce the increased armaments with which that force was to be applied.)

There is, however, one thing to be said for the people of England. Provided only that the favourite does not go down in the Derby, they remain calm. Politicians may be assassinated, terrorism may come to Westminster, India may be in the very act of bombing her way out of the Empire, the very heavens themselves may fall: but provided only that they do not fall on the pitch at the Oval, the people of England remain calm. How much one wishes that the misguided denizens of the Continent would but try to follow this devastating example.

The people of England, then, remained calm. They were interested, certainly; they were even mildly excited, though not, of course, to the same pitch as the crowd at a heavyweight boxing contest; bets were freely offered and taken on the next Minister's chances of survival. The odds, it turned out when the thing had been put on some sort of organised footing, were a shade against the Minister: five to four was the figure finally reckoned as fair. Many people thus found a new interest in politics which had been lacking before.

There was, however, some grumbling at the lack of any authoritative statement from the Government as to the measures proposed to be taken, which might have given a clearer opportunity of estimating the chances.

It has already been written that the Government of this country is not a dictatorship. Indeed, we all know that it is a democracy: the model, in fact, of all democracies. To leave the matter baldly at that is, however, to reckon without the reverence for compromise which made England what she was. Government by dictatorship has certain great and definite advantages for the governors; it also has some minor advantages for the governed, such as saving them all the pains of deciding difficult questions for themselves. It is only to be expected, therefore, that some germ of authoritarianism (if one may coin such a hideous word) should manage neatly to introduce itself into our body politic. The result is to be seen in the fact that, provided he is able to hold his Cabinet in check by cajolery, intimidation or any other means, there is nothing to stop a British Prime Minister from acting in a perfectly totalitarian way, committing his country to any course of action which, although repugnant even to a majority of its citizens, Parliament may find the greatest difficulty in reversing. The Prime Minister is always able to explain to the House how admirable his intentions were and how the country did not know what was best for it; and provided that his intentions really were admirable, sincerity will always win with the great heart of the House of Commons against any such dull qualities as wisdom, far-sightedness or statesmanship.

When, however, a suspicion of dictatorialism is mingled, as it was in this instance, not merely with sincerity but with statesmanship as well, then a Prime Minister may look out for trouble. It was not without something of this in mind that Mr Franklin had determined that he and he only must speak on the Indian Bill that afternoon; for as he frankly told Lord Arthur in a short interview they had that morning for the purpose of going through the more vital points in the Wellacombe speech, he doubted the ability of any other of his Ministers to carry the House with him.

Lord Arthur pushed his way through the usual hysterical crowd which gathers in Downing Street and Whitehall at any national crisis for the purpose of gaping at the important persons going in or coming out of No. 10 and cheering everyone indiscriminately from the Prime Minister himself to the police constable who pushes them back: the same crowd which gathers to mob visiting film stars, international athletes, or anyone else in the public news, and whose plaudits and encouragement a wise Minister does not take as representative of the genuine, inarticulate national feeling.

There were many matters awaiting Lord Arthur's attention at the India Office, now that he was acting for the Secretary of State as well as continuing with his own duties; and for the life of him he did not see what else he could do.

For two hours yesterday he had rehearsed the Wellacombe speech to Isabel. Without telling her the idea that had come to him, he had declaimed as Lord Wellacombe, as Middleton, as the Prime Minister, and even as himself, using what he could remember of the characteristic tricks of intonation, gesture and so forth affected by each; and in the end, when he had performed one or two passages, as it were, in slow motion, Isabel had realised with a little cry of astonishment what he had in mind. They had discussed the possibilities then for a further hour or more, and even then had not felt sure; there were so many difficulties still in the theory that neither could feel able to put too much faith in it, but it was the only theory they had and they hoped desperately that they might be on the right track. Isabel had undertaken to report it to her father alone and almost at the last minute, so that no hint of it should have a chance of reaching the wrong quarters too early, and to give him the warning which Lord Arthur's rehearsal had suggested.

Before they parted, Lord Arthur had taken the opportunity to raise, not without diffidence, a question which had been worrying him.

'Look here, Isabel... that chap Lacy... does he often come to see you?'

Isabel had looked surprised. 'No, that was the first time. Why?'

'Oh, nothing. I just wondered. Fellow's perfectly all right, no doubt. Decent family, and all that. But...' Lord Arthur had begun to wish he had not introduced the subject at all, for Isabel had laughed delightedly.

'Arthur, you're not asking me if Mr Lacy has been – what's the phrase? – paying me his addresses? I do believe you are. Well, rest assured. His attentions are reported to be turning quite elsewhere; and if you want any more information, try Sheila Lloyd-Evans.'

'Oh!' Lord Arthur had been too relieved to try to hide his relief. 'Is that so? I didn't know. Very good match if it comes to anything. Lacy's got a big future in front of him.'

'Yes, and Sheila's a bit negative; she'd suit him very well,' Isabel said perfunctorily. 'Her parents apparently aren't too keen, but that doesn't matter much nowadays... Why did you ask, Arthur?'

'Oh, I don't know. Silly of me. I just thought...'

'You just thought that you've heard that girls do foolish things on the rebound, and Mr Lacy wasn't any more right for me than Eric was.'

'Exactly,' Lord Arthur had said with gratitude. 'That was it, exactly.'

'Well, I wish that one day,' Isabel had retorted, with sudden asperity, 'you'd tell me who in your opinion is right.'

'I've promised already,' Lord Arthur had smiled, and Isabel had then announced that she must go; her father might be wanting her.

The conversation recurred to Lord Arthur when, his business at the Office done, he turned into Whitehall on his way to lunch. It had been clever of Isabel to tumble to the extraordinary idea he had conceived; but then Isabel was clever – clever as a monkey. How lost she would be when her father retired from political life. Somehow Lord Arthur did not like the proposal that she should stand for Parliament on her own account; Isabel would be far more use pulling the right strings behind the scenes.

On a sudden whim Lord Arthur decided to lunch in the dining-room of the House of Commons instead of at home. The loneliness of his flat appeared distasteful: he wanted company.

Before lunching he took a stroll round to see what precautions were in hand. Plain-clothes men were everywhere, in the most sacred corners and recesses. Lord Arthur wandered into the Chamber itself. A few Members were already on the benches, making sure of their seats; even the usual card seemed to be distrusted today. Several nodded to him in silence and in silence he returned their greeting. Faces everywhere were grave; an atmosphere of foreboding and uneasiness hung over the whole place. The great Chamber seemed to be holding its breath.

Lord Arthur stared at the portion of the front bench sacred to England's Prime Minister. What had that shabby upholstery with its missing button seen in the past? What was it to see today?

He shook off the fears which suddenly crowded in on him and hurried away to lunch. The Minister for the Dominions was there, and beckoned to him. Lord Arthur had never been conscious before of any particular affection for Mr Lavering, but he accepted the invitation with pleasure.

At lunch Mr Lavering imparted a piece of information. Seven Cabinet Ministers had decided to call upon the Prime Minister at the very last moment and try to persuade him not to speak. If he persisted they would resign on the spot, as a last resort. Lord Arthur learnt with some surprise that Mr Lloyd-Evans was among the seven. On his asking how the belief had arisen that it was the Prime Minister himself who was to speak, Mr Lavering had divulged that a process of elimination among the Cabinet had left this as the only logical conclusion.

After lunch Lord Arthur was bereft of his anchor. Having deliberated with himself at considerable length in his rich, fruity voice, Mr Lavering had decided to add himself to the seven and make an eighth, giving his reasons at considerable length. Lord Arthur refused a tentative invitation to accompany the deputation to No. 10 and add his moral support. He could not disapprove of any effort to make the Prime Minister change his mind, but hardly thought this one was likely to be successful. He contented himself with telling the Minister for the Dominions that he had already pressed to be allowed to make the speech himself and that this offer still held good: a piece of news which the Minister received with undisguised relief and gratitude.

With an hour or more before the House would assemble, Lord Arthur found himself too restless to remain. The Prime Minister had hinted already that he wished to see no more of him at No. 10, and Lord Arthur hardly liked to intrude upon Isabel's anxiety. In the end he walked quickly over to the India Office and manufactured some work for himself there.

It was a lucky choice. He had not been in his room for ten minutes before a telephone-call came through from the Treasury.

It was the same official whom he had already consulted about Mansel. 'I don't know if you're still interested in our friend, dead as well as alive,' he said at once, 'but I thought you might like to hear the news.'

'What news?' Lord Arthur asked.

'Panic,' replied the other laconically. 'Or something so near it as makes no odds.'

'Panic?' Lord Arthur repeated, puzzled. The crowds had seemed orderly enough, more interested than frightened.

'On the Stock Exchange,' the other explained. 'There's been the usual rush to unload any stock that had Mansel's name attached to it. Very silly, because a lot of his concerns are still sound. Of course the Indian ones have suffered most. There's not a buyer. That isn't surprising, as most of the Indian shares aren't fully paid-up. There've been three suicides reported to date; I dare say there'll be a dozen before the day's out.'

'Good Heavens!' Lord Arthur was horrified.

'Oh, it's the usual thing; when a big man crashes, he brings hundreds of small ones down with him. This crash is going to be a bit worse than usual, because not only was his position in India thoroughly unsound with an enormous amount of capital tied up in it, but he was murdered. You may say that shouldn't affect the financial situation, but believe me, it does. It's no good looking for logic when a panic's in the air.'

'This looks pretty bad,' Lord Arthur muttered.

'It's certainly bad. I shouldn't be surprised if it turns out the worst crash on record in this country. Mansel always was spectacular. And to add to the irony, I've a report through this morning from a highly reliable source that platinum has been discovered in the hinterland of Barghiala in remarkable quantities; in fact, the reports suggest that the deposits may be the richest in the world. If Mansel had lived to bring off that deal, not only would everything have been saved but most of the people now committing suicide would have been something like millionaires. He was conducting negotiations in the name of his Indian company, we've heard, not in his own. A pretty stroke, eh?'

'It's all on a par,' said Lord Arthur.

So the Terrorists had not only the murders of two British Cabinet ministers to their credit, but the indirect murders of half a dozen harmless British investors. It had hardly seemed possible that such a bad business could become worse, but…

Putting off his return as long as possible, he found the House already in session when he got back to Westminster. Only two or three questions were down on the list, and these were answered perfunctorily, in lowered tones by the Under-Secretaries concerned. From the thinned-out aspect of the front bench as Lord Arthur slipped into a seat directly behind the Prime Minister's own, he gathered that the Cabinet deputation was still urging its case.

If the atmosphere of the House had been tense three days beforehand, when Middleton rose to speak, it had been nothing compared with the painful rigidity in which every Member seemed to be held now as in a vice. Hardly a whisper was to be heard, and Lord Arthur wondered if everyone else was finding the same difficulty as himself in breathing. On either side of the Speaker's chair, against every rule and precedent, a little group of detectives watched the scene with worried eyes. The lobby, the galleries, and every approach to the Chamber was packed with them.

Lord Arthur tugged nervously at his small moustache and stared round. On every face he saw the reflection of his own fears.

Before the Questions were quite concluded, there was a small diversion. Lacy, looking more or less unperturbed, rose from his seat on the front Opposition bench and crossed the floor towards Lord Arthur. Leaning over the vacant seat he whispered:

'If there's anything our lot can do, even as late as this…? Move the adjournment or something…?'

Lord Arthur noticed that the other's voice was not quite steady in spite of his affected calm, and in equally uncertain tones replied:

'I don't think so. We've got to go through with it.'

Lacy waited for a few seconds, as if wondering whether to say more, then went quietly back to his seat.

Lord Arthur looked up at the clock. It was already a minute over the time, and still no one came. He felt he could not bear the suspense much longer.

Resting his elbows on the back of the bench in front, he leaned over them and stared down at the blank upholstery, trying to make his mind a similar blank. He tried to force his attention to concentrate on ridiculous trifles. There was a tear in the leather exactly the shape of the letter P; one of the flat buttons was nearly an inch out of alignment; the leather had been polished by the Prime Ministerial trousers to within six inches of the back of the seat but no further...

Then suddenly there was action.

Half a dozen Ministers came tumbling into the Chamber, looking both scared and excited. The Minister for Labour stopped to have a word with the Speaker; the others hurried to their places. Comstock dropped into a vacant seat beside that of the Prime Minister, the other side being already occupied by the Chancellor of the Exchequer, and then twisted round to Lord Arthur.

'Lloyd-Evans knocked him out!' he whispered, excitedly. 'Knocked him clean out, in front of all of us. He's going to make the speech himself.'

'*What?*' Lord Arthur could not make sense of this extraordinary communication.

Comstock explained, more or less incoherently. They had all pleaded with the Prime Minister, who had remained adamant. Finally Lloyd-Evans, convinced like the rest of them that it was hopeless to persevere, had stepped forward and, under the eyes of his astounded colleagues, had knocked the Prime Minister unconscious with as neat a left to the chin as ever Mr Comstock had seen. He had then announced that he was going to make the speech himself, had removed the manuscript of it from the Prime Minister's breast pocket, and summoned the Commissioner of Police to the room. Lord Arthur gathered that Sir Hubert Lesley, with remarkable quickness of decision, had accepted the situation, called up Sir William Greene, who was already in attendance below, to make sure that the Prime Minister was not seriously hurt and, on receiving his report that it appeared to be no more than an ordinary knock-out blow and the Prime Minister when he came round in twenty minutes or so would be perfectly well except for a headache and a sore jaw, had then undertaken to escort Lloyd-Evans to the House in place of the unconscious Prime Minister.

Scarcely had Lord Arthur grasped these facts when Mr Lloyd-Evans himself appeared, attended by Sir Hubert as far as the Speaker's chair, paused for a moment, white and breathless, to exchange a quick interrogative glance with the Speaker and receive a nod in return, and then dropped heavily into the Prime Minister's place.

A buzz of speculation which had already broken out with the somewhat helter-skelter entrance of the Ministers, redoubled when it was seen that the President of the Board of Trade and not the Prime Minister had occupied the latter's seat; but there was little time for discussion. Pausing only for a minute to confer hastily over the side of his chair with the Commissioner, the Speaker called in a low voice upon the President of the Board of Trade.

There was no response.

Slumped in his seat, Mr Lloyd-Evans seemed to be ignoring the summons. The Speaker called upon him again, more clearly.

And then a horrible thing happened. Mr Lloyd-Evans slumped down still lower, and then very slowly rolled off the Bench on to the floor and lay there, prone and motionless.

For a moment the House stared at him in horror. Then Sir Hubert, with a bark to his men, darted forward, Sir William Greene close on his heels. While the House sat petrified a quick examination was made. Then four detectives gently lifted the inert body and carried it out of the Chamber. Sir Hubert, as he followed, bent towards the Chancellor of the Exchequer. Lord Arthur heard the one word he muttered:

'Dead!'

Still the House sat as if turned into stone.

Lord Arthur was never conscious that he had made a decision. Acting almost without thought, he scrambled over the back of the Bench in front of him and, even as the Speaker's trembling lips were about to pronounce the adjournment of the House, reached the Chair.

'Don't adjourn,' he whispered, urgently. 'Call on me.'

The Speaker stared down at him for a moment, then moistened his lips and complied.

Lord Arthur stumbled back to the front bench and, in a low, flat voice, began without any preamble or explanation the late Secretary of State for India's speech.

Gradually the House unfroze, gradually Lord Arthur's voice gained power. He stood quite rigidly, making neither gesture nor movement, his eyes fixed on vacancy as he recited the rounded periods which he knew so thoroughly by heart. The House listened in utter silence, holding its breath.

The minutes marched on. The point at which Lord Wellacombe had collapsed was reached and passed, then the point where death had overtaken Middleton. Ten minutes… twenty…half an hour…

Lord Arthur warmed up. More life came into his voice. It seemed an age now since Mr Lloyd-Evans had been carried, a sagging mass, out of the House. Behind the façade of words another part of Lord Arthur's brain could contemplate that tragedy now almost with detachment. Poor Lloyd-Evans! It had been a gallant gesture, but the physical frame of the man could not have been equal to the strain for his heart to have given out so suddenly – pouf! like that, the very instant that strain was momentarily relaxed. Funny, no one had ever known Lloyd-Evans had a heart. He must have kept very quiet about it. And that was odd, too, for there is no one more fussy about his health than an ex-athlete. Funny, to think of Lloyd-Evans as an athletic undergraduate, with a blue for rowing as well as for boxing. People changed so much…

Lord Arthur's hand crept towards his tie. Some men are button-conscious when they are speaking in public and fumble continually with coat or waistcoat buttons as if to make sure that everything is still in order; some are tie-conscious, and some have a different trick; but all speakers possess some favourite gesture or action which seems to make the sentences flow more freely. It was Isabel who had fastened on Lord Arthur's habit of pulling at his tie, during the rehearsal yesterday afternoon. Lord Arthur himself had been almost unconscious of it, but recognised the propensity when Isabel pointed it out.

He was nearing the end of the speech now.

But the end was not to be reached without drama. At the exact moment that Lord Arthur's hand was about to reach his tie a shriek rang out from the Ladies' Gallery.

Lord Arthur, his sentence cut in half, stared up. In the shadows he could make out the figure of Isabel. She was gesticulating at him wildly.

Lord Arthur paused for a moment, swallowed once or twice, and then, with the same rigidity of pose as at the beginning, began to speak.

For eight minutes more his voice filled the high chamber. And then, with a slight bow to the Chair, the speech was finished.

Instantly pandemonium broke out. Cheers and shouts from every side echoed through the House; order papers were waved, even hats flung hysterically on to the floor. For the moment Lloyd-Evans was as forgotten as if he had never existed.

Lord Arthur lifted his hand, and the pandemonium was cut off as if by a chopper.

'Before we proceed with the debate,' he said, 'I move that the House adjourns for half an hour, but that no Member moves from his or her place, and that the Commissioner of Police be requested to carry out such investigations here and now as may seem fit to him.'

He glanced at the Speaker.

It was no time for precedent.

'The House is adjourned,' said the Speaker, firmly. 'Honourable Members will please keep their seats.'

Sir Hubert came hurrying forward. He grasped Lord Arthur's hand and muttered a fervent word of congratulation.

'Lloyd-Evans?' asked Lord Arthur.

'Dead. Apparently heart failure.' He bustled away.

Lord Arthur turned, scrambled over the vacant seat behind him and regained his own. He sat down thankfully. His job was done, he was still alive, and... he felt weak at the knees.

Sir Hubert was busily instructing his men. The House buzzed with excitement and anticipation.

Lord Arthur hunched himself forward over the back of the bench in front. How was it that he was still alive? Had his fantastic idea been right after all? Did he actually at that moment carry on his person some unknown, hidden weapon of death which had missed its mark – or had his immunity been due to his sudden inspiration, unforeseen by the enemy, to take Lloyd-Evans' place literally over that unhappy man's dead body? He wished Sir Hubert would hurry up. He wanted to be searched, and quickly. It was a disturbing thought that even at this moment…

He pushed the thought away from him and tried, as an hour ago, to concentrate on trifles. That P-shaped tear was still just as it had been, but the loose button had been dragged off by Lloyd-Evans' sliding weight; Lord Arthur bent and retrieved it from under the bench. As he straightened up, his hand, still in the gloom under the bench, knocked against some obstruction and he was conscious of a sharp prick.

For once in his life Lord Arthur gave way to something like panic. For a moment he stared stupidly at a tiny speck of blood on his thumb: then, remembering in a flash what Sir William had said about the curious properties of curare, he began feverishly to suck at the spot.

One of his neighbours grasped the situation.

'Sir Hubert!' he shouted. 'Here – quick!'

The reader is now in possession of all the clues which enabled the Commissioner of Police, five minutes after the events narrated, to make an arrest.

Readers are invited to answer the following questions:

1 *Who killed the murdered ministers?*
2 *How did the poisoned thorns reach the victims?*
3 *What were the hidden facts behind the murders?*

These questions were set to those who read the book in serial form. In spite of a very large number of entries, no fully correct set of answers was received. Readers of this book may like to amuse themselves by pausing at this point, and reflecting what answers they might have sent in.

chapter twenty-one

Postscript to Politics

'I was wrong,' the new Secretary of State for India admitted, handsomely. 'Utterly and completely wrong.'

'It was a brilliant idea, though, darling,' consoled his fiancée. 'And I was even more wrong than you.'

'No, no,' the new Secretary for India demurred. 'I was the wronger – I mean, the more wrong.'

They had only been engaged for twenty-four hours, and were still in the maudlin stage.

His fiancée selected a lock of the new Secretary for India's hair and rolled it with considerable care into one of the new sausage curls. She poised the curl on the top of the Secretary's head and regarded it with loving admiration.

'You look sweet like that,' she pronounced.

The Secretary for India kissed her.

'I should never make a detective,' he resumed, some moments later. From his tone one might have gathered that to make a detective had always been his real ambition; the India Office was only a stop by the way.

'You *would* make a detective, darling,' retorted his fiancée with indignation.

'I was too clever.'

'But you are clever.'

'I ought to have listened to the experts. Both MacFerris and Greene couldn't understand those thorns. They told me dozens of times that they didn't see how a fatal dose of curare could be injected even by three or four thorns. I ought to have tumbled to it that the thorns were a blind.'

'If Scotland Yard didn't, why should you?' demanded his fiancée hotly. 'I think you did awfully well, Arthur, and you *would* make a detective.'

Lord Arthur smiled up at her. Even he found difficulty in recognising in this delightfully affectionate, clinging person the old self-sufficient Isabel. He thanked his stars for the thousandth time that he had had the wit to realise at last who was the right man for Isabel, and had wasted no time in telling her. The wonder still was that Isabel should have agreed. Love makes altruists of us all.

It was just one week since the final scene in the House, and by a series of emergency measures which had left the old Parliamentarians gasping, the India Bill had received the Royal Assent that same morning and was now law. Lord Arthur had been rewarded for his share with the vacant Secretaryship, and was now finding himself, to his bewilderment, the most popular man in the country. The Government press agents were confident, too, that they could maintain him in that position for a whole week, till a visiting American film star who could dance the tango with unusually sinuous lusciousness was unfortunately due to arrive.

Lord Arthur had come that afternoon from a final conference at Scotland Yard in which the last threads of the mystery had been unravelled and the full body of evidence at last assembled. He had already made a brief report to the Prime Minister and now, over an early glass of sherry, was making a much fuller one to his fiancée.

Isabel suddenly began to giggle. Lord Arthur had never even guessed that she was capable of giggling.

'That shriek of mine in the House. I shall never forget it. Nor, I should think, will the House.'

Lord Arthur smiled, then looked serious. 'If we'd been right, it might have saved my life.'

'You really forgot about your tie?'

'Completely. I never thought I could get *so* carried away by my own oratory.'

'And you thought that there might be thorns in your tie all the time? Darling, how awful. What did it feel like? You were terribly brave.'

Lord Arthur thought. 'No, I couldn't believe it. I didn't see how there possibly could be. They wouldn't have been expecting me to speak, for one thing. No, I'm afraid I wasn't really so brave.'

'You were. Terribly.' Isabel changed her position on the arm of his chair. 'So it's really all cleared up at last. I can hardly believe it. Even about poor Mr Lloyd-Evans?'

'Yes. Most probably hydrocyanic acid. Apparently almost indetectible.'

Isabel shivered. 'And it was meant for father! I shall never be able to forget that when… when there's a discussion about the death penalty again. I know it's all wrong, but the personal aspect does affect one's views.'

There was a little silence. Then:

'How were the police able to eliminate Mr Frith?' Isabel asked. 'Eric was on the other side of Mr Lloyd-Evans…'

'The button was there before he came into the House,' Lord Arthur put in. 'I saw it myself, though, of course, I didn't know what I was looking at.'

'Yes, but how did they know Mr Frith hadn't put it there? He was sitting beside Lord Wellacombe and Mr Middleton, too, you see.'

'Oh, I don't think there was ever any suspicion on Frith. He was much too cut up over Wellacombe. Besides… no, except for that one point there were no grounds against him at all.'

'They certainly took everyone in with thorns,' Isabel mused. 'The button idea, after all, was so much simpler.'

'A tiny hypodermic syringe made up as a button, just holding the right amount and, of course, acting through the pressure when anyone sat on it. Yes, it was clever. But for all that I ought to have realised that the exact place to be occupied by the intended victim was important. Lloyd-Evans told me as much, but neither of us realised what it meant. And I saw for myself that there was a button missing from the seat where both Wellacombe and Middleton had sat.'

'The police had searched the benches beforehand?'

'Oh, of course. A permanent arrangement would have been detected at once. The button was simply plugged in each time just in advance. It's been established now that Lacy was in his seat each time before questions, crossed the floor to speak to Lloyd-Evans in a pause just as he did to me, and then went out into the lobby, to follow the speaker in quite innocently.'

'If the police had searched people before the speeches instead of after, they'd have caught him.'

'I don't think so,' Lord Arthur objected. 'He only had to plug the button in beside his own place. No one would have noticed it.'

'Mr Lacy!' Isabel murmured. 'It's extraordinary that we never suspected him. It's so obvious now that he must have put that last letter in the box downstairs when he went down to get that Indian newspaper.'

'Well, you know, I did vaguely suspect him. I admit I forgot all about the newspaper: it was so natural and ordinary it simply didn't register. But I'd always thought there was something queer about the fellow. I can't say I'd ever realised that he really is an Indian, but I should never have been surprised to learn it.'

'It's astonishing. He admitted it in the end?'

'He exulted in it. Of course, we ought to have spotted it. I felt at the time that there was something fishy about that accident in 1912, with only Colonel and Mrs Lacy killed and the ayah disappearing directly afterwards. Of course, they were murdered. What a plan, with twenty years to wait before it could even begin to work!'

'It really was planned as long ago as that?'

'According to Lesley, it must have been. The substitution for the Lacy infant of another child of North Indian stock, which is white enough to pass as a European so long as no suspicion is aroused; the means taken to ensure that the child would be brought up as an Englishman; and then the revelation which must have been made to him round about his twenty-first birthday of the purpose for which he had been chosen and the duty that had fallen on him.'

'The duty being to work for the independence of India by any means in his power?'

'Exactly.' Lord Arthur paused. 'The evidence is plain enough, now we know. Lacy did undergo a remarkable change when he was twenty-one. From that time he worked for nothing but a position in our political system which would enable him to push ahead with his plans. It's funny how the blood persisted, in spite of his upbringing: scent and all that.

And from the way he enamelled his fingernails, obviously to cover the dark half-moons, he must have been terrified all the time of being found out.'

'He really did feel strongly about his own country,' Isabel put in. 'You remember how bitterly he spoke that afternoon here.'

'Certainly he did, poor devil. And he never doubted that the end justified any means. You understand his motive, don't you? He was anxious to stop the passage of the Bill, which would certainly have been a big block to the Separatist campaign, but he also hoped to push on a Labour Government here which would mean the India Office for himself. As Secretary he could do vastly more for his people than as a mere member of the Opposition. He came within an ace of it, too.'

'But India as a whole doesn't want Separation.'

'That doesn't matter. Lacy's lot wanted it. And so do people like the Maharajah of Barghiala.'

'By the way, what was Lacy's connection with the Maharajah?'

'There's no evidence of any, so far as I know. Lacy visited Barghiala in his travels, and certainly he learned of the platinum deposits there, but I don't know of any other connection.'

Isabel was still considering the personal side.

'Did he really intend to marry Sheila Lloyd-Evans, Arthur?'

'I dare say. She'd have been of great use to him. The fact that Lloyd-Evans wouldn't hear of it accounts for Lacy's enmity and the attempts to incriminate Lloyd-Evans with the box of thorns and the delivery of the Brown Hand letter.'

'Mr Lacy delivered that letter himself, in disguise?'

'Oh, no. He wasn't the same build at all. The police have got hold of some seedy actor who admits having done it, for a pretty substantial reward. People like that will be turning up. Lacy had a big organisation, as we knew he must have, and plenty of money at his disposal. Probably half the people working for him didn't know what they were doing. It will all disintegrate quietly now. Scotland Yard believe the foreigners have skedaddled already.'

'It's extraordinary that he never gave himself away,' Isabel commented.

'Well, he did in a way, to me,' Lord Arthur had to admit. 'Either he got careless, or he didn't think I mattered. Over Ghaijana's birthplace, for instance,' Lord Arthur went on, disregarding his fiancée's snort of indignation. 'He told me that Ghaijana was born in Barghiala, but I've seen his birth certificate and the place was Benares. And do you remember how he said to us, "Once a native always *a* native"? He was talking about the Native States, but it held all right. I don't think it was he who spoke to Lloyd-Evans on the telephone; that would have been an unnecessary risk; but Lloyd-Evans recognised something familiar about the voice, though he couldn't place it. It was the intonation, of course. Lacy had the Indian's rather high voice.'

'Poor Mr Lloyd-Evans!'

Lord Arthur nodded. 'I dare say it was the best thing that could have happened. No one will, know his secret now, whatever it was.'

'Mr Lacy – I must still call him that – got on the track of it through Sheila?'

'That seems obvious, though no doubt Sheila has no idea of it herself. It would be some discrepancy in dates or something like that no doubt, which gave Lacy his clue; and he was astute enough to follow it up.'

'And Dr Ghaijana had nothing to do with it?'

'Nothing at all. Lacy's motive there was obvious. Ghaijana had actually begun to suspect him; and where could Ghaijana do less harm than in prison, where all that he said about Lacy would be disbelieved? Actually, everything he said was true. Lacy did plant the thorns in his room.'

'Those thorns! How they took us all in.'

'There was no excuse,' Lord Arthur maintained, honestly. 'We were told again and again that even four thorns couldn't hold thirty milligrams of curare. I admit I thought of Lacy in connection with the thorns, but there was no possibility of him planting them on Wellacombe and Middleton in the lobbies; they were much too well guarded. And, of course, any attempt to do so across the floor of the House itself would have been seen instantly. Lacy started the hare of sleight-of-hand in the lobby for his own purposes, but even at the time I thought it impossible, and so did the police.'

'Well, you were right there, darling,' Isabel said, fondly.

'On one point, yes,' Lord Arthur smiled. 'Not a very good bag. I even saw Middleton give a kind of start when he sat down on the needle, but that never registered either.'

'You mean, he felt the prick?'

'Well, it was probably a reflex action. The doctors say he wouldn't have consciously felt the prick, not expecting it – any more than they themselves found the puncture.'

'They should have found it, surely?'

'They say it would be almost impossible. It's not a smooth-skinned part of the body, you see. And, naturally, they were concentrating on the exposed parts.'

'I shall never forgive our ingenious idea for not being right,' Isabel said.

'That the poison was introduced from the thorns through the characteristic gestures on the part of the speakers – Wellacombe pulling at his lapels, Middleton stroking the back of his head, and so on. Yes, it was ingenious. But it still left us with the worse problem of how the thorns could have been fixed so conveniently in the right place under the eyes of the police; and, of course, that was impossible. By the way, it was something MacFerris said that gave me the idea. He referred to a curare-smeared scratch on the ball of Wellacombe's thumb. Why, I wondered, just there? And, of course, I remembered how Wellacombe always used to tug at his lapels.' Lord Arthur meditated a moment. 'There are still one or two curious points. Why that scratch on Wellacombe's thumb after all? There was only one thorn found in his case, you remember. Yes, and for that matter why only one thorn?'

'Do you know,' Isabel exclaimed, 'I believe we were *meant* to think that, about the gestures. To put us off the scent. That's why the thorns were at the back of Mr Middleton's neck.'

'You've hit it, my darling,' agreed Lord Arthur. He looked at her with fond admiration. Isabel could see farther with one eye than he could with two. 'Of course, that's it. And I tumbled plump into the trap.'

'And I shouldn't be surprised,' Isabel went on, 'if they left only one thorn in the first case out of sheer ignorance. After the ball of the thumb had been scratched with it, of course. When the doctors began making a fuss about the size of the fatal dose, the number of thorns was increased.'

Lord Arthur considered the point.

'Yes, that's possible. On the other hand, I've always suspected that they didn't intend to kill Wellacombe, only to frighten him; but he was an oldish man, and a dose that might not have proved fatal in other cases was too much for him. That certainly would explain Mansel's participation better.'

'I haven't really grasped yet how Mr Mansel did come into it. You know I've hardly seen you this last week.'

'Except for a couple of minutes I snatched to propose to you,' Lord Arthur smiled. 'Well, the Mansel connection puzzled me at first, but I think it's fairly clear now.

'The essential thing to remember about Mansel is that he wasn't a crook financier. His companies were honest, and he did really feel a big responsibility to his shareholders. He told me so himself more than once, and I believed him. That, combined with his knowledge of the platinum deposits in Barghiala, was his sole motive for mixing himself up in the plot.

'He was in touch with the Terrorists, we knew, and somehow he got on to Lacy. They laid the plot together; but I'm quite sure Mansel never intended murder. Lacy led him up the path there.

'Mansel, you must remember, was desperate. His huge organisation in India was wrecked; he must have known some of his small shareholders were in despair. If the Company had to be wound up, there would be a crop of suicides, just as there has been since his death, and any number of worthy people would be ruined. Mansel was ready to go to pretty far lengths to stop that happening. I don't know, he may even have been reconciled to the murder of a Minister or two, setting it as a lesser evil than the suicide of a dozen humbler folk. But I think he only meant to frighten the Government out of the Bill. So he and Lacy concocted this plot by which Lacy should be responsible for the button which really did the work, while Mansel should plant the misleading thorns on the victims in the rush and confusion afterwards; and, of course, we know that Mansel was one of the first to reach both Wellacombe and Middleton.

'Whether they were equal partners, whether Lacy was the dominant one and double-crossed Mansel by killing instead of paralysing and then using Mansel's connivance to blackmail him into helping with the next case, whether Mansel all the time was no more than Lacy's tool, we shall probably never learn. It doesn't really matter very much. But what brought about Mansel's death was almost certainly his reluctance to kill your father. He was terribly upset over Middleton's death; and he signed his own death warrant when he refused to co-operate in your father's. I'd worked on him a bit, you know, and I'd actually brought him to the point of talking. I don't know what he'd have told me at that interview we arranged, but probably quite a lot. What I can never forgive myself for is the fact that it was I who tipped Lacy off about Mansel's intention to spill the beans.

'Lacy must have had his plan ready. It was quite simple. He must have known, or guessed, that Mansel's telephone was being tapped. He simply rang him up, held him in a cunning conversation designed to show on the records that he must be a comparative stranger to Mansel, and thus established his own alibi for the actual moment of killing, while one of his Indian accomplices stuck a hypodermic full of hydrocyanic acid into Mansel and strolled away at his ease, with a few thorns left behind just to mislead the police again.'

'I see,' Isabel said, slowly. 'You know, darling, it's absolutely unethical of me but I can't help being sorry for Mr Mansel.'

'Nor can I,' Lord Arthur admitted.

There was another pause, while Isabel absent-mindedly unrolled the curl on top of the Secretary for India's hair and tried the effect of another above his left ear.

'We may have fallen into their trap over the thorns,' she said at length, 'but as soon as you picked up the button you saw the truth.'

'As soon as it pricked me,' amended Lord Arthur, with a little shiver. He still had only too vivid a memory of that unpleasant minute when he had not been at all sure that he was not to follow the fate of his three predecessors.

'It was wonderful of you to understand its significance, just in a flash like that,' Isabel said, fondly.

'Oh, I don't know. I ought to have seen it before. I'd noticed before that there was a button missing from that seat, just as there had been from the one where Wellacombe and Middleton had sat. But even when I saw another button there, and out of alignment at that, I never spotted the truth. When I did, of course, I realised at once that no one but Lacy could have put it there, when he came across the floor to speak to me. But there I was again. I wondered at the time why Lacy should take it on himself to make that offer. It wasn't his job; it was his chief's.'

'It was the most dramatic thing I ever saw,' Isabel said, with conviction, 'when you pointed to Mr Lacy and shouted to Sir Hubert to arrest him, that second, before he could make a move.'

'Lesley wasn't quick enough, even so. Of course, it was impossible. Lacy only had to drop back on to that other button he had ready, and he was dead within ten seconds. Hydrocyanic acid acts quickly enough when it gets the chance.'

'I wonder if Mr Lacy had a second button ready like that each time?'

'I should say, certainly. He was taking no chances, and he didn't intend to be hanged. I dare say he knew the odds were against him all the time.' Lord Arthur sighed. 'He was a brave man in his way.'

'I'm thankful he... took that way. His trial would have been too terrible.'

'Yes,' said Lord Arthur. 'Now, as things are, the whole thing's cleared up and done with.'

'And now I know all I want to know, I hope we never speak of it again. Oh, Arthur, when I think you might have... have been...'

'Well, we've got lots of other things to talk about, Isabel,' Lord Arthur interposed, hastily. 'Lots and lots. That is... well, for instance, where shall we go for our honeymoon?'

Isabel understood her fiance thoroughly.

'Mr Secretary,' she said, 'you're very sweet.'